GUARDIAN

Guardian

TJ Kang

Teresa J Kang

Contents

"For He shall give His angels charge over you,

To keep you in all your ways.
They shall bear you in their hands,
Lest you dash your foot against a stone."

Psalm 91

1

Choices and Consequences

Rich Wright knew as soon as he swung his fist that he was making a huge mistake. As an unashamed action movie fanatic (if Dwayne Johnson or Vin Diesel was in the starring role, you could count Rich in), he had seen more than his share of slow-motion scenes – cars exploding, bridges collapsing, gunshot victims flying through the air, and the oldie but goodie: lives flashing before the eyes of mortally-wounded heroes. He had seen them all in the movies, but he never thought he would experience his very own slow-motion scene in real life. Yet, here he was, his clenched fist moving inch-by-inch closer to the waiting jaw of the prick who had just insulted his boyfriend. He could even see the smirk blossoming on the prick's face as if to say, "Gotcha!".

In the split second from drawing back his fist to connecting with its target, Rich thought about his athletic scholarship, his so-so grades, and what his mother would do (forget Mom – what would Lonny do?) if he blew his chances to make the NFL all because of a provocation anyone with the IQ of a woodchuck could have seen coming from a mile away. An image of Lonny's face appeared in his mind, looking simultaneously disappointed and pitying. The image opened its mouth to speak just as the fist met the jaw, and time resumed its usual speed. Rich was almost relieved.

In terms of physical strength, the prick was no match for Rich, who could easily have stunt-doubled for Chris Hemsworth as Thor. His six-foot, four-inch, two hundred forty-pound frame, along with his ice-blue eyes and blond hair, attested to his Viking heritage. Daily trips to the gym in any weather and despite any crisis short of loss of limb didn't hurt either. Nonetheless, the prick was wiry, fast, and slippery as a buttered weasel. For every punch Rich landed, another one missed its mark a split second after the prick ducked out of the way.

The exchange of blows went on long enough to launch four YouTube videos. It might have continued indefinitely if it wasn't for the arrival of the Varsity Assistant Football Coach, Mike Kussler, or as he was known by the team behind his back, "Coach Ass Kisser". As soon as Kussler entered the locker room where the fight was taking place, several athletes who had been standing around in various stages of transition from practice uniform to towel to street wear, watching the fight and cheering on their favorite, jumped to attention and pulled the combatants apart.

Rich's ears were ringing from a couple of solid head shots from the prick, so he missed a lot of the specific content of the lecture that Coach Ass Kisser was screaming at him, but he got enough of the gist of it to know he was in very hot water and that his fate would be decided by Coach and communicated to him later. For now, Rich was to get his sorry ass out of Kussler's face and go home and think about his future. Rich uttered several "Yes, sirs" at appropriate intervals and waited for the Assistant Coach to wind down. Kussler had turned to the onlookers and was screaming at them about team loyalty and brotherhood when Rich saw his chance for escape. He picked up his gym bag and slipped out of the building into the blinding late-afternoon sunlight.

He sat inside his black Dodge Charger with both doors open and the air conditioning running full blast, cursing himself for being so easily manipulated, along with being stupid enough to drive a black car in the desert. "Just add it to my list of failures," he said to the empty car. He unzipped his gym bag, which bore evidence of being trampled on by someone's size 13 Chuck Taylors – possibly his own – during the fight, and took out his cell phone. The screen was shattered. With a sigh, Rich tossed the phone back in the bag, pulled the doors shut, and put the car in gear.

****

Lorena Cuevas sat on a bus bench and checked the time on her phone: 9:25 PM. Still plenty of time to get home, take a quick shower, get dressed, and make it to the club in time to meet up with her friends. She would be the last to arrive, and her *chicas* would be at least two rounds of drinks ahead of her, but that was okay. Lorena wasn't much of a drinker. She went out for the atmosphere, the dancing, and the conversation and laughter with friends. No matter how tired she was from a busy shift at the restaurant, going out and having fun with the girls always raised her spirits. The fatigue and stress would melt away for those few hours, and it was well worth waking up hungover the next morning.

Lorena looked down the street for the headlights that would signal the approach of the eastbound city bus. No sign of it yet. She was about to check her social media for the fifth time in the past ten minutes when she heard a familiar voice calling her name. She involuntarily cringed. At first, she ignored the voice and intentionally quashed the urge to turn around. With a huge dose of wishful thinking, she told herself that maybe it was someone else calling some other Lorena, but then the source of the voice appeared around the side of the bench and looked down at her with a peeved expression.

"I've been calling you from like five feet away. Are you asleep or something, or just ignoring me?" Oscar Urias growled.

"I'm not ignoring you, Oscar. I just didn't hear you," she said innocently. What are you doing here anyway? I told you that I was going out with my friends after work tonight. Are you checking up on me?"

Oscar scowled at her. His facial expression and general appearance warned of danger ahead like a sign post in front of a collapsed bridge over a thousand-foot drop. He was of average height, but he made up for his stature with heavily muscled arms and shoulders, every inch of which were covered in intricate tattoos of a fanged snake slithering through a skull, a heart encircled with barbed wire, and various names and phrases in Old English lettering. A spider web covered part of his neck, with a bulbous spider suspended under his right ear. His head was shaved, and he wore a folded bandana tied low over his thick, black eyebrows.

"Lower your voice," Oscar barked. "Do you want everybody coming out of the restaurant to know our business? Come on, get in the truck. I want to talk to you." The small gathering of people waiting for the bus turned at the menacing tone of his voice and then looked quickly away, anxious to avoid drawing his attention.

"No, Oscar, I don't want to get in the truck", Lorena replied, but he was already walking away toward the parking lot, looking straight ahead, confident that she would be following along after him. She stayed on the bench and called out, "Like I said, I'm going home and changing my clothes and then I'm going out with my friends. We can talk tomorrow."

Lights flashed and a single honk came from a new-model king cab pick-up as Oscar pressed the remote to unlock the doors. "Just get over here and get in the god-damn truck," he shouted without looking back. When Lorena failed to appear at his command, he turned his head toward where she still sat on the bus bench and lowered his voice only slightly. "I'll give you a ride home," he said. After a pause, he added, "I just want to talk to you."

Lorena stood up and hesitated beside the bus stop. In the distance, the headlights of the city bus finally appeared. It would be easy to hop onboard and watch Oscar's face as the bus pulled out from the curb and took her away. She played the scenario out in her mind, then sighed and shook her head before turning her back on the bus and traversing the short distance to the truck where Oscar stood impatiently holding the passenger door open.

"Alright," she said. "I'll let you drive me home, and we can talk on the way." She hesitated before getting into the vehicle. Tilting her head up to look him straight in the eye, she added in a firm voice, "But I swear, Oscar, don't you start your shit tonight. I had a long shift and I don't want to get in another argument with you right now." She put a foot inside the door frame and hoisted herself up and into the seat. Oscar slammed the door shut behind her and walked around the front of the truck. He climbed into the driver's seat and started the engine.

They rode along in silence until they came to a red light. Oscar turned to face Lorena and picked up the conversation where it had left off, as though no time had passed since leaving the parking lot. "You're the one talking shit," he said. "I pick you up and offer to give you a ride but instead of being grateful, you're all pissed off and defensive. You sure sound like you've got something to hide to me."

"Oh my God, Oscar," Lorena answered wearily, raising her hands to her face to rub her eyes. "I really don't want to argue with you right now. I just want to go home and spend a little time with my girlfriends. I swear to God, I'm not hiding anything from you." She took a deep breath, let it out, and turned toward him. "What is it you wanted to talk to me about anyway?"

"I think it's time you moved out of that apartment," he said, looking intently at her to judge her reaction. "I don't like you living with another guy."

"Rich is *gay*! How many times do I have to tell you that? He has a boyfriend." She said the word "boyfriend" slowly and distinctly, as though speaking to a small child or someone with limited intelligence.

"Yeah, that's what you keep telling me, but where is this boyfriend, huh? I've been to your apartment a dozen times and I never see anybody but you and Muscle Man Rich. Are you sure about this so-called boyfriend?"

"Yes, of course I'm sure! I've met Lonny, and he's a really nice, sweet guy. Richie is totally crazy about him. Damn it, Oscar, you and I have been over this before, like a thousand times. I'm tired of it, and I'm tired of your accusations and your paranoia and all the rest of it. You treat me like a liar and a whore, and I haven't done anything wrong. Nothing! I go to work and then I go home, and every once in a while, I go out with my friends – my female friends – for a little fun. You're the only guy I talk to besides Richie. You scared away all my other male friends a long time ago. I'm sick of trying to convince you that I'm telling you the truth, so why don't you just pull over and let me out, huh? I'm done."

"You're done when I say you're done!" Oscar snapped, his eyes flashing. "We're going to talk about this right now, and you are going to come clean about what's really going on with your 'gay' roommate and his 'nice, sweet' boyfriend. Maybe you're doing both of them, eh? Is that why you don't want to move out of there? I've asked you over and over again to come stay with me, but you always say 'no'. Maybe you're afraid I'll catch you cheating on me with your gay boys. Is that it, Miss I'm So Innocent?"

"You are out of your fucking mind, Oscar. You really are." Lorena suddenly fell sideways and slammed her shoulder against the passenger door as the truck made an unexpected right turn. "Hey!" she cried. "What the hell?" She massaged her bruised arm and looked anxiously out the window at dark and unfamiliar streets. "Where are you taking me? This isn't the way to my apartment. What are you doing?"

Oscar ignored her and drove down several side roads, finally pulling over onto the shoulder of an empty frontage road beside the freeway overpass. "I told you, we need to talk, so we're going to stop right here where it's nice and quiet with no distractions, and we're going to talk."

"No! Where is this place? I don't like it here. Besides, I can't talk to you when you're like this. No matter what I say to you, you'll just turn it into an excuse to be angry. Please, just take me home now, or at least take me to a bus stop or a 7-Eleven or somewhere I can call for an Uber. It's too dark here. I don't feel safe."

"You don't feel safe? What is that supposed to mean? What are you afraid of – me?" Oscar glared at her, his dark eyes glinting red in the reflected light of the instrument panel.

Lorena broke eye contact and looked out the side window. In the distance, the headlights and taillights of vehicles passing on the freeway above looked like strings of Christmas lights, the kind with chasing lightbulbs. Lorena's father had hung up that kind of lights the Christmas before she left home for good and moved by herself all the way from Florida to Arizona.

She had been overflowing with hopes and dreams then. She would go to college and get a business degree. Then she would save up to start her own beauty salon catering to the needs of multiracial women like herself. Two years later, and here she was, struggling just to pay rent and take a few courses of community college each semester. At this rate, it would take five more years to graduate. Even worse, she was stuck in this dead-end relationship, knowing Oscar was bad for her, but too scared, ashamed, and maybe just too tired to leave him. What happened to that self-assured, independent girl, she wondered?

"You know what?" she said, still facing the window. "It's fine. I'll get out here and walk. I'm sorry, but we've had this same conversation before, too many times, and I'm just not in the mood to do it again. We had a good thing going for a while, but I've had enough of your controlling bullshit. It's not worth it anymore. Goodbye, Oscar."

Lorena grabbed her purse and pushed the door open. She jumped down from the truck to the gravel below and started walking in the direction she thought they had come in from, although she wasn't sure after the many turns they had made down dark side roads. She prayed that Oscar wouldn't follow her. She would rather take her chances alone on a strange road than deal with him when he was in one of his moods.

Oscar stood in the light of the open truck door and watched Lorena walk awkwardly in her platform sandals along the gravel road. She was going the wrong way, but it didn't matter. She wasn't going to get very far anyway. He let her walk on for a while, then caught up with her in a few quick strides.

"Where do you think you're going?" His voice was like ice. Lorena paused briefly, then quickened her pace. With a chuckle, he grabbed a hold of her arm and yanked it hard so that she fell back against his chest. He spoke into her ear, his lips so close that she could feel the spittle on her skin. "Get your ass back to the truck," he hissed. "I'm not done talking to you yet."

Lorena tried to pull her arm away, but he held fast. "No, I'm not going back to your fucking truck!" she said with a firmness that masked the growing fear she felt inside. "You know why? Because you actually are done talking to me. And I'm done too, for good this time. I have nothing else to say to you. Now, let go of my arm. I'm leaving." She tried again to pull her arm free and was opening her mouth to scream at him when she felt the first blow strike her face. Her head flew back, and she was looking up at the stars and the Christmas headlights and taillights on the freeway. Another blow hit her in the temple, and all the lights went dark.

2

Awakening

Minerva Short awoke suddenly from a dream that began with dozens of crows taking flight from a barren field and ended with the birds transforming into burning embers rising into a sky choked with ashes and smoke. Disoriented, she looked around at the unfamiliar room. Her pale eyes took in a number of objects made of sleek white-enameled metal or a dull gray alien substance like a hardened rubber, scattered around the room. All were sparkling with red, blue, and yellow lights, like something from the imagination of H.G. Wells. One such object extruded long worm-like tentacles toward a young woman who was lying asleep in a bed. The object made a continuous beeping sound that coincided with flashes of its multi-colored lights. Minerva shuddered and drew her shawl more tightly around her bony shoulders.

Tearing her gaze away from the futuristic machinery, Minerva quickly inspected the rest of the room and was surprised to find it quite bland, with white walls, a tiled floor, a simple straight-backed chair, and a modest night stand with a pitcher of water and a cup. On the side rail of the bed where the sleeping girl lay, near her left arm was a panel of buttons. Minerva peered at the buttons and was tempted to try pushing them to see what would happen but stifled the urge. She was not here to press buttons or play with machines.

Minerva took note of the needle taped to the girl's arm and the tubing snaking up to a bag of clear liquid hanging on a metal stand. She observed that small round disks were adhered to the girl's flesh and attached to the worm-like tubes coming from the alien machine. Some kind of medical equipment then, she concluded. It was certainly nothing she had ever seen before in any hospital she had visited during her lifetime. It had been many years since she was last inside a hospital, though, and much had changed since then.

Minerva bent over the bed for a closer look at the girl. The small patches of skin not covered in bandages were bruised and swollen, but in spite of her injuries, she was pretty in an exotic sort of way, with long red curls and skin the color of café au lait. She slept fitfully, as though dreaming disturbing dreams, and there was a sheen of perspiration on her forehead. Minerva lifted a corner of the bedsheet to dab the moisture from the girl's face as she moaned and muttered softly in her sleep.

Leaning forward so close that her beaky nose almost touched the girl's softly rounded one, Minerva opened her mouth and breathed into the bandaged face. Tendrils of gray vapor, like the smoke of a snuffed candle, were inhaled into the girl's nostrils. She choked and turned her head away. Suddenly, her eyes opened, and she gasped and tried to push herself up and away from the face hovering inches above her own.

The face was that of an extremely elderly woman. It was as wrinkled as a dried apple and so pale as to be nearly transparent. It was framed by long, charcoal gray hair, shot with thick streaks of white, pulled back in a severe bun and tucked beneath a wide-brimmed black hat. A veil of pointelle lace was pushed up over the brim of the hat to reveal a high forehead and startling silver eyes that seemed to burn with an inner fire.

Seeing the terrified look in the girl's eyes, the old woman smiled kindly and rose up to stand at the bedside with her hands folded politely in front of her. She stood tall and straight-backed, despite her obvious advanced age. She wore a long, dusty black dress that was at least a century out of fashion, with a high collar buttoned tightly around her throat. What little flesh was visible above the collar and below the lace-trimmed cuffs of her dress was unnaturally white and parched, like the crumbling veneer of an ancient and weathered clay statue. When she moved, small puffs of a powdery substance lifted briefly into the surrounding air and disappeared just as quickly as they settled back onto her form.

"Who are you? What are you doing here?" The girl attempted to shout, but her voice came out as a thin rasp. Her hands, encased in plaster casts to the elbow, grabbed at the bed sheet, but she lacked the strength to sit up or call for help. Her head swiveled franticly around the sterile hospital room in confusion, her brain still muddled from sleep and medication. She looked back at the old woman, still standing tranquilly at her bedside, and blinked rapidly to clear her vision. Besides being a complete stranger dressed like a character from Downton Abbey, there was something off about the old woman's appearance. She seemed to be standing in front of an almost imperceptible cloud of mist or smoke that softened and blurred her edges, so that her extremities faded into shadow and flickered in a swirl of fine gray points, like dust in a shaft of sunlight.

The old woman smiled, showing a set of horsey teeth nearly the same dull, ashen tone as her face. She patted the girl's hand, which still clutched at the white cotton bedsheet. Her touch was cool and dry. "I'm Minerva, my dear," she said gently, "and I must confess that I don't quite know what I'm doing here. Not yet anyway. But don't you worry, child," she said, patting her hand again. "I'm sure I'll figure it out. I always do."

****

Nurse Monique Green made her rounds on the hospital's fourth floor east wing without incident. It was a quiet night on the ward. Even elderly Mr. Preston, who had awakened the previous night with severe gastric distress after overindulging in two trays of Salisbury steak and creamed corn, was snoring peacefully. As she made her way to the end of the hall, her white rubber-soled clogs thudding dully on the tile floor, she noticed a drop in the temperature. The hallway had already been too cool for comfort, but the icy air that hit Monique in the face was like stepping into a walk-in freezer. Goosebumps rose on her skin. She shivered and rubbed her hands up and down her arms to warm them. "Drafty old place," she said. "It's a wonder we don't have more patients leaving here with pneumonia than coming in with it."

Monique paused in front of room E-414 and listened. She thought she had heard voices, or at least one voice, through the door, but that was highly unlikely. The patient in E-414 hadn't spoken a word since she was brought in two nights ago, broken and bleeding, by the paramedics. It couldn't be the TV either, because the girl hadn't been conscious except for fleeting moments since she arrived. Monique opened the door.

The patient was propped up on her elbows, her eyes wide and staring fixedly ahead at a point somewhere between the bed and the wall. She didn't react to the sound of the opening door, but continued to stare into nothingness. As Monique looked on, she nodded briefly, as though in answer to a question. She raised an arm with its white cast and shielded her face with it, then quickly drew it back. When Monique came across the room to her bedside and touched her arm, the patient startled and stared at her silently before glancing once more at the empty space over the nurse's shoulder. Monique turned to look behind her but saw nothing out of the ordinary and certainly no one else in the room.

"Is everything alright, honey?" Monique asked as she coaxed her patient gently back down onto her pillow. "Did you need something? I thought I heard you talking to someone." The girl said nothing, but turned her face toward Monique. Her hand shot out from the bedsheet, and her fingers grasped Monique's arm with unexpected strength, digging into the nurse's flesh. She opened her mouth to speak but no words came out. She glanced surreptitiously at the room beyond, and then her eyes seemed to become unfocused. Her grip loosened, and her lashes fluttered shut.

Monique checked the patient's vital signs and stayed a few extra minutes in the room, watching the girl's face to see if she was going to wake up again. When she was satisfied that the girl was sleeping soundly, Monique made a note on the chart at the foot of the bed. She lingered for a moment, worry lines pinched between her eyebrows. With one last look at the patient and around the otherwise uninhabited room, she walked out the door into the brightly lit hallway.

Minerva Short went with her.

3

Voices

"Spare change? Can you help a veteran who's down on his luck?" Bobby Crocker repeated the two questions on a continuous loop, triggered by any man, woman, or child passing within ten yards of his bus bench. He suspected he had uttered the questions at least once at the passage of a stray dog. Depending on the response or lack of one, they were followed up with, "Thank you, God bless", or "Have a nice day anyway". Sometimes the voices said far less polite things, but since no one could hear them but Bobby, that was alright.

Today's earnings had been slim. The sun had set at least a couple of hours ago, and there were few people still boarding or exiting buses and the nearby light rail trains at this time of night on a weekday. After a quick glance around him to make sure no one was watching, Bobby furtively removed a zippered sandwich bag from under his baseball cap and counted out three $1 bills and $3.25 in change. It was enough to get a meal from the value menu at one of the fast food joints down the street, but Bobby decided to save it instead. Maybe tomorrow, if it was a good day, he would end up with enough to buy a baggie of weed, or at least a couple of joints, from one of the high school kids who took this bus route to school. Weed tended to mellow the voices out, take the angry edge off of them. Alcohol had the opposite effect. It just pissed the voices off and made them louder and more agitated. Too bad, because alcohol is cheaper.

"Have a nice day anyway." Bobby got up from the bench, wincing at the sharp pain in his lower back from sitting in one place too long. His knees crackled and popped as he took the first steps toward the alley behind the nearby Dos Sombreros Mexican restaurant. "I'm getting too old for this shit," he muttered to himself while he kneaded the muscles in his back with his fists.

Dos Sombreros was very generous with their tortilla chips. The servers placed a heaping bowl of chips on each table, along with bowls of red and green salsas. Bobby wasn't sure if the salsa portions were too small or the chip portions too big, but the dumpsters behind the restaurant gave evidence of the quantity of chips left uneaten on the paying customers' tables. He only hoped the owners never caught on to this wasteful practice. He had filled his hollow stomach many times because of it.

The restaurant was still open, but business was slow, and the staff had already taken out the trash. The door to the kitchen was propped open with a rock to let some fresh air in, and the overlapping scents of roasted meat, fried tortillas, and sizzling fajitas wafting through the open door made Bobby's mouth water. After a quick glance to make sure no one was around, he moved quickly to the dumpsters and away from the light spilling out of the restaurant.

The trick was getting to the trash before it started to look and smell like trash. Opening the lid of the first dumpster, Bobby was pleased to find a Styrofoam container with half a burrito and leftover rice and beans. "God bless the forgetful," Bobby said to the container as he scooped up chips to add to his meal, squinting in the dim light from the open door to select only relatively clean-looking ones. He owed many a decent meal to diners who asked for a to-go box for their leftovers and then left it behind on the table.

Bobby slid silently into the deeper darkness behind the dumpster at the sound of voices coming through the open doorway. He peered around the side as two young women in festive Mexican tiered skirts and off-the-shoulder blouses came out and leaned against the wall. One lit up a cigarette and took a long drag, blowing out the smoke with a sigh of pleasure. "Why do you come out here, Lo?" she said, looking through squinted eyes at her companion, who had seated herself on an upturned bucket and was massaging her feet. "You don't even smoke".

"If I say I need a smoke break, Mr. Trujillo is like, 'Sure, go ahead'," the second girl replied. "If I say I just need a break, I get 'You already had your break. Get to work!'. I'm telling you, it's a case of discrimination against non-smokers."

The girl who was smoking chuckled and shoved a pack of menthols and a lighter into her skirt pocket. Mercy Olivares was shorter and heavier than her non-smoking friend, and she wore makeup that was artistically but thickly applied, like the work of an expressionist painter. Her friend Lorena wore very little makeup but still managed to look beautiful. It was reason enough to hate her guts, but she didn't. Under smoky eyelids in shades of mauve and charcoal, Mercy looked closely at Lorena through clumped black eyelashes. Her expression grew serious as she exhaled a small cloud of smoke.

"Lo, is everything okay?" she asked cautiously. "I mean, I know it isn't my business, but that bruise on your shoulder doesn't look like a hickey. And last night when you came in late, it looked like you had been crying."

Lorena seemed to freeze momentarily. She self-consciously pulled her blouse up to hide the bruise. "I'm fine," she said, still turned away from her friend. "I must have bumped into something. It's nothing."

"What about last night?" Mercy persisted. "You looked really upset. I wanted to talk to you, but we were so busy that I never got the chance."

Lorena turned to face her friend and gave her an irritated look. "You know what, Mercy? You're kind of nosy. And I say that as a friend."

There was a pause. In a quiet voice that Bobby had to lean forward to hear, Mercy said, "I know I'm nosy. And I know you were just kidding, so don't say anything. I'm just worried about you, that's all. I've been worried about you for a while, but I was afraid to say anything because you might get mad."

"Why are you worrying about me?" Lorena's voice had lost its flippant tone and her words were almost too soft for Bobby to make out.

"You know." Mercy said. She hesitated before saying more and watched her friend's face for a reaction. She took a deep breath and spoke rapidly as if to say her piece before either she lost her nerve or Lorena could cut her off. "It's that guy you're with. He's no good for you. Anybody could see that. I mean, even his own friends are afraid to piss him off! He's cold-blooded and hot-headed at the same time, and he's nothing but trouble. You might think you can change him, and I'm sure he does love you because, well, who wouldn't love you?" At this, Lorena smiled faintly, then lowered her eyes to stare at the ground.

"The thing is," Mercy continued breathlessly, afraid to give her friend an opening to argue with her. "Once a guy puts his hands on you, you have to know that it won't stop. He's just going to keep hurting you, and one day… Look, Lo, I'm serious. You're smart and beautiful and you don't need that macho asshole dragging you down, okay? There, I said it, and I won't regret saying it even if you get mad at me."

Mercy crossed her arms over her chest and looked defiantly at her friend. After a long silence with no response from Lorena, Mercy dropped her hands to her sides, and her expression changed. "Are you mad at me?" she asked.

"No, I'm not mad at you. Stop worrying about me. I'll be fine. I can take care of myself." Lorena leaned forward and gave Mercy a quick hug. "Come on, break's over. We need to get back inside before Mr. Trujillo comes out here and starts yelling at us about how much money we're costing him. You and I can *not* talk about this some more some other time." Bobby leaned back, away from the light, as the door creaked open and then slammed shut again, blocking out the sounds of Spanish pop music, the clinking of glasses, and the laughter of diners on their second or third Margarita.

Bobby stepped around the dumpster and leaned back against its rusted metal wall to chew thoughtfully on his burrito.

****

Francisco Alfonso Veracruz-DeLeon, once known to his friends as Al, leaned back against the seat of his two-toned 1972 El Camino, which rested on its hood at the side of the road, just beneath the Interstate-10 overpass. His eyes were closed. Dark stains were spattered across his clothes and one polished wingtip shoe. The other shoe was missing. Thick, wavy black hair and a coating of gelatinous gore hid a silver-dollar sized dent in his head, just above the hairline.

Al was not concerned about his head or his missing shoe, nor was he aware as he tapped his fingers rhythmically on the dashboard that his right arm was broken several inches above the wrist and lying at a right angle, giving him the appearance of having two elbows on one side. It didn't occur to him to wonder how he could be sitting in the driver's seat of an overturned car, in defiance of gravity. All of Al's attention was acutely and exclusively focused on his senses and what news they might bring him tonight.

He listened to the sounds of traffic passing overhead and tried to decide if anything felt different this time. Did the traffic maybe seem just a little farther away? Did his hands and feet feel just a little numb? He wriggled his fingers and toes. They felt pretty much the same as always. A truck horn blared, answered by the high-pitched beep of a compact car horn.

Al sighed and opened his eyes. He pushed the car door open and tumbled out into the dirt. Heaving himself up from the ground, he brushed away the debris from the backside of his acid-washed Jordache jeans with his good arm. Far above, white headlights and red taillights rushed past in a never-ending line. Al turned toward the lights and sounds of traffic and began climbing slowly up the incline toward the overpass. He scaled the concrete pillar with ease and soon was perched on the guard rail, eighteen feet above the ground.

As he had done each of the hundreds if not thousands of times that this scene had played out before, he bowed his head and said a prayer to the Virgin Mary to intercede for him. "Please, holy Mother of God, have mercy on me. Let my soul find rest. If not in heaven, then even hell would be better than this."

Al turned his back on the freeway and leaped from the guard rail. In the brief seconds of free fall before he hit the ground, he had one thought: *Please, just let me stay dead this time.*

4

Regrets

Minerva Short stood behind the nurse's shoulder as she typed, and watched the words appear as if by magic on a lighted glass screen in front of her. Minerva found this quite astonishing and would have been content to linger and watch this interesting new device at work, but she forced herself to focus on the task at hand. The future never ceased to amaze her, but duty called. In a stroke of good luck, the nurse paused to read notes about the admission through the emergency room of a 22-year-old woman found unconscious with multiple fractures, lacerations, contusions, and a severe concussion. Minerva read with her.

The young woman had arrived by ambulance after police were called by a dog-walker reporting an unknown female, unresponsive and bleeding, lying on the ground in a neighborhood park, concealed by some vegetation. She was fully dressed and still had her purse looped cross-body over her neck and shoulder with a wallet inside containing her ID, along with $34 and some change. Her phone, if she had one, was missing. According to the police report, although her clothes were torn and bloodied, she did not appear to have been sexually assaulted. She had, however, been brutally beaten and had broken bones in both wrists, her left humerus, and four ribs on her left side. She had received a massive blow to the head and had arrived at the hospital comatose.

She had since regained shallow and fleeting consciousness but had not spoken a word. The police had been by a couple of times to interview her, but thus far had been turned away empty-handed.

Nurse Monique Green's attention was drawn away from the screen by the arrival at the nurse's station of a young Asian woman holding the hand of a small boy. While the woman inquired about the room number of a Mr. Wu, the little boy stared at Minerva. Minerva stared back. The boy held up an Iron Man action figure like a talisman and gave her the scariest expression he could muster. Minerva held her hands to the sides of her face in mock terror and smiled at him. The boy giggled, and his mother turned to him and said, "What are you laughing at, silly boy?" He shrugged, and Minerva winked at him as his mother led him away down the corridor.

While the nurse directed the woman and child to Mr. Wu's room, Minerva continued reading the report on the computer screen. She took note of the girl's name, Lorena Cuevas, and her address. She observed that under "Emergency Contact", the record read, "Unknown – Patient unable to provide". Two days had gone by since the girl's admission to the hospital, and Minerva wondered why no one had been found yet to claim her as their daughter or sister or friend. "All alone in the world, are you, my dear?" Minerva whispered, close to the nurse's ear. Monique shivered and pulled her cardigan tighter across her chest. "Drafty old place," she said. "I'm probably coming down with pneumonia myself."

****

Rich Wright released a long sigh as he lowered himself into the steaming bathwater. He winced as his scraped knuckles hit the water. He leaned back and closed his eyes, listening to the pop of Calgon bubbles and breathing in the scent of lavender. Classical music played softly and soothingly in the background.

Despite the carefully choreographed ambiance, Rich was far from relaxed. The fight replayed in his mind like a video loop. He hadn't gone looking for a fight. He hadn't started it, not really, even if he *did* take the first punch. He had been defending Lonny, which was what he was supposed to do, right? How would it look if he had let that bastard Lance say those sick things about him in front of everyone in the locker room and not done anything? So, why did he feel so guilty?

Maybe he had punched a little harder than necessary. Maybe he could have – *should* have – ended the whole thing a lot sooner. Or maybe the uncomfortable truth was that he had enjoyed the pain he had inflicted on that prick. He had enjoyed it quite a lot. If Mike the Ass Kisser hadn't shown up, who knows how long he would have kept fighting. Probably until one of them was knocked out and couldn't fight anymore. What kind of person likes fighting that much? Some kind of sociopath? Is that what kind of person he really was?

Rich opened his eyes and looked at his reflection in the bathroom mirror. The face looking back at him was boyishly handsome despite the bruises blossoming in reds and purples across his nose and under his left eye. His carefully messy blond hair gave him an almost angelic quality. No one could tell by looking at that face that Rich Wright had enjoyed every single punch he had thrown, that he had relished in the blood and violence and pain, cleansing him of a portion of the years of repressed anger and shame. The naked truth was that if he had today to do over, he would do the very same thing again without hesitation. "Oh, Richie boy," he said to the face in the mirror. "You are so very fucked up."

Someone pounded on a door somewhere beyond the Bach and the bubbles and the noise of Rich's own thoughts. He lay back against the tub with his eyes closed and listened with detachment to the pounding, which paused briefly and then began anew. Finally, as the water began to cool, Rich pulled himself up from the bath and wrapped a towel around his waist.

****

Bobby Crocker's worldly possessions fit neatly into his old army rucksack which, along with his bedroll and collection of bottled water, he kept concealed in a ditch on undeveloped county land near the freeway. The bottled water came from people who didn't trust him not to spend their money on booze or dope, but who felt guilty enough to want to help keep him alive. They meant well, and having bottled water saved him a trip to the water spigot outside the 7-Eleven, so he was grateful and said, "Thank you. God bless," just as if they had given him money. If he was honest, though, he preferred money.

With a bellyful of Mexican food and a head full of voices clamoring for his attention, Bobby headed out of the bustle of downtown toward his ditch and his waiting bedroll. The sun's corona had already disappeared below the horizon, but the sky held a lingering gray light. The rising moon had been full two nights ago and was beginning to wane but was still bright enough to allow Bobby to carefully pick his way through the gravel and dried brush. He didn't like waiting until full dark, when even the lights of the nearby interstate weren't enough for him to find his way without risking twisting an ankle or stepping on a rattlesnake.

As he walked away from the bus bench and the street lamps just blinking on as twilight turned to darkness, he halfheartedly asked a few late evening pedestrians if they could spare change for a veteran down on his luck, but he knew from experience that people were even less likely to want to get near a homeless person after the sun went down. "Oh well," he sighed. "Tomorrow's another day."

"Fuck you," said the voice in his head.

"You too, and the horse you came in on," Bobby replied. A couple strolling past on their way to a late dinner heard him and crossed to the other side of the street.

On the opposite side of the overpass, less than a quarter of a mile from where Bobby added another water bottle to his collection and began to spread out his bedroll, Al DeLeon opened his eyes. Sighing heavily, he tumbled from the car and rose slowly to his feet. He grasped his dangling right hand with his left hand and bowed his head. "Holy Mother of God, have mercy..." Moments later, he wearily began to climb toward the lights and sounds of passing cars.

5

Distractions

"Richie! Richie! Come on, man, wake up and open this door!"

A crack appeared in the window blinds of the next-door apartment. A pair of faded gray eyes made larger than life by the thick lenses of tortoise shell-rimmed bifocals looked out from a wrinkled face and stared disapprovingly at the muscular, dark-skinned young man standing just outside Apartment 214. "Richie, seriously. You need to get your ass up and open this door before your charming neighbor lady calls the cops about the suspicious-looking Black man."

The door opened. Rich stood in the doorway with a towel wrapped around his waist and dripped water onto the welcome mat. The blinds in the opposite window opened wider, and the eyes moved to a better vantage point. "Are you going to let me in, or are you just going to stand there and give a free show to Mrs. Peeping Tom over there?" The visitor gestured toward the gaping blinds in the next-door window. The eyes withdrew, but the gap remained.

"Alright, alright, James, I guess you had better come in." Rich stepped back into the apartment and opened the door wider. In a nearby tree, a single crow settled silently onto a branch. Its beady black eyes tracked the movements of the two men on the landing.

"What took you so long coming to the door, and why haven't you answered your phone?" James asked as he followed Rich inside. "I've been trying to call you all morning."

"I was in the bathtub, obviously," Rich said, waving his hands over his wet body and towel for emphasis. "As for the phone, sorry about that. I had to drop it off to have the screen repaired yesterday. It got kind of messed up after practice. What are you doing here, anyway?"

"Your phone's not the only thing that got messed up after practice. Have you seen your face?"

"Ha, ha, very funny," Rich said, sounding more tired than amused.

"Look, I heard about what happened yesterday," James continued, "and I just wanted to check in with you, see how you're doing. When you didn't answer your phone, I got kind of worried and figured I would drop by, make sure you weren't dead. From the looks of you, it was a close call. Man, you've got bruises on top of your bruises."

Rich looked down at the black and blue blotches across his chest. "Ordinarily, I would be flattered that you're looking," he said with a wink, "but I think I'll go get dressed. Are you hungry? You can make yourself something out of the fridge if you are. I'll just be a minute."

Rich retreated to the bedroom, and James went into the kitchen and poked his head in the refrigerator. A pitcher of water was flanked by a neat row of protein shakes and a pair of plastic containers that seemed to hold pureed fruits and vegetables, but looked to James like someone had vomited into Tupperware. On the shelf below, more plastic containers held cut vegetables and mysterious lumps of something vaguely brown. "What is all this shit?" he asked loudly enough to be heard from the next room.

"What?" Rich's voice coming from the bedroom was muffled by the towel he was rubbing briskly over his hair.

"Nothing, Man. So listen, I heard about what happened. I felt kind of bad because I wasn't there. I mean, if I was, it would have gone a lot differently. My man Lance wouldn't still be walking around with all his teeth still in his ugly mouth, for one thing. And seriously, Richie, what the hell is this green shit in your fridge with the celery sticks? Is it supposed to be that color?"

"Green...? Oh! That's a pesto humus I found at Trader Jon's. It's not bad. They were out of the spicy humus that I usually get. And, don't worry, you couldn't have done anything about it anyway."

"About them being out of spicy humus?"

"No, you idiot, about me getting my ass kicked by that Neanderthal yesterday. It's been coming for a while. I shouldn't have let my guard down. It was stupid of me to let Lance get under my skin like that. I'm pretty sure he knew exactly what he was doing and that he was baiting me on purpose in front of everybody. Once he started challenging me, I couldn't just back down and look like a sissy."

"Man, you *are* a sissy. No offense."

"Yeah, okay, thanks for that. Anyway, what set me off was when he threatened Lonny. I didn't see that coming, and I guess I wasn't ready for it. I'm used to the name-calling, the innuendos, the keeping me at arm's length like I've got something contagious. I just had no idea he even knew about Lonny, and when he said he would "make that wetback scream 'no mas', well I just lost it. I even threw the first punch, which is probably exactly what he wanted."

"Is this brown thing meat?"

"What?" Rich stepped into the kitchen, tousling his blond hair to evenly distribute the marula oil hair product on his palms. He was dressed in pale blue shorts and a white tank top that showed his muscles and tanned skin to fine effect, or would have, if not for the bruises peeking out around the neckline. "No, it's tofurky. Like turkey, only it's tofu. Are you even listening to me?"

James emerged from the fridge, gripping a carton of almond milk. "Yeah, I'm listening. It's just that you have the scariest damn refrigerator I've ever seen in my life. I'm trying to imagine what it would be like to live on that stuff, and I just can't. Tell me you at least have some cereal."

"There's some muesli in the pantry. The bowls are in the cabinet over the sink."

James shook his head sadly as he poured himself a bowl and leaned over the kitchen counter to eat. "So, okay, I hear you. Lance pushed your buttons, and you reacted, and yeah, I'm sure that's exactly how he meant for that to go down. He isn't really a Neanderthal, you know. He just looks like one. He's smart enough to keep his grades up at least enough to keep his eligibility to play, right? But you have got to get a hold of that temper of yours. Just look at you, man. This isn't the first fight you've got yourself into, and you're starting to get a reputation as a hothead. You can't afford that label to get around, not if you want to have any chance at all of making pro."

"I know, I know..."

In the living room, just beyond the doorway to the kitchen, an orange tabby cat named Effie startled from her nap on the sofa and jumped to the floor. Hackles rose on the cat's back. She stared in the direction of the wall and let out a long hiss, then lowered her body to the floor and scooted backwards under the sofa. From her hiding place, she watched the creature that stood near the wall, like a shadow in the otherwise sunny room. It peered into the kitchen where Effie's male human and the other male human were talking. The creature looked like a human too, but it didn't smell like one.

The cat opened her mouth and engaged her Jacobson's organ to pick up any scent coming from the thing that wasn't a human. The odor of moistened grain and milk wafted in from the kitchen, along with the familiar scent of the human men. At first, it seemed that the creature in the room carried no scent at all, but then Effie picked up the faintest whiff coming from where it stood still quietly observing. The scent was almost imperceptible, but unmistakable. It was the essence of decay.

6

Hesitation

"Take care of yourself, Bro. Just try to keep a cool head and look humble when you meet with Coach, alright?" James held out his right hand. Instead of shaking it, Rich pulled him into a bear hug and squeezed him hard enough to push the air out of his lungs.

"I will. Thanks for checking on me. I appreciate your support, James. I really do."

James patted Rich awkwardly on the back and pulled himself out of his friend's embrace. "Don't get all mushy on me, Man. It's all good. I'll see you in practice, okay?"

"Yeah, if Coach doesn't kill me first, I'll be there."

"Alright, then. Say 'hi' to Lo-Lo for me. Tell her I'm still waiting for her to dump that loser and go out with me. Where is she anyway?" James leaned to the side to look past Rich's shoulders, as if expecting Lorena to be standing in the hallway eavesdropping.

"I assume she's still in bed," Rich said. "I haven't seen her. She must have come home pretty late last night, though, because I didn't hear her come in. I'll be sure to tell her you're still delusional, okay?"

James chuckled and turned to leave. Rich leaned out through the doorway and watched as he trotted down the stairs. "See you soon!", he called after him and then stepped back into the apartment and closed the door. Without his friend's constant banter, the apartment felt suddenly empty and quiet except for the ticking of the vintage Felix the Cat clock hanging on the kitchen wall. And there was one other sound – a low growl, barely perceptible, coming from the living room.

"Effie?" Rich walked into the room and looked around. There was no sign of the cat at first, but following the growling sound led him to peek under the sofa. A furry face stared wide-eyed up at him before retreating backward into a dark corner.

"Hey, Effie, what's up? What's wrong with you, huh? Here, kitty, kitty. Come on out of there, you little weirdo." Rich reached a hand under the sofa to coax the cat out and was rewarded with a hiss and a scratch to the wrist. With a string of curse words, he yanked his arm out, accidentally knocking his elbow into the sofa leg.

Rich rolled onto his back and uttered a longer, more emphatic string of curse words. Clutching his elbow and groaning, he lay on the floor with his eyes closed, waiting for the pain to subside. Without warning, a pair of cool hands touched his face and covered it with a soft material, like a knitted scarf. A body, too lightweight to be James sneaking back in to play some bizarre prank, knelt over his chest and held the material gently but firmly in place while pinning his arms to his sides with its knees.

"Lo?" Rich spoke in a muffled voice through the yarn pressing into his mouth. It tasted old and musty, like cast-off clothes stored in some long-forgotten trunk in an attic. "Ith-that you?" He tried to pull his arms free, but the legs encircling his torso pulled tighter, and he found himself unable to move. "Damn, guhl, 'ou're throng! 'Ave ou en urkig out?"

The only response was from the hands, which pressed down harder on the material and forced more of the yarn into his mouth so that he could no longer speak. It tasted moldy, and the smell, like an animal's carcass left to bake in the sun, triggered a gag reflex in his throat. The pressure against his teeth was painful, and it was getting harder to breath as more layers of the material were bunched together and concentrated on his nose and mouth. He began to see tiny white lights through his closed eyelids, and he felt himself drifting toward oblivion.

Putting aside his fear and confusion, Rich marshalled one last burst of energy and pushed outward with all his strength to free his arms, but it was like pushing against concrete. At the exact moment that he lost consciousness, an unearthly shriek, high-pitched and drawn out like a banshee's wail, pierced the air. To Rich, it was no more than a momentary ripple in the silence that carried him away from the living room floor of his apartment to places unknown.

****

Minerva was never one to hesitate when there was a job to be done. She took her work extremely seriously. After all, she was performing God's work, and what could be more serious than that? Yet, she *had* hesitated. She had held back from quickly dispatching the young man after his friend left him alone in the apartment, unaware of her presence. It would have been a matter of seconds to drive her fist into his chest until his heart ceased beating, or to come up behind him and throttle him with her bare hands, although admittedly he had an unusually large neck. Nonetheless, she had opted to slowly suffocate him with her shawl. It seemed ridiculous in hindsight. Still, had it not been for the cat, the man would be dead by now instead of just unconscious.

The cat. Minerva was quite embarrassed. Her mission on this mortal plane was a solitary one, and sometimes she missed the comfort of having someone to talk to, but today she was grateful that there had not been an audience to see her leap up and squeal like a 12-year-old girl when the blasted cat shot out from under the sofa with an ear-splitting scream loud enough to wake the… Perhaps not the best metaphor.

She looked down upon the unconscious man on the floor and wrung her hands together over her chest in a nervous gesture habitual to her since adolescence. As she watched him breathing slowly and evenly without the encumbrance of the shawl, which she had removed from his face and tied neatly back around her own shoulders, she pondered where her uncertainty might be coming from. He was the obvious suspect, after all. The girl in the hospital's address led her to this apartment, where this man clearly also lived. He was certainly big and strong enough to have inflicted her injuries, and he had injuries of his own – bruises and scrapes that could have come from a young woman defending herself, fighting for her life against the beating he gave her.

But what about the conversation between this man and his visitor? It had sounded like they were talking about a run-of-the-mill fist fight between men, not a brutal attack on a young woman. Names were mentioned: Lance, Lonny, Lo-Lo. Had she misheard, or had they been referring to Lorena Cuevas, the girl in the hospital bed, by some other name? Minerva frowned. She had made mistakes in the past. Not often, but enough to know that mistakes have consequences.

She needed time to think before taking further action. The big man on the floor would keep for now. It was imperative to get this right. A young woman's life was at stake. She left the man where he lay and glided through the apartment wall onto the balcony, where she sat down on a folding chair with a cracked and faded vinyl seat. A ray of sunlight fell through her insubstantial body. It failed to warm her cold fingers which twisted together absently in her lap.

She leaned back in the chair and closed her eyes. She had always found a little nap quite conducive to problem-solving. Almost immediately, she drifted into a dream state of velvety darkness, broken by images and voices from the past and the future, carried on a puff of smoke to brush the old woman's awareness with a warm caress. Minerva dreamed of another time and place when there had been consequences, some unintended, from her swift justice. A smile twitched briefly on her pale lips as she dozed. Not all unintended consequences were to be dreaded, she thought through her dream haze. Who but God could say if a man struck by a stray bullet might have deserved it more than the man at whom the shot was aimed?

7

Mistakes

Minerva awoke to the sound of a train whistle. She brushed an accumulation of snow off her shoulders and wide-brimmed hat before looking around to get her bearings. It was nighttime, and a three-quarter moon shown down on the blanket of snow covering the ground, reflecting off ice crystals on the cleared roads like ghost lights. Gas lamps behind the bench where she sat illuminated a train station with a weathered sign that read "Morgan Park". Before her, railroad tracks ran parallel to the station and were visible as black horizontal lines against the pale snow. A train had just departed from the station, leaving a cloud of steam in its wake, a denser darkness against the moonlit night.

"Morgan Park," Minerva said thoughtfully to herself. "It sounds a bit familiar. Cleveland? No, no, not Cleveland. Syracuse? No... Oh, I think I have it. Chicago!" She clapped her hands together in triumph and smiled. "Yes, I'm fairly certain this is a Chicago station. A rather picturesque part of the city, but not without its troubles, if memory serves. There doesn't seem to be much going on at the moment, however. Oh well!" she said lightly with a shrug of her shoulders. "I'm here, so there must be a reason."

Minerva folded her hands on her lap, leaned back against the bench, and waited. In the eastern sky, the night slowly but inexorably gave

33

way to day as the warm glow of the sun began to rise over the horizon. Minerva took no notice of the cold or the fresh snow piling up on the brim of her hat. She would remain where she sat, unmoving and unperturbed by time or weather, untouched by hunger or thirst, until more was revealed. She had always been a patient woman.

****

Lucius Brown stamped his feet to get the blood flowing. It was cold enough inside his small apartment to see the mist of his breath with each exhalation, despite the small coal fire he permitted himself in the early morning hours. Lucius was used to the cold. His job delivering blocks of ice to restaurants and fish markets all over town required a pre-dawn start in all kinds of weather. Between the icy streets and the ice he carried, Lucius was cold most of the time, but he didn't mind. The work was steady and put food on the table, and he was grateful for it.

He whistled a tune as he carefully poured strong coffee into a thermos which he placed in a battered metal lunch bucket, along with two salted pork and cheese sandwiches wrapped in waxed paper. Still whistling, he pulled on his hat and coat and a pair of oiled leather gloves and went out the door, breathing in the brisk, biting air of the dawning day.

To make the three-mile journey to the ice house to pick up his wares and his schedule of deliveries for the morning, Lucius did not have the luxury of an automobile. Instead, he piloted an old but lovingly maintained bicycle with a custom-made (by Lucius Brown himself) trailer hitched to the back. He opened the door of the trailer, which was essentially an oversized wooden crate mounted on a metal frame, and strapped his lunch bucket onto a small shelf designed for that purpose. Stenciled onto the door in bright blue paint were the words, "Brown Ice Delivery". A hasty freehand addition in black paint of an apostrophe and the letter "s" after "Brown" bore witness to the unfortunate misinterpretation of the business's original name by a number of customers.

The sun was just peeking above the horizon when Lucius reached the West Side Ice Company. He peddled around to the back of the building where the steel door was raised in anticipation of the deliverymen's arrival. A burly red-haired man with flannel sleeves rolled up over freckled forearms waited, oblivious to the cold, smoking tobacco from a small pipe and squinting through the pungent smoke into the distance.

At the sight of the bicycle-drawn cart coming around the side of the building, the man waved impatiently for the rider to approach the ramp leading up to the doorway. "Good mornin', Mr. McLeery!" Lucius called out as he peddled up the alleyway.

"And what is good about it, eh, Lucius?" McLeery replied with a distinctive Irish brogue. "Is it a good morning when half of my deliverymen report with the influenza, Lucius? And me with orders from two new customers starting this very day. What is good about that then, I ask you?" McLeery folded his beefy arms across his chest and glared down at Lucius as if he had directly and maliciously brought the flu upon his fellow deliverymen.

"I'm very sorry to hear that, Mr. McLeery. I hope everyone is going to be okay..."

"May the cat eat every one of them, and the Devil eat the cat!" McLeery turned his back and headed through the open doorway. Not having a suitable response to that pronouncement, Lucius smiled weakly and pumped his legs to bring the bicycle and trailer up the creaky ramp and inside the warehouse for loading.

Several minutes later, Lucius emerged from the warehouse into the dawning day with a loaded trailer and a troubled mind. He wheeled carefully down the ramp and onto the pavement, feeling the additional weight of the double load of ice. Under other circumstances, he would have been thankful and pleased to have the extra work, which would result in extra pay and better meals over the coming week, maybe even the rare indulgence of a beef roast (just a small one, of course – Lucius was not an extravagant man). Today, however, Lucius found himself tempted to stop the other delivery man – a skinny white kid who looked about 13, who was just now making his way to the ramp and the waiting scowl of McLeery – and offer him part of his day's assignments.

Instead, he silently watched the boy ascend the ramp, his young, strong legs pumping to pull the weight of his own handmade cart up the incline.

Lucius shrugged, turned his back on the warehouse, and began peddling his way towards the business district.

****

Billows of steam arose from the waiting train and mixed with the cold air to produce miniature clouds that floated briefly above the tracks before dissipating into the chilly morning air. From her perch on the snow-covered bench, Minerva peered intently through the clouds of steam at each passenger as he or she disembarked and crossed the deck, slippery with muddy, half-melted slush, toward the station doors. Most were business men in suits, heavy overcoats, and hats, with just their begloved hands and faces visible, their cold-nipped noses stuck in outspread newspapers or leaning over pocket watches as they trotted into the station.

A few solitary women stepped carefully down from the train. They too were dressed for business, in modest dark wool skirt suits, hats, and gloves. They watched the ground in front of their feet as they walked across the icy platform to avoid slipping on their slick-soled pumps and boots. One woman, an elderly lady in an enormous coat that overwhelmed her short, plump frame and nearly tripped her as she descended to the platform with a helping hand from the conductor, briefly arrested Minerva's attention. The woman had tears streaming down her face, but then began to smile widely and hurry her pace toward the station. Waiting there was a much younger woman with the same bushy hair and stocky stature. She and her two small children waved as the elderly woman approached and then broke into a run to meet her halfway. By the time they embraced in the middle of the platform, Minerva had lost interest and was looking in another direction, searching the thinning crowd with a discerning eye.

Nearly last to exit the train was a couple who were in mid-argument as they disembarked, wrestling each other for control of a large suitcase. The woman looked younger by at least a decade, but her face was drawn, pale, and prematurely aged with worry lines around her eyes and thin lips. She wore a shabby lightweight coat with a ratty fur collar over a summery floral dress, and she held a handbag and a train case in one hand while pulling on the handle of the large suitcase with the other. The man was florid-faced and paunchy, and his pin-striped suit was shiny with age and tight around his middle, the buttons straining to hold against the press of his girth as he hefted a duffle bag over one shoulder. The man was attempting to yank the large suitcase away from the woman, but his efforts pulled him off balance and caused him to stumble and nearly fall to the floor.

"Give it to me, damn it!" he hissed loud enough to turn the heads of several other passengers making their way across the platform.

"Edgar, please!", the woman said pleadingly, lowering her voice as if to make up for his much louder one. "Just let me get it. You've been drinking since we left St. Louis, and you're none too steady on your feet. I just want to get inside without making a scene. Can't you see that people are staring at us?"

Without hesitation, the man slapped the woman hard across her face, throwing her head back and causing her to fall backwards over the suitcase into a puddle of dirty slush. Her train case and handbag clattered to the ground as her arms flew out to the side. She quickly leapt back up and held a trembling hand to her reddened cheek. Intensely aware of the disapproving glances of the people milling around on the station platform, her eyes filled with tears, and she brushed ineffectually at her soiled clothes.

"Shut up, woman!" the man brayed in a slurred voice. "Make a scene? I'll make a scene, you stupid bitch. I should have left you in that seedy shithole of a town where I found you, you worthless whore!" He paused long enough to notice the shocked expressions and scandalized mutterings among the spectators. "What are you looking at?" Spittle shot from his lips as he shouted and swayed drunkenly, legs widespread to hold himself upright.

He turned back to the woman and said in an only slightly lowered voice, "Now, pick up that shit and go inside and look for a newsstand, if you can handle that. I want a copy of the *Times*, and a race schedule, if they've got one. There might be just enough time to play the ponies before the next train. And I told you I've got this suitcase, so just leave it, will you?"

The woman gathered up her small baggage and turned without a word, her head bowed and her hand covering her face as she walked as quickly as she could toward the station door. He watched her go, still swearing under his breath, with his back turned to the suitcase and the now-departing train.

Minerva silently arose from the bench and walked up behind the man. She lifted the suitcase effortlessly and tossed it onto the train tracks, then turned and casually tapped the man on the shoulder. He pivoted, ready for a confrontation, then looked around, confused. When he realized his suitcase was missing, he balled his fists and scanned the area. "Alright, who's the joker? Somebody must want their ass kicked… Come on, get back over…" Edgar stopped in mid-snarl as he looked down from the platform and saw the suitcase lying there, only a few yards from the train building up steam as it pulled away from the station. He turned away from the tracks and opened his mouth to should for help, but then froze. His jaw dropped, and he uttered a whimper, too soft for anyone to hear.

Inches from his face stood a hideous corpse dressed in a tattered, old-fashioned black dress. Its face was little more than a skull, with withered chunks of desiccated flesh clinging to the forehead and cheeks. A flap of skin, yellowed and dry as parchment, dangled from the bony chin. The eyes and nose were gone, revealing deep black sockets. On its head were patches of charred flesh covered with clumps of stringy gray hair tucked obscenely under a jaunty feathered hat. Worst of all, the mouth had no lips but yet seemed to be smiling, a slow, triumphant smile.

The man took a step backwards, then another, still whimpering. He held his hands up in front of his face to block the sight of the horror standing before him. The smiling corpse slowly advanced, matching Edgar step for step, driving him back with raised bony hands protruding from rotted lace cuffs. He could smell her rank breath as she opened her mouth wide and exhaled a foul smoke into his face through unhinged jaws. He choked on the taste of ashes and soot and tried to take another step back, but his foot found no purchase. His center of balance shifted backwards. With a cry of terror, he stumbled over the edge of the platform onto the tracks and into the path of the oncoming train. The train was not yet moving quickly, but its weight and momentum prevented it from stopping in time to avoid running over the man who had suddenly appeared in its path. As the engineer looked on in horror, the train's cow-catcher knocked the man over onto the tracks, and the locomotive rolled slowly over his body, crushing the life from him. Edgar had plenty time to scream before his throat was flattened under a wheel.

The train ground to a halt. On the side facing the platform, a pair of legs in pin-striped trousers stuck out from beneath the wheels. One leg slowly toppled over and slid from its trouser leg to rest its toes in a pool of blood and snow, like a timid bather testing the water before a swim. Before the body had time to stop twitching, a crow, and then another, landed on the tracks. The first hopped onto the tip of a scuffed leather boot and began to pluck at the shoe laces. The other stepped lightly over the trouser-less leg and pecked at the edge of the torn limb, pulling off bits of flesh. On the opposite side of the train, the head of the former Edgar rolled briskly away from the tracks, down a hill, and into a snow bank, where it would remain until the Spring thaw.

The people on the platform gasped and screamed in alarm and ran to look over the edge at the body below. Those who had already entered the station came pouring back out to see what the commotion was all about. Among them, pushing through to the front of the crowd was the young woman in the floral dress. Upon reaching the platform edge, she looked down at the crushed remains of her husband and fell to her knees. She covered her eyes with her hands and began to rock back and forth, wailing in shock and grief.

Minerva observed the young woman's anguish with a mixture of annoyance, disappointment, and resignation. Too often, those she saved from exploitation and abuse resisted being freed from their oppressors. Over the rolling decades of her existence, she had puzzled over this, trying to understand the complexities of human love. She had been human once. Had there been a time when she had loved selflessly, without judgment or logic? If there had been such a time, she couldn't remember it now. It didn't matter. What mattered – the only thing that mattered – was bringing justice: punishing those who would do evil and protecting the innocent, even though the innocent were rarely grateful for her efforts.

With a sigh and a shake of her head, Minerva returned to her bench and sat down. She tidied her skirt and clasped her hands primly on her lap, then leaned her head back and closed her eyes.

****

"See you next time, Lucius!" the fragrant fishmonger called out as he waved cheerfully toward Lucius Brown's departing delivery cycle before returning to artistically arranging perch, bass, catfish, salmon, and other fishes great and small on their bed of ice. Lucius waved back over his shoulder and smiled. Turning to face the road ahead, Lucius's smile quickly faded. Sighing deeply, he glanced at his delivery schedule, weighted down by a small river rock in his bicycle basket. Each location had a black check mark in grease pencil next to the address – all but two. Lucius had checked off each delivery of ice to local businesses, mostly familiar locations like the fish market. Only two items on the list were for places where Lucius had never before delivered ice. Lucius didn't think they were the new customers that Mr. McLeery had mentioned. They were most likely established customers usually handled by other delivery men. Other *white* delivery men.

Earlier in the morning, just after he left Mr. McLeery's warehouse, Lucius had decided that he would get those two deliveries out of the way first. The two locations were close to one another, just across the railroad tracks in west Morgan Park. One was an inn that served breakfast and lunch in a small attached restaurant. The other, across the street and a couple of doors down, was a sweet shop that sold ice cream along with a wide variety of candy and homemade fudge. Lucius had never visited either establishment. For one thing, he had neither the time, the money, nor the inclination to buy sweets or eat a meal in a fancy restaurant. For another, black folks in general were rarely seen and not very welcome on the streets and in the businesses of the upper middle-class white neighborhood of west Morgan Park.

It wasn't that black folks weren't *allowed* to be there. There was no law against it, and Lucius didn't expect to be questioned by the police or any trouble of that sort. No, it was more that black folks just didn't have any business to be there, and they tended to stick out like the proverbial sore thumb. On the rare occasions when Lucius had found himself in that part of town, he had experienced the uncomfortable feeling of eyes staring at the back of his head, and people whispering about him as they looked disdainfully at his dark skin and shabby working man's clothes.

Lucius told himself that maybe it was just his imagination. After all, he thought charitably, it isn't often that rich white folks laid eyes on someone like him, unless they were shining their shoes or digging their sewage ditches. They certainly didn't expect to see a black man riding around in their neighborhood like he belonged there. He tried to take their uneasy stares in stride, but it still made his skin crawl, and he would rather make twenty other deliveries in familiar territory up steep hills and over icy roads than make even one delivery in west Morgan Park.

He decided he would hit the inn first. He figured that since they opened for breakfast, they might need their ice earlier than the sweet shop, which didn't open for customers until eleven o'clock. Lucius checked the address on his list and pedaled a couple of blocks farther before turning right into a narrow alley that serviced the businesses on the streets to either side. The sun had risen above the horizon, and the sky was beginning to brighten into day, but the rows of buildings kept the alley in shadow. Drifts of dirty gray snow and half-melted ice crunched under the wheels of Lucius's delivery cycle as he made his way carefully in the semi-dark toward the back entrance to the inn.

He spotted the inn's delivery dock and parked his ice wagon close to the painted metal doors. He knocked firmly, and after a few minutes, the right-hand side door was opened by a stocky middle-aged white woman in a starched housekeeping uniform. Her graying blonde hair was pulled back severely from her round face into a tight braid that was coiled and stuffed under a white cap. Ruddy patches on her cheeks failed to give her a cheerful appearance due to the stern set of her mouth and the suspicious look in her small eyes. The name "Angelique" was embroidered onto the right breast pocket of her blouse.

Angelique gave Lucius a quick once-over, then frowned with obvious displeasure at what she saw. "What do you want?" she said in the gravelly voice of a chain smoker.

Lucius was immediately reminded of his landlady, Mrs. Stanton. All of her tenants secretly referred to her as "Mrs. Satan" because she was mean as a snake and smelled like the sulfur matches she used to light the tiny brown cigars she smoked constantly. Lucius was so struck by the resemblance that he stood there with his mouth hanging open and a blank look on his face until she spoke again.

"Well, what is it then?" Angelique growled. "We're not handing out food or drink to hobos, so you can just go bother somebody else if you haven't got any business here." She took a step back and began to pull the door closed.

"Wait!" Lucius snapped out of his momentary trance just in time. "Please! I'm sorry, Mrs. Stanton. I mean, I'm sorry Miss…um…Angelique. I've come here with your ice delivery. Your regular man is out today with the influenza, so they sent me in his place. If you can show me where you want it, I'll bring your ice in for you."

Angelique's frown never wavered, but she stepped aside and permitted Lucius to unload the ice from his trailer and follow her into the inn's kitchen area where he filled the ice box under her critical eye. Not another word was spoken between them, and when Lucius exited the inn and heard the door close and latch behind him, he breathed a sigh of relief. "One down, one to go," he said as he checked off the box next to "Beverly Inn" on his list with a flourish of his grease pencil.

Lucius remounted his bicycle and pedaled toward his final delivery destination, just ahead and across the alley. He was looking straight in front of him and humming softly to himself when he thought he heard a sound coming from the opposite side of the alley. He stopped pedaling and held very still to listen. There it was again: low and rhythmic, like someone crying. It was a woman's voice, and she was sobbing as though her heart had been ripped asunder.

Lucius peered into the shadows, squinting to see where the sound could be coming from. "Hello? Is anyone there?" he said. The sobbing sound stopped abruptly. Still straining to see anything in the darkened alley, Lucius said in a louder but still gentle voice, "It's okay, Miss, I didn't mean to scare you. Are you okay? Is there anything I can do? Tell me where you are, Miss, so I can go over and talk to you."

The figure of a woman arose from a wooden stair leading up to the back door of one of the businesses lining the alley. She was dressed all in black, which had helped to conceal her in the gloom. As she took a step forward, Lucius caught the motion out of the corner of his eye and turned in her direction. She raised a handkerchief to her face and moved into the light. "I'm right here," she said.

8

Second Chances

Rich felt a heavy weight pressing down on his lungs. As he regained consciousness, the memory of suffocating came rushing back, and he heaved his body up from the floor in a panic, gasping and taking in huge gulps of air. The cat that had been sleeping on his chest was sent flying across the room. She rose to her feet with affronted dignity and stalked behind the TV stand.

"Lorena?" he called out. "Are you still here?" Rich was alone in the living room, and the apartment was silent except for the ticking of the clock. He remembered the hands pressing the foul yarn into his nose and mouth and almost wretched again. He felt more surprised and confused than angry at Lorena's behavior. He wanted to know why she had tried to suffocate him, of course, but even more he wanted to know how in hell a hundred-pound girl like her had been able to subdue him like that. If she was taking some kind of martial arts self-defense class, he wanted in. Those were some effective moves she had, for sure.

He got up from the floor and walked down the corridor to stand outside the closed door to Lorena's bedroom. "Hey, Lo, are you in there?" There was no answer. He knocked on the door. "Lorena?" Still no answer. She must have left while he was still passed out on the floor. It just didn't make sense. He thought about calling her, but then remembered that his phone was still sitting in the repair shop. He would have to wait until she got home from work to ask her what this insanity was all about. In the meantime, he had other business to attend to.

Rich slipped on his boat shoes, grabbed his car keys, and headed out the door. On the balcony, the sound of the door slamming shut went unheard by the old woman dozing in the chair. She dreamed on.

****

Minerva opened her eyes to the sight of train tracks against a landscape of patchy, yellowing snow. With a twinge of alarm, she looked around her at the platform, the station, and the brightly painted "Morgan Park Station" sign. The sun had risen above the rooftops of the town and was shining down in cheerful rays over the gathering of police officers and railway officials talking with one another and scribbling on clipboards. A teenage boy in a thin canvas jacket whistled a tune as he attempted to clear away the remaining debris around the tracks. He turned over the gravel and earth to cover the red-black stains that marked the spot where Edgar had breathed his last.

"Oh dear," Minerva said, wringing her hands nervously in front of her. "And I was so sure."

A few blocks away, Lucius Brown dismounted from his bicycle and walked slowly toward the figure in black. "Miss?" he said gently. "Are you alright? Do you need help?" A woman with milk pale skin, made more pallid by the contrast with her cropped black hair and black dress, approached cautiously from the shadows. She was young, in her late teens or early twenties, and her cheeks were red and blotchy from crying. She blew her nose into her handkerchief and, snuffling a last sob, regarded Lucius with big brown eyes rimmed with thick black lashes, glistening with tears.

"Who are you?" she said in a quavering voice.

"Oh, Miss, I'm not anybody. I'm just the ice man. My name is Lucius Brown. You can call me Lucius." He reached out a hand to shake hers, but stopped himself when she startled and took a step back. He raised both hands, palms outward, and leaned away from her.

"I'm sorry, Miss," he said gently. "I didn't mean to scare you. I heard you crying, and I thought I should make sure you weren't in need of some assistance. I'll be on my way now, but if you don't mind me saying so, Miss, I think you might want to go back inside. It's not safe for a young lady to be out alone in a dark alley, even in a nice neighborhood like this one. You don't need to worry about me, I'm harmless enough, but there are evil people in this world, just waiting for a chance to take advantage of an innocent young lady like yourself."

The woman's face underwent a transformation. With tears still glistening in her eyes, her cheeks flushed, her lips twisted from a frown to a half-smile, and a hoarse laugh erupted from her mouth, followed by a flood of giggling, bordering on hysteria. As Lucius looked on in confusion, she took a few deep breaths to steady herself and wiped the tears from her eyes with a silk handkerchief she pulled from the neckline of her dress. "Innocent young lady!" she said with a final chuckle. "That's actually funny. Thank you, Sir, for giving me a good laugh. God knows I haven't laughed much lately."

Lucius hesitated, unsure of how to respond. Whatever had made the young woman cry as though her heart was breaking, she seemed better now, and really, it was none of his business. He couldn't have explained exactly why he felt this way, but his instincts were telling him to flee this place and this emotional white woman before something happened. Something bad. With a tip of his hat and a bob of his head, he began stepping backwards toward where he had left his bicycle and wagon across the alley.

"Wait, don't go yet!" the woman said. "You said your name is Lucius. Is that right?

"Yes, Miss. Lucius Brown. Pleased to meet you." He tipped his hat again and smiled, but sneaked a quick glance toward his bicycle. It took all of his strength not to make a run for it. All he wanted was to get on with his last delivery and get out of this neighborhood. While his face was turned away for only a second, she darted forward and grabbed his hand. She shook it and then held on to it with both of hers.

"Hello, Lucius! I'm Lucía Margiata. My friends call me Lucy. This might sound strange, but I was praying just now for a sign from God – anything to tell me what I should do. I'm in some terrible trouble right now, you see. Anyway, then you came along with a name so close to mine. Lucius, Lucía – what are the chances? I don't believe in coincidences, so you must have come in answer to my prayer. Won't you come over and sit down with me for a minute or two?" She turned and started walking up the steps, still holding onto Lucius's hand. She didn't give him a backward glance to see if he would follow.

As Lucy pulled him along behind her, Lucius looked to the left and to the right to see if there were any witnesses to this encounter. He dared not think what would happen if someone saw him there in the dim alley, holding hands with a pretty, young white woman. He had heard all about the lynching of black men that went on down South for crimes as innocent as speaking to a white woman the wrong way. He wistfully pictured himself getting back on his bicycle and pedaling away as fast he could, his last ice delivery be damned, but before he knew what he was doing, he had followed the young woman up the steps where she was now seated.

"Is there something I can do for you, Miss?" he asked nervously.

"It's Lucy", she said. "You can listen if you have the time, Lucius. I could use someone to talk to right now. Would you like to sit down?"

"No, Miss Lucy, I'm fine to stand. I would be more than happy to listen to what's troubling you and to help if I can," he said, his character and upbringing overcoming his fear.

"I can tell you're a nice man, Lucius. You have kind eyes. And it's just Lucy, not Miss, okay?" Lucius nodded and shuffled his feet nervously while stealing a quick glance around. Still no one else out and about, which was a relief. Lucy continued, pointing with her thumb to the building behind her. "This is my father's restaurant – *Mangi Margiata*. Homemade pasta and the best marinara sauce outside of Sicily. We're Italian, obviously." She smiled weakly. "It's just my father and me now. My mother passed away two years ago. She had a bad heart. My father was always protective of his only child, his baby girl, but since Mama passed away, he's been more like a jailer than a father. I'm a grown woman now. I turned 21 in August, and I want to go out with friends and dance and meet people." Her voice was becoming stronger and somewhat petulant. She looked dreamily into the distance as she spoke. Lucius wondered if she even remembered he was there. As she went on with her story, he had to quell a strong urge to sneak back to his bicycle and creep away.

"There's a dance club on 5th, near the bank but on the other side of the street. It's called 'The Sophisticated Feline'. They play all the new sounds there, like jazz music. I absolutely love jazz! Do you know the place, Lucius?" Her eyes flicked briefly in his direction, nearly catching him looking for an escape route.

Lucius shook his head, "No, Miss. I mean, no Lucy. I'm not from around here."

"Oh. Well, never mind. It's not important. A couple of months ago, I was at The Feline with some friends – Papa thought I was helping out at St. Mary's to get ready for the annual rummage sale – and I met the most wonderful man." A smile lit up Lucy's face, transforming it from splotchy to luminous. Lucius began to see how a face like hers, framed by her modern, short bobbed hairstyle, could get a girl into all sorts of trouble.

Lucy went on, looking off into the distance as she pictured the scene. "He was so handsome and exciting, and so talented too. He played saxophone for the jazz band."

Alarm bells began ringing in Lucius's head. "He was in the band?" he asked quietly.

"Oh yes, and he played so beautifully that I couldn't keep my eyes off of him. I hardly danced or talked to my friends all night. I just sat there watching him play. He saw me looking at him too, and then he started looking into my eyes while he played, as if he was playing only for me." She sighed deeply and touched her crumpled hankie to her eyes. "I wanted to talk to him that night, but I was afraid my friends would talk and it would get back to Papa, so I waited until I could go back another night on my own. I was so worried that I would get there and a new band would be playing and I would never see him again, but when I walked in The Feline the next time, there he was, looking even more handsome than the first time I saw him. He spotted me right away too, and he smiled at me and winked. It gave me a thrill like I've never felt before."

Lucius was feeling warm around the collar, despite the cold morning. He pulled at his collar and shifted from one foot to the other. Lucy took no notice of his growing discomfort. "I waited until the band finished their last set for the night, and then I slipped through the door that leads to backstage. There is a space there where performers store their gear and a couple of small offices used as dressing rooms. I walked right in like I belonged there, and no one tried to stop me.

"Now, don't think badly of me, Lucius! I know that a nice girl shouldn't chase after a man like that, but what else could I do? He wasn't likely to come out and talk to me in front of the other people in the club, and I just had to meet him!" Lucius smiled politely and opened his mouth to say that he was no one to judge her, but she wasn't looking at him and went on, speaking more rapidly in her excitement at the memory of her romantic encounter.

"He was waiting for me backstage, just like he already knew to expect me. We went into one of the dressing rooms and talked until the club closed, then he gave me a ride home. I sneaked in through a window so my Papa wouldn't know I was out so late. Nothing happened that first night. Joshua was a complete gentleman. That's his name, by the way – Joshua. I started sneaking out and going to the club every chance I got, and Joshua and I began meeting up at coffee shops and other places far enough away where no one would be likely to recognize me.

"I could listen to him talk for hours about his music and the places he has traveled with the band. They're from Louisiana originally. Not New Orleans, but somewhere a ways north of there, someplace I'd never heard of. Anyway, we would meet whenever we could, and he would talk about his life, and I would talk about mine. I told him about my mother dying and about how hard it was on both my father and me.

One evening, we were talking like that, and I think I had started to cry a little, thinking about my poor Mama, and Joshua reached out to comfort me. Before I knew it, we were in each other's arms. He told me he loved me that night, and I realized I was in love with him too." Lucy paused, and the tears began to well up again in her eyes as she gazed into the distance and the memories played in her head.

"Miss Lucy?" Lucius asked softly. "Can I ask you a question that you might take as offensive?"

She turned to look at him and gave him a radiant smile that went all the way to her eyes, sparkling behind her tears. "Yes, of course. If you really were sent here in answer to my prayers, I shouldn't refuse to answer your questions, now should I? No matter how offensive they might be."

Lucius hesitated, then said carefully, "Well, um, I don't really know about that, but… This Joshua of yours – does he maybe look something like me? Not old and ugly like me, I don't mean that, but is he, you know…?"

"Do you mean, is he black?" She laughed a quick, unhappy laugh, and a tear rolled down her cheek. "Yes, he is. That's just the problem. Don't get me wrong – it isn't a problem for me, but it is for a lot of people. I'm sure I don't have to tell *you* that! Besides, there is a lot more to my problem right now than just the color of Joshua's skin. You see, someone found about us, and it was just about the worst person that could have ever found out. His name is Santoro. He works here at the restaurant. My father adores him and is always hinting to me that he would make a great husband." She shuddered at the thought.

"Santoro is in love with me. I know he is because he tells me all the time. He has asked me to marry him more times than I can count, and I keep telling him 'no,' but he doesn't give up. He says that I'll come around some day and that I could make my father and him both happy and that he would always take care of us. I'm sure he would too, but I don't love him. I can't marry someone I don't love. Tell me, Lucius, does that make me selfish?"

Without waiting for an answer, Lucy continued. "I don't care if it does. This is the twentieth century, and I'm an independent woman. If I get married at all, it's going to be to the man that I love, not someone that my father or anyone else chooses for me. Anyway, where was I?

"One day about a week ago," she went on, "Joshua and I were sitting in a restaurant on the South side of town. It was one of our favorite meeting places because no one took much notice of us and served us just like we were any other couple. We were relaxed, holding hands, enjoying each other's company, when I heard the bell hanging on the door knob jangle. I looked up, and there was Santoro, coming through the door with a case of olive oil. Sometimes we sell some of the olive oil that we ship in from Italy to other restaurants around town. Anyway, we locked eyes, and even from a distance I could see the heat rising in Santoro's face. I dropped Joshua's hand and shouted at him to leave, to run away as fast as he could, and not to look back, not to stop for anything.

"Joshua and I had talked about what we would do if we ever got caught together, so he figured out what was going on immediately. He jumped up out of his seat so fast that he knocked over his chair. He looked me in the eyes for just an instant, then turned and ran through the kitchen toward the back door. I think what saved him was that case of olive oil Santoro was carrying. He had to set it down before he could run after Joshua, and that slowed him down just enough for me to get between him and the kitchen. He pushed me out of the way and ran to the back of the restaurant, but by then Joshua was nowhere to be found."

Lucy was starting to cry again, tears running down her cheeks, and her voice faltered as she spoke. "Santoro was angrier than I've ever seen him. He called me terrible names and threatened to tell my father. I begged and pleaded with him not to tell. He said the only way I could stop him would be if I agreed right there on the spot to marry him. He said I was lucky that he still wanted me after what he had just seen and that I should be grateful. Grateful!" She laughed a bitter laugh which turned into a series of loud sobs.

Lucius looked nervously around. He took a step closer and awkwardly patted the young woman on the back. In a quiet voice, hopeful that Lucy would lower her own voice before her crying attracted attention in their direction, he asked, "What did you do?"

Lucy took a few shuddering breaths and steadied herself to answer. "I did the only thing I could think of to do. I stalled for more time. I told Santoro that I needed a week to think it over, and that at the end of the week, if I didn't accept his proposal, he could tell my father and I wouldn't try to deny it. I told him that if he went to my father sooner, I would deny everything, and it would be his word against mine. He agreed to my terms.

"Every day since then, I've been trying to find Joshua to ask him to take me away from here, to marry me himself somewhere where no one will judge us for the color of our skin. Maybe Canada, or… I don't know. There must be somewhere we could go. But, he's gone, Lucius! He's gone! I've looked and looked and asked about him everywhere – at the Sophisticated Feline, at all our favorite meeting spots, but either no one knows where he is, or no one is willing to tell me. And the worst part…" Her words were punctuated by sobs. "The worst part is… I think I might be…. Oh, I can't even say it!" She moaned loudly and buried her face in her hands. "What am I doing to do? It has been one week today, and Santoro is going to demand an answer. I'm so confused and scared. What am I going to do?"

She began to cry more vigorously in great, anguished wails that carried down the alley in the still, cold morning air. Lucius reached out to pat her again and say "Shh" or "There, there" or whatever it might take to get her to quiet down, but at the touch of his hand on her shoulder, Lucy sprung from the step and threw herself into Lucius's arms, where she continued to sob loudly as she clutched his neck in an iron grip.

At that moment, the door above the steps slammed open, and the biggest, hairiest, angriest man that Lucius had ever seen in his entire life erupted through the doorway. The man bellowed something in Italian, and Lucy released her grip on Lucius. She turned toward the man and exclaimed "Santoro!" before launching into a stream of what Lucius assumed were Italian expletives delivered at high volume. Santoro ignored Lucy's verbal assault and attempted to reach around her to grab Lucius, but she stood her ground and shoved him hard in the chest. He stepped backward from the force of her blow and stumbled over the doorstop, then lost his balance and fell hard onto his backside. Stunned, he sat there motionless for a moment.

Lucius saw his chance to escape and took full advantage of it, running for his bicycle as though he was being chased by all the demons in hell. He jumped onto the seat and started pedaling like his very life depended on it, and he suspected that it did. He shot past the sweet shop where he was supposed to deliver his last load of ice and kept pumping his legs toward the light at the end of the alley.

Behind him, he heard the crunch of the big man's feet pounding on the icy gravel. The safety of the sunlit street was just a few yards ahead, but Santoro was gaining on him. He pictured the huge Italian catching up and putting his enormous hands on him, and he peddled harder. In the background, Lucy's stream of Italian curses became more distant. One of the wheels of Lucius's cart hit a rock and nearly caused him to overturn. As he struggled to regain his balance, he thought he could feel hot breath on the back of his neck. He held his breath and braced for the moment when the hands would grab him and pull him to the ground.

Just then, he heard a loud thud and a stream of cursing. He risked turning his head just long enough to see what was happening. No more than two yards behind him, Santoro had slipped and fallen on the melting ice. As Lucius briefly met his eye, he struggled back onto his feet and shook his fist at the fleeing ice man. "If I ever see you around here again, nigger, I'll kill you! I'll kill you! Do you hear me?" Lucius heard the words echoing in the narrow alleyway, but his eyes were fixed straight ahead, and he continued peddling madly and didn't stop until he cleared the alley and emerged into the blessed sunlight.

****

Lucius realized he had been sitting there looking at his delivery schedule and its last unchecked box for at least 10 minutes. Sighing deeply, he returned the schedule to its place in his bicycle basket. The way he looked at it, he had two choices: one, he could go back to Mr. McCleery and confess that he had failed to make one of his deliveries, which would probably cost him his job, or two, he could risk going back to Morgan Park and that alley and hope to heaven above that Santoro and Lucy had taken their quarrel indoors by now. Because if they hadn't, Lucius figured, it could cost him more than a job.

9

Decisions

Rich breathed in the familiar odor of the gym: sweat with a hint of steroids. The place was a favorite among serious bodybuilders, and the free weight benches were all occupied with grunting, perspiring men. It wasn't his usual gym, but he hadn't gone there to work out. He was looking for someone.

Rich looked appreciatively over the glistening bodies of the weightlifters, but the man he wanted wasn't among them. He was turning to leave when he spotted him across the room, seated at the lat pull-down machine. His back was to Rich, so he didn't see him approach from behind. "Hey man, we need to talk," Rich said.

The man startled at the sound of a voice inches from his ear and let go of the bar, causing it to fly upwards with a loud clang. A few heads turned at the sound and smirked at the amateurish move before getting back to their own workouts. The man whipped around, ready to lash out at whoever dared to interrupt his flow and make him look foolish in front of his peers. When he saw who was standing there, his anger cooled to a slow simmer, and a brief smile twitched at the corners of his mouth. "Hey, Ritchie, what a surprise!" he said. "I'm sorry to let you down after you came all this way, but as you can see, I'm busy right now. Say whatever you need to say to me at practice tomorrow."

The smile flickered again. "You will be at practice tomorrow, won't you Ritchie? Or did you get your fairy ass kicked off the team this time? Mike seemed awfully peeved at you."

Rich held his breath and mentally counted down from ten, like Lonny had advised him to do when he felt like punching someone. Too bad he hadn't remembered back at the locker room. "Look, Lance," he said in as casual of a voice as he could manage, "I don't like it any better than you do, but we're on the same team and we've got to find a way to get along."

Lance laughed and shook his head. He took the hand towel from his shoulder and wiped the perspiration from his head and neck without taking his eyes off Rich. There was no humor in his eyes, despite the laughter, and his voice when he spoke again was like cold steel. "Listen to me carefully, Sugar Plum, because I don't like having to repeat myself. We may be on the same team, but it won't be for long. I'm going to do whatever it takes to get you booted out. We don't need some homo staring at us in the shower, okay? So, just fuck off." He tossed the towel back over his shoulder and turned back to the machine. He immediately gripped the bar and started pulling it down, resuming his workout and making it clear that the conversation was over.

"Lance," Rich tried to keep his voice calm and reasonable, but he could feel the anger rising up through his body and settling in his neck, which grew hot and flushed a deep red. His fists clenched and unclenched at his sides, and he struggled to control his breathing, which was coming in quick, short huffs in time with his increasing heart rate. He was one step away from losing it, and he knew it but wasn't sure if he could stop himself.

As he looked on from behind, the lat pull-down bar came down and rose again with a steady, unbroken rhythm. Lance had dismissed him as though he didn't exist. Rich knew he should just leave. He knew it was his only option to keep this encounter from ending very badly. Yet, somewhere in the back of his brain, a little voice spoke up and suggested trying one more time to reason with the asshole. If he could just convince Lance to agree to a truce, everything would be so much easier. If there was another voice competing for Rich's attention, telling him that Lance was never going to agree to a damned thing, he chose to ignore it.

Rich waited until the bar was at its highest point before reaching over and putting his hand on Lance's shoulder to pull him around to face him. Lance grabbed the hand, flung it away as if it were leprous, and spun around. He was no longer smiling. "Don't touch me, you fucking faggot," he said through clenched teeth. "I have nothing else to say to you, so why don't you get out of here and go play ass tag with that spic boyfriend of yours?"

Rich took a deep breath and counted to ten in his head again, faster this time. With a colossal effort, he nearly succeeded in keeping the anger from his voice. "Look, I only have one other thing to say to you, Lance, and that's to leave Lonny out of this. You can say whatever homophobic, small-minded, hateful bullshit you want to me. I've heard it all before, and I seriously doubt you have the brain power to come up with anything new. But I draw the line where it comes to Lonny. He hasn't done anything to you. You don't even know him. So, I'm asking you…no, I'm telling you, you fucking Nazi throwback, to lay off my boyfriend."

Lance rose from the bench and stood so close to him that Rich could smell his breath, which reeked of fried onions. The smile was back on his face, but it didn't reach his eyes, which glared with unmasked hatred into Rich's own. "Listen to me, Richie boy, because this is the last time I'm going to waste my time talking to you. You don't get to tell me what to say or what to do or who I can fuck with. If I want to call your little butt buddy a spic, I'll call him a spic. And if I want to show up in a dark alley when he's walking home someday and beat the living shit out of him, I'll do just that. You people disgust me. In fact, you…"

He didn't get to finish his sentence because Rich punched him in the teeth. This time there was no slow motion. There was no counting to ten, or even to three. One second, Lance was spouting his onion-steeped hatred into his face, and the next, Rich was staring at a shiny white fragment of a tooth sticking out from his own bleeding knuckle.

Almost immediately, a trio of well-muscled personal trainers appeared from nowhere and hauled him away from where Lance stood with his hand over his mouth, a narrow rivulet of blood trailing from the corner of his lower lip and down his chin where it fell to the floor in tiny, perfect droplets. One of the trainers opened the door for the other two, who threw him bodily out onto the hot asphalt. As he fell to the ground and rolled, one of the trainers shouted, "You've got thirty seconds to get your ass off the property before the cops come."

Rich took this as fair warning and hurried to his car. He glanced back at the open doorway as he fumbled for his car key. The trainers stood just inside and watched him. One held a phone to his ear and was speaking rapidly to someone on the other end of the line. Lance was nowhere to be seen. Rich spun the car around and peeled out of the lot as quickly as he could in hopes that the goons at the door wouldn't be able to read his license plate. The knuckles on his right hand throbbed as he gripped the steering wheel and sped away. "That could have gone better," he said out loud, followed by a sigh and, "Lonny is going to kill me."

10

A Good Night

Al DeLeon looked in the full-length mirror and smiled. From his shiny black hair, slicked back in wavy locks with a healthy dose of Tres Flores hair oil, to his polished Stacy Adams wingtip shoes, he was the ultimate lady's man. Al adjusted the gold chain around his neck, took one last satisfying look at his reflection, and headed for the door, grabbing his car keys on the way and shoving them with some difficulty into the pocket of his skin-tight jeans. Thinking of sweet Annabelle and the way she looked on the dance floor in her low-cut red dress, the perspiration on her cleavage sparkling in the light of the disco ball, he turned back one last time and sprayed on a couple more spritzes of Opium for Men. He then checked his watch and hurried out into the night, whistling a tune.

Thirty minutes later, Al opened the door of the El Capri Dance Club and was hit with a blast of air-conditioned air, loud music, and the blended odors of sweat and alcohol. Breathing it in with relish, he gave his eyes a moment to adjust to the lowered house lights and then headed for an open table near the dance floor. He looked around at the small clusters of people hovering around the other tables and at the few couples on the dance floor. No Annabelle. It was still early, so he wasn't too concerned. She and her two girlfriends had been there every Saturday night for several weeks, and her parting words the previous Saturday as she gently freed herself from his embrace when the last song of the night faded to a close, were "See you next time." Al smiled at the memory.

Tonight was going to be a good night. Al was confident of that. He had thought about Annabelle every day since their last dance together. She was a special lady – petite and curvaceous with big, sparkling brown eyes in her pretty round face and clouds of curly black hair. He knew he wanted her from the moment he spotted her walking into the club the first time, weeks ago. She had been laughing with her girlfriends, and the sound of her laughter, like the tinkle of glass chimes in a summer breeze, had broken through the hubbub of conversation in the crowded bar and made him turn around on his barstool to look in her direction. He remembered how she had struggled to climb onto her barstool in her tight skirt and the dainty way she had pulled down her hem when it slid up over her thighs as she sat down.

He wasted no time buying her a drink that first night. He had stolen glances at her from across the room as she drank and chatted with her friends and noticed that she drank only white wine, which she sipped lightly while her girlfriends gulped down beer from the bottle. From the start, she stood out from the crowd as a true lady. When he ordered a round of drinks for her table, she had rewarded him with a shy smile and a wave from across the room, which gave him the courage to ask her for a dance.

That first dance was magical. He couldn't remember the song that had been playing, only the scent of her perfume and the sound of her voice, soft and sweet, when she lifted her chin to look up at him and tell him her name. He almost forgot his own name, he was so spellbound by her full red lips, so close to his own as she spoke. He didn't notice when the song ended, and Annabelle had laughed her musical laugh and teased him for still swaying on the dance floor even though there was no more music.

He got to know her little by little over many dances that night and the Saturday nights since then, and his estimation of her had only grown. He had looked forward to tonight all week with equal measures of excitement and fear. Tonight was the night he was finally going to muster the *cajones* to ask her to go home with him. For that, he was going to need some liquid courage. He waved the cocktail server over to his table and ordered a pitcher of Budweiser. As he waited for his beer to arrive, he idly spun the paper coaster around on the table and smiled. Yes, tonight was going to be a very good night.

****

Al was just starting in on his second pitcher of Bud when he heard a familiar sound. Three women in colorful cocktail dresses and high heeled shoes were silhouetted in the open doorway as they entered the club, all giggling and talking at once. One voice stood out immediately. Al had heard that sweet laughter in his dreams. He smiled and raised a hand to waive at Annabelle and her friends, but they were looking back towards the still-open door.

Close behind the women, a trio of young men entered the lounge. The women looked away quickly, still whispering amongst themselves as they moved toward an open table near the bar. They gathered around the table, and Annabelle sat with her back toward Al. The three men went straight to the bar and ordered drinks. The bar was getting crowded now that the night was in full swing, and there weren't three vacant bar stools together, so two of the newcomers had to settle for leaning against the bar while the third seated himself on the last bar stool.

Al breathed a sigh of relief. For one awful moment, he had thought the men and women had come in together on a group date. In that brief instant, his heart had dropped into his stomach to founder in the rising pool of Budweiser. It took him a full five minutes to recover from the false alarm, aided by a few deep breaths and several long swigs from his beer glass.

Al chuckled, chiding himself for having such an overactive imagination. He rose only slightly unsteadily from his chair, intending to flag down the cocktail server and order a round of drinks for Annabelle and her lady friends – one white wine and two Coronas with lime. He spotted the server and had just begun to raise his hand to get her attention when he saw that she was carrying a tray of drinks in the direction of the ladies' table – one white wine and two beers with lime wedges stuck in the mouths of the bottles.

Al watched with confusion as the cocktail server made her way to Annabelle's table. How had they ordered their drinks so quickly? They had only just walked in, and they hadn't gone to the bar or flagged down a server. He was sure he would have noticed if they had ordered drinks, so what was going on?

A horrible thought began to dawn in Al's mind. Still standing in front of his table with his hand halfway raised, Al slowly shifted his gaze toward the bar. The three men were talking animatedly to each other and drinking glasses of beer. One of them turned briefly toward the women's table and smiled. Was that a wink? Al couldn't be sure in the dim light. He looked back at the women to gauge their reaction, but Annabelle's back was still toward him, and her friends were talking and laughing together as before.

Al realized he was still standing and awkwardly sat back down. He took several gulps of his beer to steady his nerves. His initial shock had shifted into embarrassment and was threatening to turn to anger. Al didn't want to lose his cool, especially not in front of Annabelle. He needed to pull himself together, think this through, and not overreact. After all, he wasn't sure that the man had winked, and if he did, he could have been winking at one of Annabelle's friends and not at her. He wasn't even sure that the men had bought the ladies' round of drinks. Maybe one of the other ladies had ordered while his eyes were focused on Annabelle's round derriere in its skin-tight pink satin skirt. It was definitely distracting enough. Or maybe the cocktail server recognized them and brought their drinks without waiting for them to order. Yes, that's probably what happened. Al let out a breath he hadn't realized he had been holding.

The dance floor began to fill up as a trendy Mexican pop song started to play. Taking one last, long drink of his beer, Al stood up, adjusted his shirt collar to optimally frame the gold chain resting on a patch of dark, curly chest hair, and strode confidently toward Annabelle's table. Her friends spotted him before Annabelle did, and one of them lowered her head conspiratorially and said something that brought their chatter to an abrupt halt. Three pairs of heavily made-up eyes followed Al as he came around the table to face Annabelle.

She looked as beautiful as ever, and she smiled up at him with her lovely wide mouth. Al grinned back, but he felt some of his confidence leak away, stabbed by pinpricks of doubt. Was there something different about Annabelle's smile – did it seem just a little forced? Had she hesitated, just for a split second, and darted her eyes to the side before greeting him?

Al shook off his doubts and reached out his hand. "May I have this dance, *Chaparrita?*" Annabelle nodded and took Al's hand, allowing him to help her up from her chair and lead her toward the dance floor. Al felt the warm, small hand in his, smiled and gave the hand a light, affectionate squeeze. As he pulled Annabelle gently forward, he didn't notice her turn back to direct a meaningful look toward her friends and a swift glance in the direction of the bar.

11

Too Late

Between football practice and the one-to-one discussion with Coach that followed (a discussion in which he was made to understand in no uncertain terms that he needed to shape up or he would soon find himself shipped out), Rich Wright didn't make it to the phone repair shop until two days after he dropped it off there with a shattered screen. In all that time, Lorena had not come home. The first night, a Friday, Rich was not too concerned. She often stayed out late on weekends and crashed at one of her friends' apartments. Sometimes she spent the night with that asshole Oscar, but after the second night away without stopping by even long enough for a change of clothes and a shower, Rich was beginning to worry.

After paying the outrageous price for his new phone screen, Rich sat in his car in the strip mall parking lot with the air conditioning running and checked his messages. He had hoped that he would find missed calls from Lorena when he got his phone back, but there were none. No texts from her either, although there was a long chain of texts from Lonny. Rich decided he would deal with those when he got home. Right now, he was busy fighting a wave of anxiety as he checked his social media accounts and saw that Lorena had not posted anything since before she left for work on Friday afternoon.

Frowning, Rich tried to remember anything she might have said about her plans the last time he saw her at the apartment. To be honest, he had only been halfway listening. Alexa had been blasting an 80's pop music station, and he had been singing along to "Karma Chameleon" with Boy George while Lorena was chattering away in the next room. It had been the day before the bizarre incident when she pinned him to the floor and held something over his face until he passed out. He was still shaking his head and trying to figure out what that had been all about.

On the last morning he spoke with her, he remembered she said she hoped she would get cut early from her shift because she had somewhere to go after work. Had she mentioned a party? Try as he might, he just couldn't recall where she said she was going, if she had even mentioned it at all. He also couldn't remember hearing her come home that night. He had been zonked out on Tylenol PM, trying to recover from the locker room fight with Lance, so she could easily have come in without him hearing her.

Looking back at his phone, Rich saw that in addition to the several text messages, there were four missed calls from Lonny. He hazarded a peek at the texts. There was an increasingly terse tone to the messages that made Rich temporarily forget about his missing roommate. He quickly dialed Lonny's number, as if to try to win back points with his swiftness now after two days of silence. The call was answered almost instantly.

"Where are you? What's going on? Why haven't you answered my calls?"

Rich could only interject single words – "I..", "Sorry...", "It..", between the barrage of questions coming from the other end of the line. Several minutes and several admonishments and pleading apologies later, he told Lonny about Lorena's disappearance.

"Have you called the police?" Lonny asked.

"No, I didn't think it was that serious. She's stayed out overnight before without telling me."

"Has she stayed out two nights before without telling you? Has she texted you?"

"Well, no and no, but…" Rich was suddenly struck with an awareness of his own unmistakable stupidity. Of course, he should have realized sooner that Lorena was probably in trouble! Anyone else, anyone with half a brain, would have figured it out long before now and taken action. He was so distracted by the crashing wave of self-doubt that he almost missed what Lonny was saying to him.

"But, what? My god, Richie, what were you thinking? She could have been in an accident! She could be in a coma, or worse! She could have been abducted by a serial killer! Tell me you at least called her work and asked if they have seen her."

"No, not yet, but I just got my phone back and…"

"*Ay, Dios mio.*" There was a pause. Rich could picture Lonny closing his eyes and bringing his outward-turned hands down in a familiar gesture that Rich interpreted as "I must calm myself before I strangle this idiot." Lonny's voice resumed, calm but firm. "Go. Right now. Go to her work and see if she's been there. Then call me right back."

"Okay, I will," Rich replied. In a voice on the edge of tears, he added, "I'm sorry I didn't answer your calls. I love you, Babe. I wish you were here."

"I love you too. Now go. And don't wait two days to call me back."

Rich opened his mouth to speak, but Lonny had already hung up. He dropped his phone into the cup holder and started up the car. With a growing sense of dread, he turned west toward Dos Sombreros Fine Mexican Cuisine.

****

Miss Gladys Olsen, the tenant of apartment 216, took up her position behind her window blinds as soon as she heard the unmistakable pounding on her neighbor's door. An authoritative voice called out, "Is anyone home? This is the Phoenix Police. Please open the door." Two uniformed officers stood just outside, their backs to Miss Olsen's blinds. They knocked a second time and spoke quietly to each other. Miss Olsen couldn't hear what they said, much to her irritation. The officers stepped away from the door and started walking toward the stairs.

Miss Olsen grabbed the door knob to dash out after them. Her curiosity to know what brought the police to those brazen young people's door was overwhelming; her disappointment that they were leaving so soon was positively painful. Just in time, she looked down and realized she was wearing only a thin nightgown and no bra. She couldn't possibly go out like that. What would the neighbors think? What would the officers think? She hurried to her bedroom and threw on a robe and slippers. When she made it back to her front door and quickly stepped outside, the officers were nowhere to be seen. She craned her neck to scan the apartment grounds and the entrance to the parking lot, but no one was in sight. Regretfully, she retreated back into her apartment with a heavy sigh.

12

Broken Dreams

The last few notes of the song were still lingering, and already Annabelle was gently but firmly pulling away from Al's grasp and making her way from the dance floor in the direction of her table. "What's your hurry, *chica?*" Al purred boozily into her ear. "Come sit with me for a while."

"Thank you for the dance, Al, but I've got to get back to my friends."

She was looking away from him when he said, "I could join you." He reached for her hand too late. She was already walking toward her table and the sound of her friends' laughter.

"I'll see you later, Al," she said over her shoulder without slowing her pace.

Al watched her retreating backside, the delicious rise and fall of her hips as she moved. He watched her reach up and tug down her skirt hem, which was creeping up over her thighs. Mesmerized by the sight, it was a few moments before he refocused his vision and saw only too clearly why Annabelle was in such a hurry.

The three men from the bar had abandoned their barstools and were now gathered around the table where Annabelle's friends had been holding a place for her. She took her seat with the assistance of one of these men, who gallantly pulled back her chair and, leaning over her so close that his nose brushed her curls, pushed the chair in gently as she sat down. He must have said something to her then because she looked up into his face and smiled before looking shyly down, dark lashes fluttering, at her fresh glass of white wine.

Al realized that he was still standing alone by the dance floor staring after Annabelle. He felt no embarrassment at the realization, only anger. The heat rising from his neck to his eyes to the top of his head was one part alcohol and two parts rage. He clenched and unclenched his fists and took a step toward Annabelle's table, but then stopped. He wanted nothing more in that moment than to go over there and punch that *pendejo cabrón* in his smug mouth and maybe hit him over the head with his own bottle of fancy-assed beer. He could picture it – the crack of the bottle hitting his skull, the spray of beer and broken glass, the screams of alarm from the women. He smiled as he imagined the man with beer all over his face and clothes, humiliated in front of Annabelle and the other women.

But then a small voice crept into his head, spoiling his imagined victory. What was the point? What good would going after his rival do? Even through the fog of disappointment and too much beer, Al knew that starting a fight in the El Capri wouldn't end well for him or anyone else. It would probably get him arrested for one thing, and even worse, it wouldn't help him get Annabelle back. She would hate him for it. Tears welled up in his eyes, and he wiped them away roughly, ashamed of his weakness.

Back at Annabelle's table, the man had pulled up a chair next to her, and the two of them were leaning in to hear each other speak over the noise of the club. Annabelle had one hand wrapped around the stem of her wine glass, the other hand resting on the table. As Al looked on helplessly, the man put a hand over hers. She did not pull her hand away.

Almost blind with rage and hurt, Al stumbled back to his table, tossed some bills beside the empty pitcher and drank down the last of his glass of beer in one gulp. Grabbing his keys, he walked as fast as he could manage past the bar and to the door, looking straight ahead so he wouldn't see Annabelle (*his* Annabelle) and her new man. Even without seeing them, he could feel their eyes on him, and his face reddened with shame. He pulled open the door and emerged into the dark parking lot, away from the festive music that seemed to mock him as he staggered blindly through tears toward his car.

****

Genevieve Lopez opened the door of her battered Honda Civic and eased her tired body into the driver's seat. She quickly closed and locked the door before allowing herself to lean back into the seat and utter a long sigh that turned into a yawn. It was close to 1 o'clock in the morning, and the office building she had just finished cleaning was in an area of town that was generally safe by day, but not so much after dark. A woman alone couldn't be too careful, and Genevieve was always careful. She had to be. Her family was depending on her.

Sometimes at the end of a long day like this one, Genevieve would start to feel sorry for herself and think about quitting one of her three jobs and going back to school to become a nurse like she had always wanted. Actually, her dream when she was a little girl, much younger than her own daughter was now, was to be a doctor. She recalled telling her grandfather once that her favorite things were horses and her *abuelo*, and that one day, she was going to be a doctor and that her patients would be horses and old people, so that they would never get sick or die. Her grandfather had laughed so hard that his laugh turned into one of his long, rasping coughs. He had taken a drink of iced tea and said, still chuckling, "*Mi hija,* if you just treat horse's rear ends, you will have both pretty much covered."

Usually, this memory made Genevieve smile, but tonight, it just added to her weariness. She was just so tired, but she couldn't afford to take a break or try to follow her dreams, not with her mother in the Alzheimer's care home and her father needing her financial support to pay the bills. And of course there was Vivian, who was just on the cusp of adolescence and already starting to rebel at having to stay home and do chores while Genevieve was at one of her jobs. Genevieve felt guilty about leaving her alone so much, but she was afraid that if she didn't continue to pay the fees to keep Vivian in her softball league, she would gravitate to a rougher crowd, and Genevieve would lose the tenuous authority she still was able to leverage to keep her daughter out of harm's way.

As a single parent, she couldn't afford to be her daughter's friend. She had to be a parent and make tough, often unpopular, decisions, like telling Vivian she couldn't go to an unsupervised party with her girlfriends tonight. That had led to an explosive argument in which Vivian had told her, for the first time since she was about three, that she hated her. Genevieve understood the adolescent hormone-charged roller coaster of emotions behind Vivian's outburst, but the words still hurt.

Genevieve put on her seatbelt and said a little prayer that the car would start. It did. At least there was that to be grateful for, she thought as she backed out of the parking space and exited the empty lot. She carefully merged with the light traffic on Jefferson Street, wondering briefly what led the other drivers to be on the road at such an hour. Some were probably working night shifts like she was; others were probably on their way to or from parties or late movies. It was Friday night, after all.

As she drove toward the freeway, her thoughts drifted to tasks she needed to take care of tomorrow, like going to the pharmacy to pick up her mother's prescriptions. She also needed to go to the grocery store soon. She was pretty sure the milk was going to expire, if Vivian hadn't already finished it off with her bowl of Cocoa Puffs. She needed to get some laundry done too. She had asked Vivian to do it, but that was at least three days ago, and the overflowing laundry basket was still sitting there when she left this morning for her first job of the day as a clerk at the gas station convenience store. At least she had remembered to get gas in her car. She had filled the tank before heading over to the office building this evening, and the dashboard indicator was still pointing at the "F".

Genevieve flicked on her turning signal, even though there were no other cars on the eastbound I-10, and crossed over to the inside lane. She turned up the radio only slightly and sang along with Linda Ronstadt, "…on Blue Bayouuuu…." Ahead, the taillights of another vehicle came into view, two bright white pinpoints against the surrounding darkness. Something seemed off somehow about those lights, but it took Genevieve a moment to realize what it was. The taillights glowed lantern-bright and seemed to be getting closer faster than the speed of Genevieve's approaching car. She checked her dashboard – 67 miles per hour, and eased back on the gas pedal. The white lights were coming up faster. The white lights…

****

Francisco Alfonso Veracruz-DeLeon was glad the traffic was light tonight. He just wanted to get home and pass out in his bed and forget this whole lousy night. He turned his El Camino onto the on-ramp and headed west, pressing hard on the accelerator and racing down the freeway as though he could outrun his disappointment and shame.

The windows were rolled down, but the warm night air blowing in did little to cool the black leather interior of Al's car. He wiped the sweat from his forehead with the back of his hand and swore out loud. That bitch! She had been leading him on for weeks, and then she shines him on for some *chingado cabrón* in tight pants and a stupid oversized cowboy hat that made him look like a clown. He should have gone over and punched his stupid grinning face instead of running away with his tail between his legs. He should have told Annabelle that he could do better than a *puta* like her.

Tears mixed with the drops of perspiration on Al's face. He wiped them away savagely and shook his head, trying to clear his vision.

He had traveled half the distance home without encountering a single other vehicle. That was good, since he knew he wasn't really keeping to the center of his lane very well. How much beer had he drunk? He couldn't quite remember, but it must have been a lot because his eyes were playing tricks on him. The lane markers on the road were doubled, and there was a halo around the overhead lamps dotting the freeway and around the lights of that car coming up in the distance.

Realization dawned in a rush of adrenalin that broke through Al's alcohol-induced haze. The car up ahead was coming *this way*, head-on, and coming fast. The driver must be drunk, he thought. The car was going the *wrong way* on the freeway. Al swerved to the left to go around the car, but his unfocused eyes saw two sets of headlights instead of one, and his sluggish reflexes couldn't keep up with the El Camino's speed.

Genevieve's brain registered the headlights heading right at her, and she immediately slammed hard on her brakes. Her car fishtailed toward the barrier. She clung to the steering wheel and tried to regain control, but the car's rear end spun out into the path of the oncoming El Camino. She looked on in horror as the vehicle came at her. Time seemed suspended – the sounds of cars in the distance, the feel and smell of the night air, the lights of the street lamps and the stars above – all were gone as though they never existed. There was nothing but the headlights, coming straight at her, blinding and unstoppable.

The El Camino torpedoed directly into the Honda's gas tank before careening across all three lanes, crashing through the concrete barrier, and plummeting onto the underpass below. Just before the full gas tank exploded, consuming the small vehicle and its occupant in roiling orange flames, Genevieve thought about Vivian in her bed at home, probably sucking her thumb, a habit from infancy that still comforted her as she slept. Genevieve opened her mouth to say "I love you" to that vision of her daughter and breathed in smoke and flames and oblivion.

****

In the ambulance, Al blinked the blood from his eyes. Through the blur, he saw faces leaning over him, hands moving over his body. There were voices, but he couldn't understand the words through the ringing in his ears. His head hurt like it was stuck in a vice, squeezing his skull tighter and tighter. He couldn't feel his body or turn his head. He tried to speak, but there was a mask over his mouth. There were more faces around him now, more hands, moving quickly over and around him. One face was inches from his and seemed to be trying to tell him something. The voice was sharp, urgent. More blood dripped into his eyes, and he closed them, shutting out the faces. The voices faded, and the pain in his head faded along with them.

Al lay motionless in the soothing dark. The voices had all gone away, and he drifted in a world without sound or light or pain. A gentle warmth surrounded his body, and he became aware of a distant glow, like the moments before sunrise. He yearned to go toward the source of the glowing light and he reached out to it and felt the glow reaching back.

A new voice broke through the silence – a woman's voice, strangely muted as if coming from a distance, but clear and distinct. "I love you, Vivian," the voice said. Although his eyes were still closed, Al saw a young woman standing in front of the light, which beckoned against the surrounding darkness like the entrance to a brightly lit tunnel. The woman was bent forward, crying into her hands, but then she straightened up, cocking her head as though she had heard something. She turned toward the light, and it seemed to draw her in without her taking a single step. Suddenly, the young woman and the light were both gone, and with them the sensation of warmth and peace. Al was still reaching toward the place where the light had been, but there was only darkness.

****

On the channel 12 morning news program, the smartly dressed anchor man with glossy hair and sincere eyes reported solemnly on the fatal freeway crash that had occurred in the early hours of the morning. Video from a helicopter hovering above the stretch of freeway, shut down for the police investigation, showed the smoldering remains of the compact car in a dark pool of water that dripped like blood from the wreckage. The fire crew had fought to douse the flames in hopes of getting to the driver inside in time, but with the intensity of the explosion, there had been no realistic chance of a rescue. Several police and fire vehicles were scattered around the scene and on the underpass below, where a second vehicle lay in pieces of twisted metal and glass, strewn over several yards and sparkling in the morning sunlight.

Back in the newsroom, the anchor man's voice accompanied the video footage: "According to police on the scene, the number of fatalities and the identity of the victim or victims in the compact car are uncertain due to the explosion and intense flames that entirely engulfed the vehicle. Police say there were no survivors. The driver of the El Camino that crashed into the smaller car was taken by ambulance to a local hospital with extensive life-threatening injuries. Unfortunately, we have just learned that the driver was pronounced dead on arrival. The identity of the driver has been withheld, pending notification of family.

The investigation is still underway, but it appears that the driver of the El Camino was going westbound on the eastbound I-10 near the Twenty-seventh Avenue exit, making this the fifth wrong-way driving incident so far this year on that stretch of freeway. Police have not ruled out alcohol as a factor in the accident. The freeway closure from Nineteenth to Thirty-fifth Avenue is expected to continue for at least another hour, so commuters are advised to take an alternate route this morning. And now, back to you, Christine, for the weather forecast. I hear it's going to be another hot one..."

13

Still There

"Have a nice day anyway."

Bobby mumbled his customary response to the pudgy businessman whose polished black shoes and shiny black toupee glistened in the sunlight as he hurried by without a glance. The day was rapidly heating up, and Bobby was growing drowsy from the warm sun on his face. His chin nodded toward his chest, and he nearly dropped his battered Kansas City Chiefs baseball cap, which he held out in front of him, bottom up, like a collection plate.

Someone walked by. Bobby barely registered the man's passing, but then his head snapped up, and he was startled to attention by the appearance in his cap of a five-dollar bill. Fives were almost as rare as hen's teeth, as his grandmother used to say. He got a ten-dollar bill once, from a very drunk baseball fan who stumbled past one night from the direction of the nearby stadium, high on his team's win and feeling generous. That was a very good night. He had blown the tenner on a double cheeseburger, fries, one of those crispy little fried apple pies, and a cup of coffee. He still remembered how good that meal tasted. But, a five dollar bill this early in the day? It was definitely nothing to sneeze at.

Bobby looked up to see who his benefactor was, but he caught only a glimpse of the muscular young man striding past him toward the entrance to the Mexican restaurant. He didn't even have time to tell him, "Thank you, God bless," although he said it anyway just in case the guy was still in hearing range. If he was, he showed no sign of it and kept walking briskly ahead as though on an important mission.

Bobby watched him curiously for a moment, then shoved the five-dollar bill into his jeans pocket and stuck his upturned cap out in front of him. "Spare change?" he asked a middle-aged couple whose glaringly pale legs poked out of Bermuda shorts and marked them as snowbirds fleeing the Midwest for the desert warmth. The woman grabbed onto her husband's arm, and they scurried quickly down the street.

****

"No, she isn't here. She no-showed for work the last two nights. No call, nothing. Really put us in a bind." The manager of Dos Sombreros looked back over his shoulder as he spoke, but his pace as he moved through the restaurant, checking on his staff and customers, never slowed. "If you see her, tell her she needs to call me right away if she still wants her job. She's a good server, and the customers like her, or I wouldn't even give her that much of a chance to come back. Usually, somebody just blows off their shift – no call – they're history. But, like I said, she is usually reliable, so maybe she's too sick to call or her car broke down or she got in an accident or something. She still needs to check in, though. I've got a business to run here, you know."

The manager stopped quickly and spun around, causing Rich to nearly bump into him. His expression softened as he really looked for the first time into Rich's worried face. In a gentler voice, he said, "You're her roommate, right? If I were you, I'd be checking the hospitals or calling the police. Something bad could have happened to her." He patted Rich's arm and added, "If you find out anything, give me a call, okay?" The manager smiled kindly, gave his arm a reassuring squeeze, then turned away and trotted off toward the sound of breaking glass.

A tray of water glasses, dropped by a harried server on his way from the kitchen, lay scattered across the floor, the contents soaking into the red carpet like blood stains.

Rich looked around, hoping to spot Mercy, Lorena's fellow server and friend. He followed a plump server with tight braids and a wreath of flowers in her hair across the room and tapped her on the shoulder, but when she turned, her face was unfamiliar. "Sorry," he said. "I thought you were someone else." The server smiled and moved on.

Rich stood uncertainly in the middle of the restaurant, barely registering the smell of sizzling fajitas and the sounds of businessmen and women enjoying their lunch breaks, chatting and laughing and putting their silverware to work on plates of burros, rice, and beans. The manager's words had unsettled him. Up until now, he hadn't allowed himself to believe that something terrible might have happened to Lorena, but both Lonny and the manager had mentioned police and hospitals.

He had a class to get to in less than an hour, followed by football practice, but then, if he hadn't heard from her yet, he would go looking for the only person he could ever imagine hurting her. He hoped to God he would hear from her before the day was over, though, so that wouldn't be necessary. If Oscar gave him any reason to believe he had something to do with Lorena's disappearance, Rich wasn't sure he could hold back from beating his worthless skull against a wall until it cracked open like a ripe pumpkin.

Distracted by these thoughts, Rich made his way toward the restaurant doors. Despite the warm sunlight filtering in through the glass, he felt a sudden chill, and goosebumps rose up on his arms. As he rubbed his hands briskly up and down his arms to warm himself, he sensed someone just behind him. He caught a whiff of perfume, strong enough to overpower the pervasive odor of cooked meat. The scent was something floral, but off somehow, like cut flowers that had been left too long in a vase of stagnant water. Stepping aside, he said, "Excuse me. I'm right in the way of the door." He looked over his shoulder, and his smile faltered. There was no one standing there.

"That was weird," he said. With a shrug, he opened the door and walked out into the bright, hot day.

****

The voice Bobby thought of as Beelzebub was shouting at him, calling him a worthless, perverted worm and other less complimentary things. The only way to ignore Beelzebub's relentless taunting and commands to throw himself on the tracks and into the path of a moving light rail train was to say "Get thee behind me, Satan" 666 times. This took time and concentration and had a really detrimental impact on his ability to panhandle successfully, as people walking past him tended to think he was talking to them. He was on his 243rd repetition of the phrase when the young man who had given him the fiver emerged from the restaurant. Bobby glanced at him, did a double-take, and immediately lost count.

The young man had paused just outside the door to check something on his phone. Standing right behind him was an elderly woman in an old-fashioned black dress and hat. She was inches from the man and was peering over his shoulder at his phone screen, but he didn't seem to realize she was there. He didn't look at her or speak. The expression on the woman's pallid face was a mixture of curiosity and scorn. As Bobby watched, she appeared to flicker and disappear briefly from sight, only to return in an instant on the opposite side of the young man.

Bobby closed his eyes and thumped his palms against his head to clear the fog from his brain. When he opened his eyes again and looked toward the young man with the phone, the old woman was still there. Her feet were hovering an inch above the sidewalk, and her figure was rendered indistinct by a gray miasma, like a thin cloud of smoke, that surrounded her and blurred the edges of her dark clothing with the building behind her. As she turned her face toward the street for a brief moment, Bobby caught a glimpse of black, hollow spaces behind her eyes and nose, as though her skull was showing through her pale and paper-thin skin.

"Oh God," he said. "Not another one."

The man put his phone in his pocket and began walking toward the parking lot, the old woman following close behind. Bobby hesitated, muttering to himself, "It's none of my business. None of my business. None of my business," while rocking forward and backward and hitting himself repeatedly on the head with both hands. Finally, he blurted out, in a voice loud enough to drown out Beelzebub's incessant abuse and catch the man's attention, "Hey, buddy! You're being followed!"

Instantly, the old woman's face turned toward Bobby, and she stared at him with strange silvery eyes. As he watched, frozen with horror, her face changed into a grinning skull, covered in crumbling, scorched flesh that fell away in blackened clods that clung to her dusty black silk bodice. The eyes with their infernal light that shown through the sockets of the creature's exposed skull were fixed on the cowering homeless man.

Bobby put his hands in front of his face to block the hideous sight. As he opened his mouth to scream, she flew at him, arms raised, gnarled, skeletal hands extended. She lunged, one hand reaching for him, the other hand in front of her face with one bony finger pressed against her mouth in a shushing gesture. Bobby clamped his eyes shut, and with his arms still raised protectively in front of him, stumbled backwards over the curb and into the street.

And older model Lexus, driven by a salesman who was currently in the middle of a particularly brutal quarterly finance call on his cell phone, ran over both legs of the crumpled form lying in the street. A piercing scream arose from the asphalt as the car bumped over the obstacle in the road. Looking in his rear-view mirror, the driver saw the figure of a man in shabby clothing, writhing and clutching at his legs. He started to press down on the brakes, but then thought about that second cocktail he had consumed over lunch with a client. Instead of braking, he hit the accelerator and fled from the scene.

"What was that?" said a voice on the other end of the line.

"Oh, nothing to worry about," the salesman said with a nervous chuckle. "Some guy in front of me almost hit a hobo passed out drunk in the street. The city really ought to do something about all the hobos downtown. Put 'em all in shelters or drunk tanks or something. Anyway, what were you saying about the projections for next quarter?"

****

"Hey, buddy! You're being followed!"

Rich turned toward the homeless man who had called out to him just in time to see a look of terror come over the man's face. The man raised his hands in front of him as if to ward off an attacker and retreated backward, right into the path of an oncoming car. Rich watched in shock and disbelief as the car sped away, leaving the man lying on the street and screaming in pain.

The sound of a car horn honking as the driver swerved around the body lying in the roadway jolted Rich to action. He ran forward and grabbed the man by the underarms and dragged him up onto the sidewalk, realizing even as he did so that he could be injuring the man even worse by moving him. Too late now, he thought. A crowd of people spilling out of the restaurant and the nearby bus stop began to form around Rich and the homeless man. Rich shouted, "Somebody call 911," at the group of faces closing in for a closer look. Already, several people were talking into their phones, and a few were aiming their phones at the man and snapping photos.

Rich leaned close enough to the injured man to smell his body odor and unwashed clothes. He had stopped moaning and his eyes were fluttering closed. Bright red blood was soaking through his tattered pants legs, and there was a trail of blood where Rich had dragged him from the street. Rich put his hands on either side of the man's face and said, "Hey, man, stay with me, okay? You're going to be alright. Just stay with me. I'm going to be right here with you until help gets here. I'm Rich."

Bobby blinked and tried to focus his eyes on the young man's face bending over him. "You're rich?" he slurred. "Can you…Can you help a veteran who's down on his luck?" He let out a short chuckle that turned into a gasp of pain.

"What? No, not… Never mind that. Just hang in there, Mister, okay? Help is coming." Rich pulled off his shirt and tied it tightly around the man's left thigh above the steadily oozing blood. He looked up at the circle of onlookers and pointed at a young man in a red plaid flannel shirt who was holding his phone out in front of him, clearly filming. "Hey, you there, give me your shirt." The young man looked up from his phone and caught the look in Rich's eyes. He quickly pulled off his shirt and handed it over.

Rich was tying the flannel shirt around the man's other leg when the paramedics arrived. He gave the makeshift tourniquet a quick tug and stood up to make room for the EMTs. Before he could step back and out of the way, he felt a hand clutch his arm. "Thank you," the injured man said with an effort. "My name is Bobby. Bobby Crocker." His gaze shifted to somewhere behind Rich's shoulder, and his eyes grew wide. He opened his mouth but the only sound that came out was a thin, terrified keening.

"Please step back, sir." One of the paramedics touched Rich's shoulder and gently pushed him back. He retreated a couple of steps to join the circle of onlookers, and the paramedics closed in, blocking Bobby from sight. Rich looked down and saw that he had blood on his hands, and he automatically smeared them across his jeans. He shuddered and began to weave through the crowd to find somewhere to wash away the blood. He heard a voice coming from the ground behind the paramedics who were lifting Bobby onto a back board for transport to the hospital.

"She's still following you, man," Bobby called out. "She's still there!"

14

Resolution

Lucius Brown sat on his bicycle at the entrance to the Morgan Park alley for several minutes, catching his breath and searching with his eyes for any sign of movement. The flutter of a pigeon landing on a fence post nearly stopped his heart. Finally, when it seemed fairly certain that the enraged Italian was not about to leap out from behind a trash can and attack him, he squared his shoulders, took one quick look behind him, and began pedaling purposefully toward his final delivery target. The sweet shop was only half a block away, but it seemed like a mile.

The alleyway was much brighter than it had been earlier in the morning when Lucius had made his first attempt to deliver his load of ice. He looked quickly toward the doorstep where the spurned lover had caught him in Lucy's embrace. Lucius said a silent prayer of thanks when he saw nothing but an empty alleyway between him and the sweet shop. Arriving at his destination, he made his final delivery of the morning with a smile on his face. He was beaming so much that the shop proprietor gave him a small tip and a bar of chocolate on the way out and thanked him for being so pleasant.

Lucius hazarded to whistle a tune in between bites of chocolate as he rode back up the alley. He was beyond eager to put Morgan Park behind him. He thought about Lucy and wished her well but hoped fervently that he would never see her again. He rounded the corner and drove his boots so hard against the brakes that the trailer hitched to the back of the bicycle swung around and tilted onto two wheels, knocking the bike and its rider to the ground. Lucius ignored his bleeding palms and knees, scraped raw by the gravel he landed on when he was thrown from his bicycle. He sat motionless, staring up in shock and disbelief.

Standing no more than 10 feet in front of him was Lucy's would-be champion, Santoro.

It took only a moment for the expression on the big man's face to go from surprise and confusion to recognition and triumph. "I've got you now, you slippery bastard!" he shouted as he lunged toward Lucius, but the brief pause had been just enough for Lucius to pull himself out from under the bicycle and break into a run. With his legs pumping like those of a much younger man, Lucius ran for his life, away from the alley and toward anywhere the presence of witnesses might keep his enraged pursuer from sending him to an early grave.

****

Minerva Short stood up from the bench and paced the Morgan Park station platform for the sixth or eighth time since the incident with the boorish man and the suitcase. It had all been rather unfortunate, and she felt quite bad about what had happened, but she consoled herself that it was an understandable mistake. As far as she could tell, the man seemed to have deserved what he got. She had been a little surprised at the depth of the wife's grief, however, but then again, she had seen such irrational reactions before. Women will get attached to dreadful men, she thought, shaking her head sadly. It was true when she was a young girl, and it seemed no less true a century or so later.

Looking on the bright side, the wife would have a chance for a better life now, and sooner or later she probably would realize it. Either that or she would attach herself to another brute and continue the cycle of abuse and degradation that she most likely had been accustomed to her whole life. Minerva sighed. Really, she wondered why she bothered trying to help some of these people.

Returning to her bench, Minerva smoothed her skirt and sat down primly. She gazed toward the quiet streets of this picturesque part of town and pondered why she was still there. After the earlier bustle at the station when the train had arrived, and the excitement that followed when the train flattened that horrible man, things had quieted down considerably.

Only a few travelers stood shuffling their feet uncertainly on the platform, waiting for some clue as to when the next train would be permitted to approach the station. She studied their faces and saw nothing of interest. Nothing at all appeared out of the ordinary, apart from a boy pushing a mop which was stained red from the spattered droplets of blood he was scrubbing away from the platform's edge.

If the woman in the flowered dress had not been the one she was here to defend, Minerva wondered, and clearly she had not been or otherwise Minerva wouldn't be sitting here still, then who? Had she missed something? Should she wander around the town a bit, in case she was needed somewhere outside the immediate vicinity of the train station?

Minerva was jolted from her ruminations by the sound of someone shouting. She looked up and saw a black man running full speed toward the station. Close behind him and gaining fast was a large, olive-skinned young man who was shaking his fist and yelling at the fleeing man in at least two languages. Minerva could see that the older man's strength was starting to flag. He was panting and had one hand pressed to his ribs as if it hurt him to breathe. As she watched, the man's legs gave out, and he fell to his knees. The younger man was on him in an instant, beating him with his fists and kicking him in the gut, while his victim groaned and heaved, clutching his chest.

The people on the platform looked on with shocked faces, but no one moved to assist. A woman covered the eyes of her two small children and pulled them toward the station, while the children strained to get another look. The rest of the onlookers seemed paralyzed by the second incident of violent bloodshed in just a few short hours. They stood as though rooted in place and watched, their faces frozen with horror. Even the police officers, distracted from taking photographs of the tracks and interviewing the last handful of witnesses to the earlier tragedy, turned toward the sounds of a man being beaten within an inch of his life, and only stared.

"Ah, here we are," Minerva said.

Between the blows that struck him like hammer strokes on every conceivable part of his body, Lucius tried to speak. He wanted desperately to explain to this madman that he had the wrong guy, that it was just a case of mistaken identity, but his pleas of "Stop! Wait! Please listen!" were cut off by a vicious shot to the jaw. His mouth filled with blood, and he could feel a tooth lodged in his throat. He began to choke and gurgle, blood spilling from the sides of his mouth. A cut on his forehead was dripping into one eye, half blinding him.

Lucius curled his body into a ball and wrapped his arms around his knees as the kicks and punches kept coming, pain upon pain, without end. He prayed to God to get this over quickly. He thought about his wife Delia, who died seven years ago from a bad heart, and his beautiful daughter Delilah, who was married and living with her steelworker husband in Pennsylvania. He was sure Delilah would be well provided for and loved, and for that he thanked God in a silent prayer, a tear running down his bloody cheek.

To the spectators still gathered on the platform, including one man who had snapped out of his paralysis and was working furiously to set up his camera for some priceless shots of the action, and to the police officers who were only just coming to their senses and realizing they probably should intervene, a curious thing began to happen. The big man who had been punching and kicking in an almost rhythmic, continuous cadence, suddenly stopped and reared back, his hands clutching at his neck. Streaks of blood from his torn knuckles ran down his wrists, mixing with the other man's blood in bright red spatters on his arms and soaking into his shirt. His eyes bulged, and a look of utter terror came over his face. He took a few steps back, still clawing at his neck, and fell backwards onto the ground, where he lay writhing and gagging.

After a protracted struggle, Santoro's frantic movements ceased suddenly. His hands dropped from his neck and flopped to his sides, and he lay motionless and silent alongside the man he had beaten to unconsciousness.

As he wavered on the edge of passing out from shock and blood loss, Lucius saw a very different version of what happened to his attacker. Later, as he recovered in the hospital, he would attempt to explain to medical personnel that his blood-slurred ramblings at the scene of the assault about angels of death were nothing more than the after-effects of getting hit on the head. But in his own mind, Lucius never stopped believing that what he had witnessed that strange and terrifying morning was in fact an avenging angel, sent by the Good Lord in answer to his prayers for salvation.

After the incident, Lucius became a devoted church-goer, rising to the office of Deacon of the Fawn African Methodist Episcopal Zion Church. Although he thought often about what happened that day at the train station, sometimes waking up drenched in sweat from dreams of pain and blood, he never spoke to anyone of what he had experienced and took his secrets with him to his grave.

As he lay curled up on the ground on that long-ago morning, blood in his mouth and blood in his eyes, Lucius felt the blows to his body suddenly stop. He waited with his eyes clenched shut for the next round, assuming Santoro had stopped only to catch his breath, but nothing came. He opened his swollen eyes a slit and lifted his head just enough to look around. Through the haze of blood and tears, he saw an old woman in a black dress and hat standing between Santoro and himself. Her long, pale fingers were wrapped around Santoro's throat, and there was a silvery gleam in her eyes.

Incredibly, despite the size difference between the hulking brute and the frail elderly lady, she was pushing him backwards with apparent ease, away from Lucius. The big Italian clutched ineffectually at the bony hands and gagged for breath, a look of terror in his bulging eyes. He was powerless to pry away the fingers that squeezed his neck in an iron grip, nor could he stop the old woman from pushing him down to the ground. She knelt delicately over his body as he thrashed and tried to buck her off. She pressed one hand over his nose and mouth and kept the other hand firmly around his throat. As she leaned over him, a smile spread across her ashen face. Santoro tried to fight her off with all his strength, but it was like fighting a stone statue. Eventually, his burning lungs gave out, his crushed larynx collapsed against his cervix, and he lay still.

"Well, that's finally sorted. Better late than never, I suppose," the old woman said to the open, staring eyes as she lifted herself up from the dead man's chest and brushed the mud from her skirt.

Minerva stood there a while, looking down at the body to make sure he was no longer breathing. Satisfied, she pulled a lace hankie from her waistband, and carefully wiped off her hands. She balled up the soiled handkerchief and shoved it in a pocket concealed somewhere in the folds of her skirt before turning to Lucius and looking at him with concern.

"Well, hello, Dear," she said brightly. "My goodness, but you've taken quite a beating. I'm afraid I was a bit slow in handling the situation, and I hope you can forgive me. I'm not as young as I used to be, you know."

She knelt to the ground again and took Lucius's hand in hers. Her hands felt warm, almost hot, and her skin was dry as chalk. When she smiled, the wrinkles in her cheeks appeared to crumble into minute particles of white dust that drifted down from her face as she spoke. "I'll stay with you until those idiots over there on the platform come to their senses and bring you a doctor."

Lucius was rapidly losing consciousness again. He tried to open his mouth to say "thank you," but he was drifting away too fast, and all he could do was stare into the strange old woman's silvery, depthless eyes. The two points of light behind those strange eyes were the last things he saw before all went dark, and then he was gone into oblivion.

Minerva saw Lucius's eyes flutter shut. As a trio of policemen came running toward the two fallen men, she gave his hand a final pat and walked away, leaving no sign of her passing in the muddy slush of melted snow on the path.

Seated once again on her bench on the train station platform, she settled herself comfortably and closed her eyes. Soon, she too drifted off into a deep sleep.

There had been many dreams and many awakenings in the century that passed since Santoro Rossi lay dying on a cold winter day in Morgan Park, Chicago. This time, she awoke on the balcony of a second-floor apartment in a hot western city with the spangled rays of mid-day sunlight shining down and passing through her body like a flashlight beam through a chilly fog bank, and warming the vinyl seat beneath her.

One mustn't let fear of making mistakes get in the way of duty, Minerva thought. Things have a way of sorting themselves out in the end, and the guilty receive their due punishment one way or the other.

She rose from the chair and straightened her skirts and hat. With a final adjustment of her shawl around her bony shoulders, she held up her chin and strode decisively through the guard rail and off the edge of the balcony. In an instant, she was gone, her body dissolving into a whiff of smoke which blew away from the balcony and disappeared into the air without a trace.

15

Doubts

Rich watched as the stretcher bearing Bobby Crocker was loaded into the back of the ambulance. Before the paramedics gently directed him to back away and give them room to work, he learned that they were planning to take Bobby to the county hospital. He decided as he watched the ambulance pull away from the curb, lights flashing, that he would take a drive over there later to check on him. The poor guy's legs looked crushed, and there had been so much blood. He would be lucky to survive and would probably lose his legs. Rich wondered what would happen to him then.

In his statement to the police officer on the scene, Rich described how the homeless man had fallen backward into the street, and how the silver Lexus that had run over him had kept on going without slowing down, as if the man were no more than a pile of trash blown onto the roadway. Rich reported with regret that he hadn't seen the license plate number and couldn't describe the driver, although he was fairly certain there had been no other passengers in the car.

He didn't tell the officer about what Bobby had said to him ("Hey, buddy, you're being followed…") or the look of terror on his face as he held his hands up defensively and stumbled backwards until he tripped over the curb and fell into the path of the moving vehicle. Rich provided his contact information, and the officer thanked him and sent him on his way.

Rich stood on the sidewalk, watching the retreating lights of the ambulance. "She's still there," Bobby had said. Reflexively, Rich looked over his shoulder, half expecting to see a shadowy figure of a woman lurking somewhere behind him. Other than the rapidly dispersing crowd that had gathered around the scene of the accident, there was no one nearby.

Despite the warm weather, Rich found that he was shivering. It had all happened so fast, and he wasn't sure what was real and what was the aftereffects of shock or his own imagination. He tried to tell himself that it was nothing more than the ravings of a homeless man who was probably mentally ill and almost certainly either drunk or on drugs. He had given Bobby five bucks on his way into the restaurant, so maybe he pegged him as an easy target and was just trying to get his attention so he could hit him up for more money. That was probably all it was. Some crazy, drug-addled hobo scamming him for cash. Poor guy didn't bargain for getting hit by that Lexus, though.

Rich shook his head. It was a tragedy, but nothing more. Still, he stood as if rivetted to the spot, his gaze off in the distance where the ambulance was no longer visible, its siren no more than a thin wail echoing back from blocks away. The sensation of someone standing behind him had been so strong. Could it really be no more than a random coincidence that he had been feeling the presence of someone right there, close enough to smell them, for Christ's sake, and then some stranger on the street tells him he's being followed? Even now, the feeling of someone watching him was still there, although much diminished from before, and he felt a shiver run down his spine despite the 100+ degree temperature.

So, what to do now? Lonny would be waiting for him to call back. Rich was already late for class and he had no shirt since his had been used as a tourniquet and was now nothing more than a blood-soaked rag. He had blood on his jeans where he had wiped it from his hands. He pulled out his phone and started to dial Lonny's number, but stopped. He looked at the blank screen for a moment before putting the phone back in his pocket.

"Right now," Rich said out loud, "you need coffee." He walked to his car in the Dos Sombreros parking lot and took an extra t-shirt from the gym bag he kept in the trunk. He wiped his hands with a towel from the bag and pulled the shirt over his head. In his mind, the image replayed of Bobby backing into the street, terrified and holding up his hands to fend off some unseen enemy. Then, there was the Lexus, rolling over Bobby like he was nothing but a speed bump and then speeding off. Who could do that to another human being? What he wouldn't give to get his hands on the worthless piece of shit.

Rich gingerly pulled on the car door handle, which was red hot under the blistering mid-day sun, and climbed into the driver's seat. He immediately cranked up the air conditioner to full blast. Starbucks for sure. He could call Lonny back from there. He felt calmer just thinking about Lonny's reassuring voice over the phone. He would say that everything is going to be okay, and Rich would find himself believing it.

Lonny would want to know if he had any news about Lorena, though. Maybe he should wait to call him until after football practice, so he could make a quick stop at home to see if she had come back while he was out. He pictured her sitting on the sofa, watching TV in her yoga pants and oversized t-shirt and laughing at him for worrying about her. He would call Lonny and tell him it was all a false alarm, and Lonny would scold him for making him worry over nothing. He smiled at the image, but a glance at his phone screen showed no new calls or texts, and the chance of finding her waiting at home suddenly felt very slim.

Rich swallowed a lump in his throat, and tears began to well up in his eyes. He shook them off and allowed himself to feel the anger that rose up from his chest as he thought about that lowlife Oscar. He had to be behind this. It was the obvious solution to the mystery of her disappearance. Everyone who loves Lorena, and that is basically everyone, wants her to ditch that creep, but she was as stubborn as they come. Is, not was! God, let her be okay.

Rich came to a decision. There was no point in going home, and football was the furthest thing from his mind right now. He had made a commitment to visit Bobby in the hospital, and he would make good on that commitment before the day was over, but first he was going to hunt Oscar down and get him to say where Lorena was and what he had done to her, even if he had to put his hand down the fucker's throat and pull the truth out of him along with his lungs.

For the first time in the past 17 days since Lonny got on that plane to Colombia to visit his grandparents, Rich was glad Lonny wasn't here. If he was, he would tell Rich to handle this rationally, to call the police and let them deal with Oscar, to not risk his future over a worthless scumbag thug. In short, Lonny would stop him, and Rich didn't want to be stopped. Rich looked down at his shaking hands on the steering wheel. But first, Starbucks. He put the car in gear and coasted out of the parking lot with only one backwards glance, just to be sure no one was following.

****

Minerva stood on the pavement, oblivious to the heat as she had been to the cold in that other, long ago place, and considered her options. Being seen by the homeless man had shaken her, as very few things did. She was used to being seen by children and animals, particularly cats, but that had never posed a threat. Adults rarely listen to children, shrugging off their fantastic claims of seeing ghosts as the product of an overactive imagination, and of course, animals can't talk. But this had been a grown man, and he appeared fully conscious, not delirious with fever or on his death bed. He had not only seen her but had sought to intervene and warn her intended target. This was new to her experience and very unsettling. What did it mean? Underneath her surprise and anxiety, Minerva also felt a pang of remorse. She hadn't meant to frighten the man so badly as to send him into harm's way. He had done nothing wrong that she had observed, other than interrupting her in her work. She had only meant to quiet him down, to get him to shut his mouth and mind his own business. Clearly, he had misinterpreted her approach as a threat. It was unfortunate, but what could she do?

Minerva returned to contemplating the decision at hand. She was tempted to follow along in the ambulance to learn more about the injured man and his connection to the spirit world, but his relevance to her purpose wasn't clear, and following after him could prove to be an unnecessary distraction. The man appeared to be barely clinging to life, and if he crossed over, his unusual abilities would instantly become a moot point. Besides, she intensely disliked riding in automobiles. The sensation, like being sealed in a metal coffin while hurtling forward at break-neck speed, was not frightening, as nothing really frightened her, but disquieting nonetheless.

She considered continuing to follow after the man named Richard, but she couldn't quite shake the feeling that something was "off" somehow. The most troubling thing of all was that Richard seemed to have no idea where the girl was. At the restaurant, he had asked the proprietor about the girl. Surely, if he had put her in the hospital, he wouldn't expect her to turn up at work, would he?

Since the unfortunate incident at the Chicago train station, she had tried to be more careful in identifying her targets. Men were such beasts in general that it was easy to mistake one brute for another. They all deserved what they got, but still, she preferred to get the job done right the first time. The girl in the hospital bed was counting on her, as so many girls and women had counted on her over the years, to protect them from the violence of men, or if failing in that, to avenge them after their deaths.

Minerva had gone to the apartment shortly after she read the address on the glowing screen at the hospital nurses' station. She had stared at the address until her vision blurred, and when she finally blinked, she found herself inside the apartment. She didn't question how these things worked, not anymore, not since she began her work, and that was a very long time ago.

Minerva had hoped she would find the perpetrator of the vicious assault on the girl at the apartment, and it beat sitting around at the hospital, watching and waiting for something to happen. Once inside, she encountered Richard in the bathroom and saw the cuts and bruises that covered his body like cast-off paint in reds and blues and purples. She had a good look at him while he bathed, maybe a more thorough look than had been absolutely necessary. Minerva may be old, and she may in fact be dead, but she could still appreciate a fine male body such as this young man possessed.

She had been on the verge of interrupting his bath to mete out his due punishment, either by frightening him into a heart attack, precipitating a fall, holding his head under water until he drowned, or if all else failed, wrapping her fingers around his muscular neck – so many choices! That was when the pounding on the door began. Curious, she retreated from the bathroom and waited.

In the conversation that ensued between the young man and his visitor, Minerva learned his name and that he had been in a fight over someone named "Lonny". The man he had fought with had made offensive and suggestive remarks about Lonny. Minerva wondered if "Lonny" was an endearment for "Lorena." Perhaps the taunting had thrown Richard into a jealous rage, and he had directed it at the girl. He seemed mild-mannered now, but Minerva knew from experience that the most violent of men in private can wear a benign and gentle mask in public.

In the aftermath of the incident at the restaurant, Minerva's thoughts drifted to another time and place, and to another man who wore a blameless face to the world but was a very different kind of man in private. More of a monster than a man, really. She sat down on the bus bench which had up until an hour or so ago been occupied by a Mr. Bobby Crocker. Originally from Lees Summit, Missouri, Bobby had settled in Phoenix by way of Chu Lai, Vietnam with a host of demons that had been following him ever since, but Minerva knew and cared nothing about Bobby's demons. She had demons of her own, or at least one demon – a Mr. Augustus Short, respectable businessman, devout Christian, pillar of the community, and accomplished wife-beater.

16

Minerva

Minerva Latham was the fourth of six daughters of Mr. and Mrs. Charles Latham of Albany, New York. Although he was a loving father and would never have admitted it to God or to another human being, Mr. Latham had longed for a son and had harbored hope deep inside with each of Mrs. Latham's pregnancies that this time, it would be a boy. Instead, he had been blessed with girl after girl and never a single son. He didn't hold it against his wife – she was as good a wife as he could have ever wanted – but in his heart, his secret disappointment never stopped whispering, "What if...?"

In his defense, operating a large wheat farm like the Latham farm took an enormous amount of work day in and day out, season after season – work that could have been shared by the strong back and capable hands of a son. Of course, Mr. Latham could have put his daughters to work on the farm, and in fact, Mrs. Latham had often and quite vehemently suggested he do so, but he was resolute in his determination that his daughters were going to be ladies through and through. No calloused hands, sun-burned skin, or unsightly muscles for his girls. He made sure every one of them received a proper education and learned history, classic and religious literature, Latin, and mathematics, as well as art and piano.

While they may have differed on the propriety of girls sharing the labor of maintaining a farm, the Lathams were in complete agreement on the importance, they might even say the necessity, of finding good husbands for each of their six daughters. As soon as each girl reached seventeen, she was thrust into Albany society with gusto, attending every church social, Christmas party, music recital, wedding, baptism, and funeral for which her parents could finagle an invitation.

Minerva's three eldest sisters each charmed a suitor all the way to the altar by the time she turned 19: first Mabel, the oldest, who married the Reverend Watson's eldest son David, a tall, gangly young man who was eager to follow in his father's footsteps and start a church of his own with a pious and supportive wife by his side. Even now, Minerva chuckled at the thought of Mabel as pious. That girl played cards for money with the farmhands when her parents weren't around and picked up a variety of curse words from them that she would repeat to her sisters' delight in the privacy of their shared bedroom at night. Still, the match proved to be a good one. Mabel settled down with the young Reverend Watson in a nearby town and raised children and chickens in what seemed like equal numbers.

Next came Anna, the third daughter, who married a decorated naval officer more than a dozen years her senior, whom she met at a garden party. Captain Worthy was an old friend of the host and had come to stay for a summer holiday. The romance between the naval man and the young farm girl was swift and passionate, and the wedding took place before the autumn leaves had fallen from the trees. Their first bundle of joy arrived in a hurry as well, and his May Day birth had more than a few tongues wagging among the gentlefolk of Albany that year.

Clara, the second eldest, resenting the fact that her younger sister had married before her, quickly settled on a match with the son of a neighboring farmer, Joseph Parker, who had left farming behind to go to the city and work in the saw mills. Clara had known him since childhood, and when he came back for a visit over the Christmas holidays, she used every fluttering eyelash, demure blush, and breathy sigh in her repertoire to ensure he was snared with no chance of escape before the ringing in of the new year. It wasn't long before Clara regretted her hasty choice of a husband, as Joseph was a poor provider, moving from one low-paying job to another, and a weak and unsatisfying lover. The couple bickered whenever they spoke to each other, but silence mostly reigned in the Parker household, and they kept up the appearance of a happy marriage because it was what was expected of them.

With responsibility for their first three offspring successfully transferred to their respective spouses, the Lathams turned their sights on the next girl in line. In the case of Minerva, they knew their task of finding her a good husband was going to be particularly challenging and they feared they would get little or no help from Minerva herself.

She was an awkward girl – tall and angular, with unruly dark hair and a long, horsey face. Her first foray into society, in the form of a midwinter music recital at which she managed to choke on a chestnut and send it hurling from her throat to land squarely in the wine glass of her hostess, demonstrated a social awkwardness that was unmatched except by the awkwardness of her physical appearance.

She had a tendency to wring her hands and speak in an increasingly rapid, ascending pitch when in the presence of eligible men. She would forget her feet at the ends of her long, bony legs and trip over carpet edges and doorsteps. The barely concealed twitters of other girls watching her struggles sent burning tears to her eyes and drove her to seek out the seclusion and comfort of the home's library. There, books of poetry, romance, and chivalry spirited her away to other worlds where she could imagine herself as beautiful, graceful, and the object of desire to handsome princes.

The Song of Solomon, with its lyrical expression of love and passion, sent Minerva into ecstasies. As she was frequently spotted reading the Bible, Minerva gained a reputation as deeply religious. What her neighbors and acquaintances would have thought of her had they known the feelings running through her body as she read and re-read the bookmarked passage, *"Kiss me and kiss me again, for your love is sweeter than wine,"* can only be imagined.

In the lingering days of Minerva's twentieth winter, when the magic of new-fallen snow and the joys of the holiday season were receding memories eclipsed by relentless, bitter cold, waves of ice storms, and blinding blizzards, her dreams of romantic love, and her parents' dreams of her expeditious matrimony, were forever changed by a tragedy from which the Latham family never recovered.

****

The two youngest Latham girls, Sally and Esther, were age thirteen and twelve years respectively when Minerva was twenty. The significant gap between the Lathams' fourth and fifth children, attributable to nothing more than the will of a deity whose ways are notoriously mysterious, resulted in a division among the six sisters, with the four elder girls forming one sibling group, and Sally and Esther bonding together as though they were the only children in their large family.

The two younger girls were inseparable. They shared a bed, a wardrobe (Sally was a slight child, and Esther quickly caught up to her in size), a love for the outdoors, and all of their thoughts, dreams, and secrets with each other. Like Minerva, they also shared a love of reading, but their preference was for tales of fairies and witches and fantastic creatures that lurked in the woods or under the sea.

Minerva had given the girls an illustrated book of Hans Christian Anderson fairy tales for Christmas, and it was received with enthusiasm. On most afternoons, if the weather permitted, Sally and Esther would bundle up in coats, hats, and mittens, and set off together with a picnic lunch and the book of fairy tales into a small copse of trees that surrounded a reedy pond less than a mile from the farm. There, they would reenact the stories in the book, playing multiple parts, using different voices for each, and enlisting trees and rocks as other characters or objects important to the story. Sally once captured a hedgehog and enlisted it as a reluctant Thumbelina who was wedded to a pine cone in an elaborate ceremony in which Sally played the part of the minister, while Esther showed an astonishing range by playing the maid of honor, the best man, the mother of the bride, and the organist.

One day in late March, with the sun shining brightly overhead like a promise of Spring, the girls made their way through the fields as usual to their magical place by the pond. As they walked in the warm sunshine, they debated which story to play. Sally wanted to do The Little Match Girl, which was a favorite of hers. She was particularly fond of the part where the main character met her saintly and tragic demise. Esther argued that she was tired of Sally always getting to be the Match Girl and that there were really no other good parts for her to play in that story. Esther wanted to do The Little Mermaid, which they hadn't done yet due to the pond being frozen over continuously since Christmas.

"How many times do I have to tell you?" said Sally with a hint of exasperation. "We can't do The Little Mermaid until the Spring thaw. We can't go flopping around on the ice like a couple of fish. It just wouldn't do the story justice. When we do The Little Mermaid, I want to do it right. Besides, we didn't bring our bathing costumes. You're not suggesting we strip down to our skin in the middle of winter, are you?"

Esther stuck out her chin defiantly and said, "Why not? There's no one around, and it's a warm day. I bet the pond has already melted. And you promised I could be the little mermaid the first time and you would be the prince. If we wait too long, you might forget your promise."

"I'm not going to forget. You wouldn't let me forget if I tried." The girls walked along, and Sally paused to lift her long hair off the back of her neck to feel the cool breeze. "It really is a warm day. Look, Esther, if the ice on the pond is melted, and I say 'if,' then maybe we can dip our legs in the water long enough to act out the beginning of the story at least. But I'm not going to let you rescue the Prince, meaning me, from drowning, because I'm sure the water is still very cold no matter how warm the day is."

"Hooray!" Esther whooped. "I'm going to check the pond. I just know it's got to be melted!" Before Sally could object, Esther broke into a run and headed toward the small stand of trees, intent on reaching the pond before her sister could try to stop her. Since turning thirteen, Sally seldom ran. She claimed it was "unbecoming to a lady." Esther thought that was absurd, but she was glad of her sister's stately pace today because it would give her extra time to check out the pond on her own. She dashed through the trees and upon reaching the water's edge was barely able to stop her momentum and prevent herself from plummeting over the bank and into the pond.

Teetering on the edge, Esther wind-milled her arms until she regained her balance. She looked down toward the water and felt a stab of disappointment. The sun glinted off the sheet of ice that still covered the pond. It hadn't melted yet after all. Esther looked back over her shoulder. There was no sign of Sally yet.

Already formulating a plan in her clever, youthful brain, Esther looked around her and spotted a tree branch that had broken off during the winter under the weight of snow. There was no snow now, and the branch looked sturdy and dry – perfect in fact for the purpose she had in mind for it. Seizing the branch and returning to the bank of the pond, she poked it forcefully at the frozen surface. The ice remained solid and undisturbed. She bashed the ice with the branch a second time, still with no effect.

Sally couldn't be far off now. Esther took another quick glance over her shoulder and made a decision. It was now or never. She stepped slowly and carefully onto the ice, using the tree branch to steady her on the slick surface. With the magical thinking of a twelve-year-old child immersed in fairy tales, she reasoned that if she could just find a weak spot in the ice, she could punch a hole, retreat to the bank, and show it to Sally as proof that the ice had melted. Then Sally would have to keep her promise to let her play The Little Mermaid today. She lifted the tree branch in front of her and plunged it straight down into the ice.

As Sally came through the trees, a scolding ready on her lips, the first thing she saw was Esther standing in the middle of the pond with a large branch raised over her head. Sally's shriek of "Stop!" and the crash of a thousand fragments of ice with one little girl falling through them were simultaneous, instant, and yet suspended in a drawn-out, timeless moment of horror.

In the shock of suddenly being submerged into the frigid water, Esther let go of the tree branch. It skittered across the yet unbroken ice toward the center of the pond and came to rest against a clump of denuded reeds, the tops of which protruded a couple of feet above the surface.

Esther had never learned to swim. It was not, at least in her father's eyes, a necessary skill for a well-bred young lady. In her woolen dress, petticoat, stockings, and heavy boots, she sank like a stone. Panicking, she flailed her arms and legs, stirring up mud and debris from the pond floor and causing the water to become unfathomably murky. She had not taken a breath before she shot down through the ice, and her lungs were demanding air.

Although the water was numbingly cold, the pond was not deep. Esther knew that if she could just push herself up to the surface, she could breathe. Then, maybe she could find her tree branch or something else to grab onto until Sally was able to summon help. Despite the freezing water and her aching chest, Esther stretched up toward the light filtering down through the murk. The tips of her fingers stubbed themselves against something hard. Ice. She pushed against it, but it didn't yield. Desperately, she scrabbled across the undersurface of the ice, searching for the hole she fell through.

Something brushed against her leg. It might have been nothing more than strands of water grass or a startled fish, but Esther automatically opened her mouth to scream. She breathed in the dark, cold water, and it filled her searing lungs. Esther gagged and choked, as the last of the air in her lungs fled her body and rose to the surface in a stream of bubbles. Her hands dropped from the ice above and clawed at her throat briefly, then fell away and floated free as her struggles ceased. Her body drifted gently down to lodge in a clump of reeds.

Above the surface, Sally screamed Esther's name again and again. She watched the hole in the ice and prayed with all her might that Esther would poke her head up through it at any moment, but there was no sign of her. Sally knew that she only had a few minutes to save her sister's life. There wasn't enough time to run back across the field to the farm house to call for help. If anyone was going to save Esther, it had to be her.

She quickly removed her shoes and stockings, coat, and dress and tossed them away from the bank. Wearing only a thin cotton chemise, she stepped gingerly onto the ice, testing its strength one careful step at a time. When she was a couple of feet from the hole where her sister had fallen through, she lowered herself flat, chest-down on the ice, and pulled herself by her hands toward the hole. The ice beneath her hands began to creak, and small cracks formed a lacy path to the crumbling edge of the hole. Sally stopped where she was and began again to call her sister's name. Hearing nothing, she quickly pulled herself to the edge, took a deep breath, and plunged her head under the water.

The bright, sunny day was instantly replaced by icy cold darkness. With no sound except the pressure of water against her eardrums, it was like entering an alien world. Almost immediately, her teeth began to chatter as she held her breath in the frigid water. She had to fight the urge to shut her eyes against the cold, but she managed to keep them open and she squinted into the murky depth.

The debris that had been stirred up when Esther fell in was once again settling to the floor of the pond, increasing visibility from a few inches to several feet. Sally swiveled her head and peered through the water for any sign of her sister. Some eight or ten feet away in the direction of the center of the pond, she thought she could see something tangled in the reeds. She lifted her head out of the water, took a deep breath of air, and plunged her head down again for another look. Yes, there was definitely something there. She thought she could see a boot attached to a leg, floating in the dim water.

Sally came up for air one more time and took as big of a breath as her lungs could hold before lowering herself fully into the water. She moved slowly and with care, trying to minimize the amount of debris that would rise up again from the pond floor and inhibit her vision. Sally was only a slightly better swimmer than her younger sister, but she had once gone skinny-dipping with her big sister Mabel before she was married, and Mabel had taught her how to tread water and how to hold her breath underwater. She taught her to glide just under the surface like an otter, using her arms to propel her. She did so now, moving swiftly beneath the surface of the ice toward the bobbing boot.

When she got close enough, she could see that it was indeed Esther's boot, which was still attached to her foot. Sally could see Esther's legs and arms floating gently with the rhythm of the water, and her skirts swirling around her like living things, blocking, along with the clumps of reeds protruding from the pond floor and up toward the surface, Sally's view of the rest of Esther's body.

She reached out and grabbed the boot with both hands and pulled as hard as she could. After a few tugs, the reeds released their grip on the body, and Sally was able to grab her sister by the back of the collar and swim back toward the hole in the ice. A small stream of air bubbles escaped Esther's lips and rose toward the surface, giving Sally hope that she was still alive.

Sally's chest ached with the need for air. She struggled to hold her breath while pulling her sister's limp body toward the opening in the ice. As she kept her eyes focused on the light filtering down from above the surface, her mind drifted to the story of the Little Mermaid. In the end, they had play-acted the story after all, only Sally was in the role of the little mermaid, and Esther was the drowning prince. She prayed that she would succeed in saving her, just like in the story.

After what felt like an eternity, Sally reached the hole in the ice and pushed her face up through the surface of the water. She opened her mouth wide and filled her lungs with air. She allowed herself only a few quick, gasping breaths and then began scrabbling at the edge of the hole to gain purchase and heave herself and her sister out of the water.

The ice around the edge broke off in chunks beneath her numb fingers, sending Sally back down into the water. In a panic, she swallowed some of the murky water and choked and coughed, but she somehow managed to keep her grip on Esther's collar. She started again to try and pull herself and Esther over the edge, and again the ice broke off beneath the weight of her hands.

Despair was falling over her like the dark pond water, pulling her downward toward the shifting, muddy floor, when she realized that with each grasp of the hole's edge and the crumble of chunks of ice that followed, she was moving ever closer to the grassy bank of the pond. With renewed hope and a burst of energy, Sally pulled savagely at the edge of the hole and drove herself and Esther forward one handful at a time until the water was shallow enough for her to stand and drag her sister out onto the grass.

Her legs trembled so violently from the cold and exertion that Sally not so much knelt as fell to the ground beside her sister. Through the water that dripped from her hair and the tears that stung her eyes, Sally looked down on the small, motionless body.

Esther's lips were blue, and her flesh was cold and milky white. Water ran freely from her mouth. Her eyes were open and staring, and a small sliver of rotted wood stuck to one vacant hazel eye. Yet, Sally refused to believe that her baby sister could be gone. She turned her onto her side and pounded on her back, sending rivulets of water from her open mouth. But no air filled her lungs, and when Sally released her grip, Esther's body flopped back to the ground and lay still.

"Esther! Esther, wake up!" Sally shouted, sending a handful of ducks that had landed on the pond's surface into the air in a noisy frenzy of flapping wings. "Wake up right now, or I'm going to tell Mama what you did! She's going to get angry at you if you don't wake up. Esther! Esther, please, please wake up. Oh God, please!"

Sally slapped her sister's cheeks as hard as she could with her shivering, nearly numb hand. Esther's face whipped to the side with each strike, but her eyes remained flat and staring, and the strike of the hand raised no blush of blood to her skin. Exhausted and spent, Sally collapsed on top of her sister's body and sobbed uncontrollably.

When she had recovered enough to stand, Sally rose to her feet beside the pathetically small, sodden body. She was still shivering in her thin chemise from shock and the freezing water, but she didn't want to waste even one more second to put her dress and shoes back on. With one despairing look back at Esther, Sally took off running, barefoot and nearly naked, toward home and help.

Minerva had been the one to spot her as Sally came running toward the house, dripping wet in the cool shadows of twilight. She had run out to meet her with a blanket which she wrapped around the shivering girl. Sally refused to go inside, but instead kept pointing back across the field and gasping out Esther's name between heaving sobs.

If Minerva had insisted on Sally going inside and drying off before the fire instead of allowing the girl to lead her to the pond, she might have been able to save at least one of her little sisters. The knowledge of this haunted Minerva to the end of her days and beyond. If only... One of many "if only's." As it was, Minerva and Sally had run to the pond together, Sally dropping the blanket on the way so that she could run faster.

When they reached the grassy banks of the pond, it was clear even in the failing light that Esther was already dead. Her eyes were fixed and beginning to cloud over. Her heart was still. No breath touched Minerva's face when she leaned over the body and held her ear just above the child's chest. When Sally saw Minerva gently remove the debris on Esther's face and close her eyes, she started sobbing again, dropping to her knees in the wet grass. The enormity of her grief broke Minerva's heart, and she longed to wrap her arms around her, but instead she had shaken her and shouted at her to get up and help her.

Together, they had carried the limp, dripping body back to the farm house. In the pandemonium that followed their arrival at the house with the body of the youngest Latham child in tow, Sally's own precarious situation was largely overlooked, with tragic consequences.

On a bus bench on a hot summer's day in a place and time far removed from the events that had changed the course of her life, Minerva pondered, as she had many times before, what might have been different if only she had looked beyond her own grief and paid attention to Sally's suffering. Even now, Minerva remembered those days with a clarity undimmed by death and the passing years.

Immediately upon seeing her youngest child's lifeless body being carried, still dripping with pond water and mud, onto the porch, Mrs. Latham flung herself on the body and brought forth guttural, heart-rending wails of grief that sent the crows flying from the trees. When Mr. Latham was summoned back home from where he had been working in a distant field, he was unable to comfort his wife or persuade her to let go of the body long enough for them to bring it inside. In the end, she had to be pried loose from her child and half-dragged, half-carried into the house.

Esther's body was washed and dried, and then laid out on the bed she had shared with Sally. Minerva and her older sisters, who had come immediately upon hearing the news, dressed her in a crisp white dress and placed a blue silk ribbon in her hair. Mabel, in a gesture that did not sit easily with some members of the family, but no one dared to utter a single word of disapproval, gently applied a small amount of rouge to Esther's cheeks to make them rosy as she remembered them in life.

Mrs. Latham had taken to her bed, so the elder Latham girls took turns sitting with the body until the funeral and burial could take place. Sally did not join her sisters. Turned out of her room by the vigil for Esther, she sought empty rooms and quiet places around the farm to express her grief in solitude. No one noticed the wracking cough that appeared the day after the incident at the pond, or the flushed cheeks and alternating chills and sweats that developed over the next few days and assaulted Sally's small frame. It wasn't until the day of the funeral, four days after Esther's drowning, that the family took note of Sally's constant coughing as the body was lowered into the ground under the gathering clouds of an approaching thunderstorm.

Minerva had been jolted from her grief when Sally, after a long, wracking coughing spell, stumbled and nearly fell into the grave to join her sister. Rushing to her side, Minerva put her hand on Sally's forehead and cheeks and felt the fever burning within her. She ushered her home and called for the doctor. Sally was put to bed in Minerva's own room.

The doctor came and diagnosed an infection of the lungs, severe enough to be imminently life-threatening. He prescribed a tincture for the cough and warm compresses to break up the congestion in Sally's chest. He declared that the child was under no circumstances to get out of bed until the fever broke, and as she was now too weak to stand, there was no argument from the young patient who had been so active and full of life only days ago. Although the doctor refrained from using such accusatory words as "neglect," Minerva could feel the scorn in his eyes as he listened to Sally's labored attempts to breathe through her fluid-filled lungs.

Only when the doctor had left, after advising that someone keep watch on Sally through the night and send for him if her condition worsened, did Mrs. Latham rise from her bed of grief to attend to her youngest surviving child. Sally was burning with fever and had become delirious, at times crying out for Esther. At other times, she seemed to be reciting passages from her beloved fairy tales. "Grandmother," she whispered, quoting her favorite story, "take me with you!"

In the morning, with the sun peaking under the window shade, Sally seemed to make a recovery. She sat up on her pillows and asked for tea. After a few sips, she sunk back into sleep. Mrs. Latham, who was alone in the room with Sally, decided it would be safe to take a quick trip to the water closet. She tip-toed out, shutting the door quietly behind her.

While her mother was away, Sally had another coughing spell and choked on fluid that had risen up in her throat. She tried to call out for help, but could only gag and clutch at her throat. Her bulging eyes stared longingly at the closed door through which no help would come.

When Mrs. Latham returned moments later, Sally was lying very still, with spittle on her chin, and her lifeless gaze seemingly fixed on her mother's horrified face.

Minerva arose that morning and made a tray of toast and marmalade to take to Sally's room for her mother. When she entered the room, she saw Sally lying there and knew immediately that she was gone. Someone had wiped her chin clean and closed her eyes. Her pillows and bed clothes had been made neat, and her hair was carefully brushed and arranged in a halo of soft curls around her head. Her mother was nowhere to be found.

Minerva woke the rest of the household, and an immediate search for Mrs. Latham was initiated. Mercifully, Mr. Latham remained with the body of his second child to die in a week's time, and he was not present when the farmhands found Mrs. Latham floating face-down, dead, in the pond. She had not left a note.

When it was all over – the initial shock, the double funeral, so soon after burying the youngest Latham child, the constant flow of visitors with their hushed condolences and their raisin pies, the tears, although those were the last to go – when it was all over, there were just the two of them in the big farm house, just Minerva and her father. She attended to him and tried to comfort him, but he slipped further and further away, both physically and mentally. He stopped caring about the running of the farm and would spend long hours sitting in a chair in front of the fireplace, staring into the grate. In six months' time, he too was dead. The doctor pronounced the cause of death as heart failure, but Minerva knew her father had died from a broken heart.

With both parents gone, Minerva's sisters each in turn attempted to persuade her to come live with them. While she agreed that the farm house was too much for her to manage alone, going to live with one of her married sisters felt wrong somehow. It felt too easy, too comfortable, as though she was forgiven for instilling the love of fantasy in her young sisters that ultimately led to their deaths. No matter what Mabel, Anna, and Clara said, Minerva knew that they must hold her responsible in their hearts. How could they not? Some things were beyond forgiveness.

In the end, Minerva decided to sell the farm and use the proceeds to buy a small cottage in the city. There was enough left over from the sale of the farm for her to live on, if she was frugal, for another year or longer. After that, her fate would be in God's hands.

The months rolled by. Minerva seriously considered entering a convent. She sensed an emptiness inside herself, a hole where other people had love and hope, and she wondered if giving herself to the church might restore the parts of her soul that had been buried along with her parents and sisters. But as the time approached when she had to make a decision, with her bank account reduced to just enough to cover no more than another two- or three-months' expenses, she was forced to face the fact that she lacked the faith to join holy orders. She went to church and prayed and sang hymns, but she felt cut off, abandoned by an all-knowing God who judged her unworthy of grace. She prayed for mercy, even if forgiveness was unattainable, but she felt no comfort. God had turned His face from her. If He was listening to her prayers, His only answer was silence.

With her resources dwindling to next to nothing, Minerva applied for and accepted a position as a receptionist and office secretary for a business firm that dealt in the purchase and sale of farming equipment. That is how she came to meet her future husband, Mr. Augustus Short. Minerva was twenty-seven years old at the time. She would be sixty-eight when she killed him.

****

Minerva arose from the bus bench and started walking down the sidewalk with her back ramrod straight and her head held high. Her indecisiveness had passed. She knew what she needed to do now. As she walked briskly away from the corner, the sun dropped below the level of the high rise building to the West, casting the street in shadow.

A Siamese cat, basking in the late afternoon rays on the windowsill of a fourth-floor apartment, watched through narrowed eyes as an old woman walked by on the street below. When she vanished along with the sunlight, the other pedestrians went on with their business, unaware of her presence and unfazed by her transformation into a cloud of fine ash that drifted away in the wind. The cat uttered a low growl before jumping down from the windowsill and padding softly from the room.

17

Hospital

Rich turned the steering wheel and entered a different world from the gentrified streets of the new, trendy downtown. The old inner-city neighborhood was no more than a handful of blocks crammed between a used car lot with a somewhat ambiguous hand-painted sign ("Se habla español! No credit okay!") and a crumbling motor lodge, where Oscar lived with his elderly mother. Rich and Lonny had gone there once to pick Lorena up after Oscar passed out drunk and left her stranded without a ride home.

He slowed the car as he approached the house. He had hoped to see Oscar's shiny, red Ford crew-cab pick-up parked nearby, but the curb space in front of the property was clear. A glance up and down the street revealed no red trucks, only a scattering of aging sedans, low-end Korean compacts, and one vintage low-rider, tricked out with chrome rims that reflected the last beams of the dying sun.

Rich drove slowly around the block, looking straight ahead and keeping a neutral expression as he felt the eyes of half a dozen Latino men, some with bandanas tied around their heads, and all with cans of Bud in their hands, gathered around a primer gray Lincoln parked halfway across a front lawn. Every head turned to watch him as he passed, and their gaze followed him until he turned the next corner.

There was still no sign of Oscar's truck. Rich thought about going up to the door and asking Mrs. Urias where her son had gone, but he wasn't sure she spoke English, and despite Lonny's patient efforts, his Spanish was just short of abysmal. Even if she did speak English, she probably had a lot of practice covering up for her gangster son's activities, and there was little chance that she would just cheerfully tell some lily-white stranger Oscar's whereabouts, assuming she had any idea where he was.

Rich pounded a fist against his car door in frustration. He was zero for two. No Lorena at Dos Sombreros, and now no Oscar. He drove aimlessly now through the crumbling streets of the old neighborhood, no longer caring who watched, almost wishing for a confrontation that would at least let him vent some of the anger that was boiling just beneath the surface.

Oscar might have Lorena somewhere right now, held against her will. If she was okay, she would have called or texted him. She would never have skipped out on a shift at work either. She was too responsible for that. Lonny was right, this was bad, and he had waited too long to go looking for her. Whatever happened, this was as much his fault as Oscar's.

"I will find you, asshole," Rich said through gritted teeth as he passed the Urias house a second time. "You're going to tell me what you've done with Lorena, and if you've hurt her, so help me, I'm going to make you regret it like you've never regretted any psychopathic, *gangsta* shit you've ever done in your whole worthless life." With one last look down the narrow street, Rich accelerated and drove back toward the main road.

****

"I'm sure it was an accident! He was high on drugs and not in control. I started it, even though I know how he gets when he's had too much. I pushed him too far." Lorena looked up to see skepticism on the nurse's kind face. "I'm the one who made him angry," she continued, "so it's really my fault. He would never hurt me intentionally." Tears fell from Lorena's eyes and were absorbed into the gauze bandages on her face. Her face was still puffy and swollen from her black eyes and broken cheek bone, but she was fully awake now. She held tightly to both of the nurse's hands and pleaded, "Please! Don't make me tell them! I don't want him to go to jail because of me. He really does love me."

Nurse Monique Green freed one of her hands from the girl's grasp and patted her gently on the shoulder. "Honey, I know you want to believe that. I do. Maybe I've even been there myself, but you got to know that he's not going to stop. He's already hurt you – just look at yourself! And you want to blame the drugs, but Sweetie, didn't he take those drugs of his own free will? Didn't nobody force them on him, did they?"

Lorena's only response was to lower her gaze and shake her head slightly, while the tears continued to stream down her face. Monique plucked several tissues from the box on the nightstand and handed them to her. "You try to get some rest and think about what I said. I'll hold them off a little bit longer. I'll tell the officers to come back in the morning. But you are going to have to talk to them then. There's no putting this forever. You understand that, don't you? And I want you to tell the truth. You got to do that for yourself. Okay? Think about that, and I'll come check on you before my shift ends." She gave the hunched shoulder another gentle pat. "It's gonna be alright."

Minerva watched as the nurse walked out of the room, turning off the light switch and pulling the door shut behind her. She stood beside the bed, close enough to reach out and touch the girl who lay there, brushing tears from her face with bandaged hands, but she knew the girl could no longer see her leaning over her. Lorena's delirium had passed, and her connection with Minerva's plane of existence had gone with it.

She had hoped to get back in time to question the girl about the man who put her in the hospital, just to be sure she had the facts straight, although she had already dismissed the doubts that had briefly troubled her. The path before her was clear now. Her memories strengthened her resolve to hold accountable the man who had harmed this girl and to protect her from any further harm at his hands.

The girl looked so small and young lying there alone amidst the sterile white sheets. Minerva leaned closer to her, so close that her beaky nose nearly brushed against the girl's hair. She breathed deeply, as though pulling the air from the girl's lungs and exhaled hot vaporous breath into her face. "Sleep, child," she said. "Everything is going to be alright. I'll make sure of it."

Lorena shuddered and clutched the bed linens, pulling them up to cover herself to the chin. She looked around, confused, but soon her eyes began to flutter closed, tears still glistening on her dark lashes, and she released her grip on the blankets and drifted into a fitful sleep.

Minerva's silvery eyes glittered as she gazed at the sleeping figure. She was in no hurry to leave. After watching a while the rise and fall of the girl's chest as she slept, she walked to the window and looked out through the blinds at the darkening sky. A gibbous moon was rising through thin, wispy clouds like shredded lace. Her focus shifted downward to the parking lot in front of the hospital's main entrance where people passed in and out through the double glass doors, some carrying flowers, others pushing wheelchairs or holding the hands of small children.

She was about to turn away, back toward the dim room, when her attention was arrested by a young man walking into the pool of light spilling from the lobby and illuminating the entrance. He had blonde hair and was broad-shouldered and muscular. He ran his fingers through his hair and lifted his head up toward the building's façade, giving Minerva a brief glimpse of his face before he pushed through the door and disappeared from sight.

Minerva moved away from the window. Her eyes seemed to give out a light of their own, and her facial expression changed, like a plaster mask crumbling away to reveal the true face beneath it. Swiftly, she glided through the closed door and out into the quiet corridor.

18

Bobby

"Hi, ma'am. Could you please help me? I'm looking for a patient." Rich smiled at the front desk attendant, flashing a set of straight, professionally whitened teeth. The attendant, a retiree who volunteered at the hospital four days a week to "stay involved in the community" as she told her sister in Tampa, but more so to have a taste of the power and control she once wielded as a preparatory school teacher, looked up from the complaint form she had been filling out regarding the inexcusable condition of the floor wax.

She put her number two pencil aside, laced her fingers on the desk in front of her and looked up over the top of her half-moon bifocals at the young man who stood before her, grinning like a used car salesman. The expression on her face was both expectant and stern, the look of a woman who has seen her share of dashing young men who, on closer inspection, have all the sense of a rooster with a head injury.

"Yes?" she said, her clear gray eyes locked on his. It was less a question than an accusation.

"Oh, um, I'm looking for a patient," Rich repeated, his smile wavering slightly. The woman said nothing, but continued to look up at him. He was pretty sure she hadn't blinked her eyes even once. He stood there dumbly until his smile began to hurt, then gathered himself together and soldiered on.

"He would have come in this afternoon. The patient I'm looking for, that is. He was in an accident downtown near the Metro station on Jefferson and Second Avenue. He walked into the street and was hit by a car. I was there when it happened, and I just wanted to check on him, see how he's doing."

There was an awkwardly long silence, during which the woman behind the desk continued to watch Rich as though waiting for him to improve upon his story. Finally, having concluded that nothing further was coming, she pursed her thin lips and unclasped her hands. She reached for her pencil and a notepad. "Do you have a name?" she asked.

"Richard Wright. You can call me Rich, though, um, Amelia." He nodded at the desk plate bearing the name Amelia Finkster. He flashed his best smile, the one that lit up his handsome face like a hunky angel and melted the hearts and wills of ninety-nine percent of those who witnessed it, man or woman, young, old, or in-between.

"The patient's name," Amelia Finkster said with a slight but unmistakable tone of irritation. Her pencil was poised an inch above the notepad.

"Oh, yes, of course, the patient. Ha, ha, sorry! My mistake!" Rich could hear himself beginning to babble. He had a sudden urge to turn and run away. With considerable force of will, he stood his ground and tried again. "His name is Bobby. Crocker, I think. Bobby Crocker."

"Relationship?"

"Um, what? Relationship?" Rich shoved his hands into his pockets, an unconscious gesture harkening back to the days of Saint Benedict Catholic School when the nuns were lightning fast with a ruler against the knuckles of a boy who answered too slowly or incorrectly.

"What is your relationship to the patient, Mr. Wright? Amelia shifted her gaze to the screen in front of her. Rich felt the shifting away of her piercing stare like the removal of red-hot pokers from his face. "Mr. Crocker is in ICU," she continued. "Immediate family only. Are you immediate family, Mr. Wright?" She gave him a suspicious look over the rims of her eyeglasses.

"Please call me Rich." Rich tried another smiled, but it died a quick death. "Um, yes, Bobby is my grandfather. On my mother's side. That's why our last names are different. Not much resemblance between us either. I take more after my father." He looked away, desperate to shut himself up but unable to restrain the flood of words that poured from his mouth in the spotlight of Amelia Finkster's accusing gaze.

He took a deep breath and added, "Mom and Dad are both gone now, God rest their souls. So, yeah, it's just me and Grampa Bobby now." He settled a wistful expression on his face and waited, holding his breath.

Amelia looked at him steadily for a moment, then sighed. "Third floor. Room 312. Check in at the nurses' station." She returned to her complaint form.

"Thanks for your help, Amelia." Rich gave it one last effort to win over Amelia Finkster, but she did not look up. He had been dismissed.

He looked at the signs overhead and found the one pointing toward the elevators. He walked across the tiled floor and hopped into the first elevator that opened at his approach, dispatching a young woman pushing an older woman in a wheelchair. As the door shut behind him, he caught a glimpse of a middle-aged man in tortoise-shell glasses and a garish yellow and black plaid shirt approach the front desk and the realm of Amerlia Finkster. "Good luck, buddy," Rich muttered.

The ICU was bustling with activity. Gurneys and wheelchairs crossed paths in all directions. Doctors, nurses, and various other hospital personnel moved in and out of patient rooms, walked briskly but silently on rubber-soled shoes down the corridors, and gathered in small huddles outside doorways and against the walls. The nurses' station was attended by one harried-looking nurse. Her desk phone was ringing in an insistent, steady tone. A doctor, still in surgical scrubs and paper shoes, with his mask dangling from one ear, was gesticulating with long-fingered hands as he tried to make himself heard over the din of the phone. A line of people – Rich assumed they were family members of at least 3 or 4 patients, stood expectantly awaiting their turn to get the nurse's attention.

Rich halted in mid-stride as he spotted room 312 to his right, between him and the nurses' station. He took a long look at the nurses' station and its cloud of people. He glanced at the door of room 312, then at his watch, then at the nurses' station again. With a quick and furtive look around him, Rich dashed into the room and quietly shut the door behind him.

Compared to the busy scene on the other side of the door, the room was perfectly still, and the sudden absence of noise echoed in Rich's ears. The only sounds came from the instrument panels beeping softly in time with the patients' vital signs, and the rhythmic snores of a patient somewhere further back in the room. The four beds, two on each side, were separated by privacy screens. The lights were dimmed, and there was a pervasive smell of Lysol with a trace of something unpleasant – urine and suffering – lying beneath the surface.

As he stepped softly across the room, Rich caught another sound, soft and muffled behind a pale blue curtain that was pulled closed, blocking his view of the first bed on his right. It was the sound of someone counting in a low voice. "Four hundred and forty-two, four hundred and forty-three, four hundred and forty-four..." Rich reached for the curtain and carefully pulled it aside, just enough to peek around it and see the bed's occupant. He looked into the startled eyes of Bobby Crocker.

"Four hundred and... four hundred and thirty- six? Sixty-three? Dang it, boy! You made me lose my place!" Bobby gave Rich an irritated look before turning his face slightly to Rich's left. "And as for you, just shut your trap for a minute, would you? I have a visitor."

Rich pivoted quickly around to look behind him, his heart rate pounding in his chest even as he mentally registered that no one was there. He checked discreetly behind the curtains of the other beds, just to be sure somebody hadn't ducked behind a screen in the instant it took him to turn around. Finding only one empty bed and two beds occupied by sleeping patients, he took a couple of deep breaths and waited for his heart rate to return to normal, then turned back to the grizzled figure, now looking expectantly up at him from the closest bed.

"Hi, Bobby. Do you remember me?" he said, extending his right hand. "I was there when you got hit by the car. I'm Rich, remember? As in Richard," he quickly added, remembering their conversation at the scene of the accident. "Not rich like I've got a lot of cash."

Bobby attempted to pull himself up into a sitting position, but winced in pain and lowered himself back into the pillows. He lifted a hand that was trailing drip lines, and Rich gently shook it. "Yeah, I remember you," he said. "You gave me five bucks. I remember everybody that gives me five bucks."

Rich smiled and took a seat in the chair beside the bed. "How are you feeling?"

"Well, the food's not great, so I'm a little sick to my stomach. My legs hurt like a mother too. Could use some Pepto Bismol with a gin chaser." Bobby chuckled and then winced again. He closed his eyes and breathed through gritted teeth until the wave of pain passed. All levity was gone from his demeanor when he opened his eyes again and locked them with Rich's for a full minute before he spoke. "Yeah, I remember you," he repeated in a voice that was suddenly very serious and very sane. "How could I forget?"

"I feel really bad about what happened to you, like I should have done something to prevent it," Rich said, dropping his gaze away from the intensity of Bobby's stare. "Or like I might even have done something to cause it, although I have no idea what." He looked up to gauge Bobby's reaction. The old man was still looking at him with eyes that seemed to be searching inside him for answers to questions Rich couldn't, and didn't want to, understand.

Rich plunged ahead. "Look, Bobby, do you remember when you spoke to me back there by Dos Sombreros? It was before the accident. You said there was someone following me – a woman, I think. You said, 'She's following you' right before you stepped back into the street and got hit by that car. You looked terrified of her, whoever it was. And then again, after you got hit, you said to me, 'She's still there.' Do you remember that?"

Rich realized that he was holding his breath as he waited for the old man to answer. He imagined he could hear his own heart beating, faster and faster, and the space of time before Bobby spoke again was like drowning.

"I remember." Bobby said in an almost inaudible voice. His face had gone very still.

"Who was following me, Bobby? I didn't see anybody, and I was wondering..." Rich paused and looked away. "Look, I don't want to offend you, but I know that you have some, you know, issues. I'm not accusing you or judging you, but maybe you were drinking or taking pills, or not taking pills that you should be taking, or... I guess what I'm trying to say is..."

"What you're trying to say is that I'm as crazy as a bed bug," Bobby interrupted, shooting an irritated glare in the younger man's direction. He seemed to have recovered from his earlier fright. "Spit it out, boy. We haven't got all night. Once Nurse Ratched out there figures out you're in here, we're both in big trouble. No lime Jello for us tonight. I know I'm crazy. Do you think I'm stupid too? Let's just both assume I'm a fruitcake and take it from there, alright?"

Rich was momentarily stunned into silence, but pulled himself together with a sheepish smile and continued. "Sure, okay, let's just move on. So, yes, I was thinking maybe you were seeing something that wasn't there. Any other time, I would have been one hundred percent sure of that. But the thing is..." He paused and took a couple of deep breaths, then looked straight into the old man's eyes.

"Bobby, I could *feel* someone there. Someone standing right behind me. I felt it when I was in the restaurant, and I was still feeling it when you called out after me in the parking lot. I could have sworn it. I could even smell them. There was this strong odor, like old perfume, something floral, maybe lavender or lilac, but old and rancid. It made me think of a funeral parlor – flowers covering up the smell of a dead body.

"It sounds completely insane when I say it out loud. It had to be my imagination and just a coincidence that you saw, or – no offense – thought you saw somebody." Rich ran his fingers through his hair until it was sticking up in bunches. "I can't believe I'm even asking this question, but Bobby, can you tell me anything about what you saw and why it scared you so much that you ended up walking right into traffic? The woman that you said was following me – do you know her?"

"No, son, I don't know who she is. I've seen her kind before, though, and I've seen what they can do." Bobby reached for a pitcher of water on his bedside stand. Rich rushed to pick up the pitcher and pour water into a plastic cup with a bendable straw. His hands were shaking as he handed him the cup. Bobby took a couple of slow sips, then abruptly turned to his left and glowered at a point near the wall.

"Pipe down, would ya? I can't even hear myself talk!" Bobby shouted. He raised his middle finger toward the wall, then turned back, calmly set the cup down, and closed his eyes.

Rich was so caught off guard by the sudden outburst that he took two involuntary steps backward and fell into the visitor chair near Bobby's bed.

"*What am I doing here?*" he thought. "*This guy is off his rocker. What did I expect was going to happen? What did I think I was going to find here?*" Rich put his hands on the arms of the chair and began to lift himself up. He opened his mouth to speak, to make his excuses and get out as rapidly as he could without being a jerk, but before he could say anything, Bobby began to speak. His eyes were still closed, and his voice was distant and dreamy.

"The first time it happened was back in 'Nam. Back when the world was crazy but I was still sane." Rich leaned closer to hear his voice, which had become soft and haunting, like a medium in a trance.

"There was this young soldier by the name of Mitchell. Hell, we were all young then. But this Mitchell guy, he looked younger than the rest. He was just a little fellow, probably not more than five foot four or five, so the guys dubbed him 'Mighty Mouse'. He was always trying to prove himself, volunteering for duties, rushing in where fucking angels feared to tread, if you know what I mean.

There was a long pause, and Rich began to wonder if the old man had fallen asleep. Then, in a brief return to his normal speaking voice, Bobby said, "God Almighty, I wish I had a smoke!" One eye opened and peered up at Rich. "Do you happen to have a cigarette, kid?" Rich shook his head no. Bobby sighed and continued his story.

19

Mighty Mouse

"Listen up, gentlemen. Word on the wire is that we've got some Charlies hunkered down in some old hunter's shacks about 3 klicks out in the bush. HQ is of the opinion that they may be thinking to establish a position, and it is our duty to discourage that kind of thinking. I'm going to need four volunteers to accompany me on a field trip to do a little recon. Mitchell, I'm going to save us all some time and assume you have volunteered." Sergeant Franklin nods in the direction of the small-statured man who had opened his mouth to speak and then quickly closed it again. "Alright, who else? Jones, consider yourself a volunteer. Baker, you're in. Crocker, you too. We've got ourselves a party. Saddle up, gentlemen. We leave at oh-eight-hundred."

The sun is high overhead as the five men reach the four decrepit shacks, side-by-side in a clearing chopped from the surrounding vegetation. Despite the sun, it is raining in sudden, steamy bursts. The jungle is never quiet, but amongst the constant chatter of birds and the rain falling on leaves, there is no sound of human activity. Sergeant Franklin and his men approach with caution, observing the shacks from their hiding places in the dense foliage just beyond the clearing.

Mighty Mouse Mitchell, taking point, approaches the first shack, gun drawn and at the ready. Private Baker follows behind, head swiveling from side to side as he approaches the shack's doorless entryway. Mitchell enters first. The shack is empty. There is no sign of recent occupation, and the jungle has begun to reclaim the space, sending tendrils of vine across the dirt floor. Mitchell signals all-clear, and Baker relays the message to the hidden soldiers.

The two men move on to the second shack, repeating their approach and subsequent all-clear message. They are beginning to relax their guard. The attention of the men observing from the sidelines begins to wander. Crocker thinks about the long march ahead of them to get back to base. He wonders if they will make it in time for chow. It is corned beef hash night, and Bobby Crocker is partial to corned beef, no matter how nearly unidentifiable it is in the hands of Army cooks.

Mitchell enters the third shack. Baker stands outside the doorway, facing out toward the jungle. Mitchell begins to call out "All clear," but he is cut off at "all cl..." by a tremendous blast that sends Baker flying forward and through the wall of the second shack, which collapses on top of him in a pile of rotting bamboo. From the sidelines, Crocker sees a flaming object shoot through the roof of the third shack and land in the clearing, rolling toward the jungle's edge directly in front of him. It is Mighty Mouse's head, its eye sockets aflame and its lower jaw missing, giving the head the appearance of screaming fire.

****

Bobby paused to take another sip of water. His hand trembled violently as he picked up the cup, and the straw bounced from side to side. "I can't tell you how many times I've seen that damned head in my dreams. People say it's the drugs that made me lose my marbles, but I say anybody who can see shit like that and not go a little bit crazy, well, they are just not human." He set the cup down and leaned back into his pillows. His face was pale and sunken, making it nearly indistinguishable from the pillow case. His knuckles were white from gripping the bed sheet like a protective shield over his chest.

"Anyways," he continued, staring in Rich's direction through narrowed eyes, but not seeing him. "Obviously the whole fucking thing was a set-up. The third shack was booby-trapped by the VC. Maybe the fourth one was too. We didn't stick around to find out. We just gathered up what was left of Mighty Mouse and shoveled him into a body bag.

"Baker was in pretty bad shape. Physically, he just had some scrapes and bruises, but mentally, he was pretty freaked out. Eyes bugging out of his head, shaking like a leaf. He didn't say a word after what happened, not then, not when we got back to base, not for the next couple of weeks while they processed his transfer to a psych hospital in Tokyo. He woke up screaming sometimes, though, even with whatever drugs they had him doped up with. We could hear him all over camp. I never saw him again, never even thought of him again until today. I been thinking about a lot of things today I hadn't thought about – hadn't wanted to think about – for a long time.

"Anyways, I don't remember much about the hike back to base except that I had to practically carry Baker to keep him from just setting himself down in the jungle and checking out completely. I didn't notice anything else out of the ordinary until later, maybe because I was so focused on keeping Baker on his feet. But later, a few days or maybe a few weeks after Mighty Mouse got blown to pieces, that's when I started seeing him.

"I chalked it up at first to all the reefer I was smoking, but some of the times I saw him, I wasn't even stoned. Then I figured I must be crazy, so I kept my mouth shut about it. The first time it happened was when Sarge almost got bit by a Two-Step snake that had slipped into camp. The damn thing was hiding in the tall grass around the clearing where we had set up a homemade baseball diamond for the guys to blow off steam and have some friendly competition."

"What's a Two-Step snake?" Rich interrupted.

Bobby chuckled. "They call 'em that because if one bites you, you can only make it about two steps before you drop dead. Kraits is what their real name is. Black and white-striped bastards about three or four feet long. Not very big, but deadly as a cobra. Just one more reason to hate 'Nam. Even the fucking wildlife tries to kill you.

"So, anyways, like I was saying, on that day – the day Mighty Mouse first came back – I was sitting watching the officers playing against the enlisted men. Not much of a competition really – the officers were getting their asses kicked. Next thing you know, this private comes up to bat – I can't remember his name, but he was an athletic kid and no stranger to the game – and he hits a good one, straight to the back of the ball park, if there had been a ball park. Sarge was playing outfield and he made a run to catch the ball but he missed it, and it rolled off into the grass. So, Sarge goes jogging off into the field to get the ball, and that's when I saw him – Mighty, that is.

"The sun was shining right in my eyes, and I was holding my hand up in front of my face to block the sun so I could see Sarge go after the ball. At first, there was nothing but an empty field of grass and weeds and shit. I swear you could almost see the grass growing in that hot, wet fucking climate. So then, as I'm squinting and looking over at the field, all of a sudden there's Mighty Mouse, standing right there, big as life. It was like he wasn't there and then poof! There he was. Just like that. I could tell it was him, even with the sun in my eyes, by his size and the way he stood with his fists balled up on each hip, just like the mouse in the cartoon. It was something we were always teasing him about, that stance of his.

"When I first spied him, he was leaning down and looking at something in the grass. Sarge was running right towards him, but Mighty wasn't looking at him. Real quick, Mighty reached down with both hands, and when he raised them up again I could see that he was holding a Two-Step. There's no mistaking those black and white stripes, just like on a barber pole. He grabbed up this deadly mother-fucking snake like he wasn't afraid of it at all. He stood there and twisted that snake's head around like he was wringing a chicken's neck and then he threw it back down on the ground.

"Right about then, Sarge made it to the spot where Mighty was standing, but he acted like he didn't see him. He saw the snake, though.

He forgot all about the ball, and was getting ready to hightail it back the way he had come when he noticed that the snake wasn't moving. He took off his mitt and tossed it toward the snake, but it still didn't move. Finally, he crept up on it nice and easy and saw that it was dead. He yelled back for the men to bring him a shovel so he could bring it back without risking getting any venom on him. Sometimes even a dead snake can kill you. All this time, Mighty Mouse was standing just a few feet away with his fists on his hips and a smile on his face. At some point, I looked away for a second, and when I looked back, Mighty wasn't there anymore.

"There was a lot of talk about that snake and what could have caused its head to be twisted around like it was, but no one said a word about seeing a man in the field, and especially not about seeing a dead man out there. I didn't say anything either. As much as I wanted to go home, I wasn't looking at getting a Section 8 to get there.

"The next time I saw Mighty Mouse was when he killed a man."

****

The Army discouraged fraternizing with the locals, so Private First Class Randall Fletcher kept his war bride a secret. He told Lai that it was only until he got back to the States and could raise the money to send for her and their infant son. He didn't tell her about his fiancée back in Milwaukee whose father was holding a managerial position for him in the family-owned brewery. He wasn't going to risk his future on a Gook bar girl and her kid. He never wanted a kid anyway, and she probably got pregnant just to trap him. Women are the same all over. They act like they want to have a good time, but all they really want is to get their hooks in some poor schmuck so he can take care of them while they sit around getting fat and lazy. It's what his mother did, and his father got out as fast as he could, leaving his wife and kids to go to war and never come back.

As soon as he finished his bid here, Fletcher had decided he was going home and he wasn't looking back. Why not? He and Lai weren't even really married. He had talked one of his buddies into pretending to be a chaplain and performing the ceremony, just to get her to shut up about it and go back to meeting his needs in bed.

Private Fletcher's thoughts are far away from his troubles with Lai as he sits in the bar playing cards with his buddies. The place is old and reeks of smoke and beer. Tinny music plays on a rusty speaker older than most of the bar's patrons. The men outnumber the women at least ten to one, so when a young woman with a pretty face and a generous bust line walks in the door, heads turn in her direction and conversation falters as men take her measure. She ignores their looks as she weaves through the tables, her eyes focused on one man only. Fletcher's back is turned toward Lai as she approaches, and he doesn't see her until she taps him on the shoulder.

He turns to see her standing behind his chair, and his friendly smile shatters like a clay mask. The face beneath is off guard and dangerous. Lai takes an involuntary step back.

"What are you doing here?" Fletcher keeps his voice low, but he can feel the stares of every man at the table, and he barely manages to keep the anger out of his voice.

"You not come home for two week. I miss you. Randall Junior miss you. I need money for baby. When you come home?" Lai's voice is tentative, apologetic. She reaches out a hand toward Fletcher's shoulder, but he snatches it and holds it tightly. His voice stays soft, but there is fire in his eyes, and his grip on Lai's wrist is painful.

Fletcher forces a laugh and turns to smile and roll his eyes at his buddies. He shrugs and throws up his hands in an exaggerated "Your guess is as good as mine!" gesture.

"Look Sugar," he says, turning back toward Lai and speaking loudly enough for everyone at the table to hear. "I'm not saying I wouldn't like to come home with you and find out just how much you miss me, but I'm afraid you have the wrong Joe. I don't think we've met, and I'm pretty sure I wouldn't for-

get such a lovely..." he pointedly looks down at Lai's chest. "Face," he finishes with a sneer. He gives her hand a squeeze and then drops it.

Fletcher turns back to his card game, and Lai, stunned and confused, stands looking at the back of his head, oblivious to the laughter and stares of the other men. When it becomes clear that he is not going to acknowledge her continued presence, she covers her face with her hands and runs out of the bar. He hears her muffled sobs over the din of the crowded bar, but he doesn't turn around.

Later that night, Private Fletcher, fueled by alcohol and rage, shows up at Lai's tiny one-room dwelling and gives her a black eye to remind her never to show herself in front of his friends again. Before staggering out into the night, he tosses a few American dollar bills in Lai's direction as she sits huddled on the floor crying and saying, "I'm sorry! I'm sorry!" between sobs. On a small cot behind her, the baby is red-faced and wailing.

A month goes by before Lai again goes in search of her errant husband. The baby is sick, and she is frightened and desperate to get him medical care. She risks earning another beating and brings the baby to the Army base to ask a medic to look at him. When the medic asks about the obviously mixed-race child's father, she pretends not to understand and doesn't mention Fletcher. The medic examines the baby and gives Lai an antibiotic for him. As she is thanking the medic and preparing to leave, Fletcher walks through the door, looking for aspirin for a headache. He sees Lai and the baby and stops in his tracks.

Private Robert Crocker is also in the medical unit, getting treatment for a mild case of trench foot. He glances at Fletcher at the precise moment that he is registering Lai's presence. Crocker is so struck by the look of utter hatred on Fletcher's face that he follows him when he walks out right behind the woman and baby.

Fletcher catches up to Lai, grabs her by the arm, and yanks her around the back of the building. He doesn't see Crocker, who crouches down and peers around the corner to see what is going on. Lai begins to cry out as Fletcher *pulls her sharply toward him, jostling the baby she is carrying in a sling on her back. Fletcher puts a hand over her mouth to stifle her voice. She pulls his hand away from her mouth and begins to shout at him to stop and let her explain. He grabs her around the throat and begins to choke her. She gags and pulls uselessly at her husband's strong hands.*

Crocker jumps up and takes a step forward, intending to intervene, but he freezes when he sees Mighty Mouse suddenly standing directly behind Fletcher. It's as if he appeared out of nowhere in an instant. Crocker blinks his eyes, but the dead man or ghost or hallucination – whatever he or it is – is still there.

Mighty Mouse wraps his arms around Fletcher's chest and squeezes tight with the force of a boa constrictor. He places his fist on the left center of the private's chest, just over his heart, and presses against his breastbone with inhuman strength. Fletcher's eyes open wide, and he releases his grip on his wife's throat and clutches at his chest. His mouth gapes open but the only sound that comes out is a strangled gurgle as he collapses to the ground. Mighty Mouse goes down with him and maintains his grip as Fletcher writhes and scrabbles ineffectually at the powerful arms that encircle him.

Horrified, Lai stands with her hands still protecting her throat and looks down at her husband, who is twisting and turning and gagging in the dirt. She tries to speak, to scream, to call out for help, but her voice is gone, and she is too frightened to move. She can do nothing but watch as the father of her child is fighting for his life and losing the battle. She doesn't see his assailant, and later, she will believe it when she is told that he died from a heart attack.

While Lai looks down on her husband, Bobby is watching too, from the shadows where he is hidden from her view, but the scene he sees playing out is very different from the one she sees. Bobby watches in horror as Mighty Mouse places a booted foot over Fletcher's heart and pushes down. Bloody spittle erupts from Fletcher's mouth. He struggles, violently at first and then with little resistance as his strength wains. Moments later, he is still. Mighty Mouse removes his foot from Fletcher's chest and turns to see Bobby gawking open-

mouthed at him. Mighty Mouse winks at Bobby and then walks away around the side of the building and out of sight.

Bobby will not tell a single soul what he saw that day until nearly 50 years later when he tells the story from his hospital bed to a young man he met only hours earlier. He thought it would feel good to tell it, to get it out of his head after all those years, but in the end, it only brings back the same paralyzing fear he felt then, and his tortured mind rebels against him, refusing to relive the nightmare.

20

Guardian

"Shut up! Shut up! Shut up! One, two, three, four, five..."

"Bobby? Are you okay? What's going on?" Rich looked nervously toward the door, afraid that the old man's raised voice would get the attention of a nurse.

"Six, seven, eight, nine, ten..." Bobby was nearly shouting as he spat out the numbers, rapid-fire like an auctioneer on speed. As Rich tried to calm him with soothing murmurs and pats on the shoulder, he managed only with great effort to bring his voice down to a normal volume.

"Listen up, boy. I wish I could say more but I'm already paying for what I told you. Eleven, twelve, thirteen, fourteen, fifteen." Bobby grimaced and grabbed the top of his skull with both hands as though to keep his head from flying apart. He lowered his chin to his chest and cursed under his breath for so long that Rich began to wonder if he should call for help. Then suddenly, Bobby shot his head up and spoke quickly and clearly as he looked straight into Rich's eyes, his words racing against the demons in his head.

"They kill people, man – Guardians is what I call them, those things like Mighty Mouse and that old hag who's after you. That's what they do. They kill bad people, and they protect the good ones. Sixteen, seventeen, eighteen..."

"What do you mean, Bobby? Who are they? What are they? And why is one of them following me?"

"Nineteen, twenty, twenty-one. All good questions, but you're asking the wrong guy. I told you all I know about the damn things. An even better question, if you ask me, is which one are you? A good guy or a bad one?"

The door opened abruptly, and Rich spun around with a gasp. A formidable-looking nurse entered the room and immediately locked eyes with him. Her dagger-sharp gaze was enough to make him retreat a couple of steps and raise both hands in front of him in a gesture of surrender. She gave Rich a warning glare that dried up his charming words and excuses before they could leave his mouth. With one finger pointed at Rich, the nurse glued him to the spot.

"Don't move," she commanded before turning her back on Rich and approaching her patient. She immediately began checking the monitors and taking Bobby's pulse. She spoke to him in a voice so warm and soothing that Rich couldn't believe it came from the same person.

"It's okay, Mr. Crocker. Just relax. Lay back for me now. That's good. I'm going to give you a little something to help you rest, okay?"

As the nurse fiddled with one of the IV lines leading into Bobby's arm, Rich took a tentative sideways step toward the open doorway that beckoned just a few feet away. "You!" the nurse barked without looking in his direction. "Stay right where you are. I'll get to you in a minute." Rich froze.

The monitors beeped their rhythmic tone, and the patient in the bed by the window snored his rhythmic snore. When the nurse was finally satisfied that Bobby was calm and resting, she turned to face the intruder.

"You are not allowed in here. Didn't you see the signs telling you to check in at the nurses' station? I will not have you upsetting my patient. He's been through enough for one day. He got hit by a car, did you know that? Now, who are you exactly and what are you doing in here?" She paused but not long enough for Rich to do more than open his mouth to speak. "In fact," she went on, "I don't care who you are.

You need to come outside with me right now before you cause any more trouble." With that, she took Rich by the arm and led him firmly toward the door.

Throughout the nurse's monologue, Rich attempted several times to interject, but only succeeded in uttering disjointed syllables and sounding like a percolating coffee pot. He allowed her to pull him to the door, which she opened and began to step through, tugging Rich behind her. They both came to an abrupt halt at the sound of Bobby's voice. He cowered in his bed, appearing to Rich suddenly very small and very old. His eyes protruded from his face as he looked and pointed straight at Rich. His words were slurred from the sedative, but his voice was loud and terrified. "She's back, man! She's here! Oh God, she's right here!"

With one fluid motion, the nurse shoved Rich through the door and pulled it shut behind him, leaving him standing alone in the hall.

As the nurse rushed to attend to her agitated patient, Minerva watched from her position inside the room, near the darkened window. Her hands were folded neatly in front of her, and her eyes smoldered with an internal light like two coals in a dying fire. The old man in the hospital bed had turned his face to look directly at her. He whimpered and shook, unable to tear his gaze from those burning eyes.

"Interesting," Minerva said simply. She marveled again at the old man's unusual vision. This was the second time she had encountered him in close proximity with the young man. She wondered what the nature of their relationship was. The fact that he was attempting to warn the younger man away from her made the old man something of a threat. Perhaps she would need to circle back to him after her immediate business was attended to. Assuming, of course, that she wasn't called away to a new mission elsewhere.

Really, Minerva thought to herself, there are just too many evil men in the world for one person to be expected to deal with them all, especially someone of her age. She shook her head sadly and glided across the room and out into the hallway where she caught up with the young man, who was now walking briskly toward the elevators. She followed a discreet distance behind him.

"He has the face of an angel," Minerva said out loud, though no one heard her. "But looks can be deceiving."

21

Augustus

Augustus Short did not start out evil, only poor. As the only child of a widowed mother who supported her small family as a clerk-typist in the city, he grew up understanding the value of money and the difference between having enough to buy fresh food and having to live off canned vegetables and other hand-outs from kindly neighbors during the lean times.

When his mother passed away, she left him a savings account with several hundred dollars she had put away for him one dollar at a time, depriving herself for the sake of her only son's future. Augustus had no first-hand experience with farming or farming equipment, but he was a shrewd young man. He calculated his best opportunity for financial success and used the money to open a small shop catering to the needs of local farmers.

Although he ran his business with efficiency and frugality, Augustus treated his employees fairly and made an effort to greet each of them by name when he encountered them at the offices of Short's Sure Quality Farming Equipment. He charged fair prices for his goods, which were of good quality in keeping with the company name. He frequently accepted payment over time from farmers who had faced poor harvests and couldn't pay up front for the equipment they needed to keep their farms in operation.

In time, Augustus grew his business into a thriving hub of the farming community. His many return customers happily referred their friends and neighbors to purchase equipment from "Short's Sure," as the business was affectionately dubbed by the locals. Farmers' wives, keenly observant of Augustus's bachelor status, sent homemade baked goods to the store with their husbands and invited Augustus to social events where eligible young ladies would be in attendance. He accepted the baked goods but graciously declined most of the invitations. Likewise, he was a reliable presence in church on Sunday mornings, but rarely attended the many church-sponsored teas, bingo nights, ice creams socials, and other such gatherings.

Augustus had no interest in meeting eligible young women. His avoidance was generally attributed to shyness or social awkwardness, and he was more than pleased and relieved to go along with these explanations for his reclusive behavior. He knew from early experience that he must keep his true interests secret at all costs, and by the time he was a successful businessman, his secrets were hidden so deeply that he had nearly succeeded in keeping them from himself.

When Augustus was fourteen, he came home one afternoon to find his mother puffy-eyed from crying and red-faced with rage. As soon as he walked in and shut the door behind him, Mrs. Short lunged at him, shaking a fist in his face and screaming, "What is this? What have you been doing, you disgusting little freak?" Clutched tightly in her fist were a pair of ladies' knickers and a garter belt. Augustus felt the blood rush to his face as he stared at the garments waving back and forth in his mother's shaking grasp. He could feel drops of spittle on his face, thrown from her mouth as she shrieked at him from inches away.

"What were these doing under your mattress?"

In the end, Augustus managed to calm his mother down by saying he had found the items in an unmarked package on the doorstep. Assuming they were meant as a gift for his mother from a licentious would-be suitor, he had hidden the improper offerings until he could figure out what to do with them. Implausible as the story was, Augustus had landed on the only lie that would feed his mother's need for attention enough to overshadow her good sense.

Mrs. Short was an attractive woman for her age, with the added glamor of being an unattached widow. She pretended to be modest and pious, but she wore her dresses tight around the hips, low at the neckline, and high at the ankles, and she did little to discourage the male attention she often received around town. And so, she accepted his far-fetched explanation and banished Augustus to his room to read the Bible and pray for forgiveness, while she spent the rest of her evening happily considering the possible sources of her naughty gift.

Mrs. Short had initially assumed her son was using the lingerie to masturbate and fantasize about women. After all, he was at that age when boys did such unspeakable things to their own bodies, or so she had heard. She also had a brief but alarming thought that he might have been fantasizing about her, his own mother. She quickly dismissed this notion as simply too appalling to think about. If she had known what Augustus was really up to, she would have been appalled indeed.

At the age of fourteen, Augustus had only recently discovered the taboo pleasure of silk and lace against naked flesh. He had, in truth, stolen the knickers and garter from the bedroom of an older sister of one of his schoolmates. It would prove to be the first of a long series of such thefts, from the homes of friends, from clothes lines, and even on a few occasions (out of desperation and with extreme anxiety) from shops. After his mother's discovery, he became much more adept at hiding his purloined treasures. By the time he received his inheritance and set himself up in his own business, he was living a double life, with one identity exposed to public scrutiny and another revealed only behind locked doors to no one but his own image in the mirror.

Augustus carefully cultivated his public image as a respectable businessman, a solid but not fanatical Christian, a teetotaler, and a responsible citizen with conservative, middle-of-the-road political views, about which he was never heard to raise his voice in impassioned fervor. His routine rarely varied. Six days a week, he arrived at his office at 9 AM sharp, freshly scrubbed and clean-shaven, and wearing one or the other of his two business suits: one brown, one gray. He spoke with his managers, inspected the operations of the warehouse, greeting workers he encountered with a friendly word and a smile, and then retreated to his desk for the remainder of the morning to attend to his ledger and correspondence. He passed his lunch break at his desk with a carafe of coffee and a cold meal he had prepared himself and brought from home.

Like clockwork, Augustus could be relied upon each day to make a final tour of the warehouse at 5:45 PM and to collect his coat, hat, and lunch pail before walking out the door at precisely six o'clock. On Tuesdays and Thursdays, he stopped at Thompson's Cafeteria for a supper of sausage and cabbage. He prepared his own supper all other evenings of the week, usually consisting of an omelet or a stew with potatoes and beef. By eight o'clock, when the dishes had been washed and put away, he drew the curtains, checked the latch on his front door, and put aside his businessman persona for the remainder of the night.

From nightfall to the start of the new day, Augustus was transformed into his alter ego. She had no name. Augustus thought of his other self only as "Her".

To begin his evening ritual, he first undressed and carefully placed his suit on a hangar in his wardrobe. He then pulled a shallow trunk from under his bed and removed a pair of ladies' knickers, garters, stockings, a corset, and a wig of long red hair, which he had pilfered from the church rummage sale donation box. He caressed each item lovingly, lingering over the texture and bringing it to his face to inhale its odor. He laid out the garments on the bedspread in the positions they would occupy on a human body. He spoke to them, greeting them in hushed tones as his hands moved over his naked flesh, rubbing his nipples and traveling down his sweat-slick abdomen to his genitals. He dressed himself slowly, starting always with the wig and ending with the stockings. Once fully adorned as Her, Augustus stood in front of the full-length mirror and admired Her reflection, often for an hour or longer.

Augustus was sexually aroused not only by Her reflection or the silky feel of the feminine garments She wore. The greatest thrill he experienced was in closing his eyes and waltzing languorously around the room in the arms of an imaginary man. The man he fantasized was tall and broad-shouldered, with a strong jaw and a full, straw-colored mustache on a not-too-handsome face. Augustus had seen such a man once, many years ago.

Around the same time as the incident of getting caught with his mother's unmentionables, he had stumbled upon a man bathing in the creek where local boys sometimes went fishing. The man had a bedroll and a small bundle of threadbare clothes. Augustus assumed he was a hobo, passing through town. He had hidden behind some bushes and watched as the man removed his boots and dirty shirt and trousers and waded into the creek. He sang a bawdy tune as he lathered a sliver of hard soap and rubbed his hands through his hair and all over his body. When he reached his genitals, the boy watching from the shore felt his own penis harden.

After the man had finished his bath, dressed, and set off down the road, Augustus had to wade into the creek himself to rinse his pants so that his mother wouldn't see.

As She danced with Her invisible partner, She whispered to him about trivial things – the events of the day, stories from the newspaper, local gossip – whatever came to mind. The man would not answer, of course, but Augustus felt that he was listening nonetheless. Between dances, Augustus would pour whisky into two crystal glasses, drinking one, then the other, and filling both glasses a second time and sometimes a third. At some point, She would strip off the lingerie, savagely, as though the clothing was being ripped from Her body by a bold hand. Only the red wig remained. Augustus would then fall onto the bed and complete his erotic ritual, if he didn't pass out first from the whisky.

In the morning, Augustus collected the wig from the bed and the lingerie from the floor and put them carefully away in the trunk under the bed. He then washed, shaved, dressed in his brown suit or his gray suit, and readied himself for another work day.

For several years, Augustus pursued his daily life without change to his routine, until one morning when, as he gathered up the lingerie scattered on his bedroom floor, instead of placing the knickers with the other items in the trunk, he put them on. He did this unconsciously and only noticed when he pulled on his trousers. He paused only for a moment and then proceeded to fasten his trousers over the knickers. From that day forward, he wore the knickers under his business suit most days, eventually adding the garters and corset. He told himself the garments made him stand up straighter and approach his business dealings with greater confidence.

Augustus had no fear of his secret habits being discovered. With his mother gone, he lived alone and seldom entertained visitors in his home. The elderly woman who came in twice weekly to do light housework and laundry had been firmly instructed to leave the bedroom untouched. She was arthritic and had cataracts, so the chances of her snooping under the bed were minimal. Confident in his privacy, Augustus was completely unprepared for the event that shook up his comfortable routine and changed his life forever.

One Thursday evening, Augustus sat at Thompson's Cafeteria with his newspaper and his plate of sausage and cabbage. He had been suffering from a chest cold, which had settled into a lingering cough. As he forked a chunk of sausage into his mouth, a cough erupted unexpectedly from his throat, and he spontaneously inhaled the bite of food into his wind pipe. He grabbed at his throat with both hands. His eyes bulged in panic, and his face turned red as he gagged, unable to breathe.

A couple sitting at the table across from Augustus saw him struggling and shouted for assistance. Within seconds, a small crowd had gathered around him. A burly, bearded cook lifted him from his seat like a rag doll and struck him sharply between the shoulder blades. The waitress loosened his tie and began to unbutton his shirt. As the crowd of employees and guests looked on, with Augustus powerless to intervene, the shirt was pulled open to reveal the lace-covered bone work of his corset.

The ensuing shocked silence was unbroken for a full ten seconds until a hearty smack from the cook sent the hunk of sausage flying three feet to land on the shoe of a diner on his lunch break who was also a longtime member of Augustus's church.

For the first few days after this incident, Augustus allowed himself to believe that his explanation to the crowd gaping and staring in the cafeteria – that he suffered from a bad back and wore the corset for support on days when it was especially painful – had been sufficiently convincing. The sermon given the following Sunday, and the knowing looks and whispered conversations as he passed through the congregation, quickly dispelled that delusion. Reverend Whitaker chose the topic of Sodom and Gomorrah for the morning's service, even though he was squarely in the middle of a series of sermons on the parables of Jesus. When the Reverend reached the part of the story dealing with destruction of the sinful by fire and brimstone, Augustus felt his eyes burning directly into his own.

That afternoon, Augustus returned home, removed the lingerie and wig from the trunk, and shoved them into the fireplace, tears gliding down his cheeks as he watched them burn. He stayed up late that night, staring into the fire and drinking before falling asleep in his arm chair with a single glass and an empty bottle of whisky at his elbow.

The next day, before his usual late afternoon inspection of Short's Sure operations, he approached his secretary, a plain spinster he had never before given more than a passing glance, and proposed marriage. Minerva Latham, after a moment's silent contemplation, said, "Yes Sir, Mr. Short, that would be acceptable."

22

Oscar

Oscar Urias liked blood – the smell of it, the taste, even the color – such a powerful, in-your-face red. It was impossible to ignore blood. He enjoyed watching boxing matches at his local boxing club or on Pay-Per-View at the sports bar. One solid hit to the face, and the blood would fly from the boxer's nose or mouth in a crimson arc. Beautiful. The only thing better was mixed martial arts. The opponents grappling, slick with their intermingling blood and sweat. Even better than watching MMA was actually participating in it. The feel of the blood oozing from his torn knuckles, the smell of it dripping from his nose, the taste of it in his mouth – this is what Oscar lived for.

When he started running with the Diablos Locos gang at the age of fifteen, it wasn't for the prestige or the girls or even the promise of easy money from slinging *chiva* to desperate junkies. For Oscar, the main appeal of joining up with the DL's was the fighting. When some dumb kid wanted to be jumped in to the gang, or some asshole got on the DL's bad side and needed their ass whipped, Oscar was right there, ready for duty.

An assault charge at age nineteen introduced Oscar to the John Lewis Correctional Facility where he served two years for the initial charge and another five for biting the earlobe off a wannabe White

Pride piece of shit who served him a tray of pasta and meatballs with a side of spit in the chow line. He had spat out the earlobe but licked the blood from his lips, relishing the warm, salty taste. He might have gone back for more if the guards hadn't taken him down.

Oscar learned the trade of air conditioning and heating repair in the penitentiary. With the help of an incentive program for hiring ex-cons on parole, he got a job a few months after his release with a small a/c and heating company that was barely bringing in enough cash to keep its trio of beater vans running and pay its employees a hair over minimum wage. He was called out to an apartment building on one of the hottest days in July to fix a tenant's broken a/c. That was how he met Lorena.

She had met him at the door and immediately launched into him in a mixture of English and Spanish – Why was he late? Did he know how long she had been waiting in the heat? Did he know how hot it was? Did he even care that she was going to be late for work because of him? He heard the words but barely registered them. He was too dazzled by the sight of her. She was the most beautiful woman he had ever seen. Her hair – like a wild tigress, her skin – smooth and silky as melted caramel, and her body – *ai Dios mío,* what a body!

Oscar had never cared so much before or since about fixing an air conditioner. He gave that ancient, rusted-out unit every bit of his knowledge and skill and somehow got the thing to start working again. Her smile when the first gust of cold air hit her flushed cheeks was like the sun coming out from behind the clouds. He seized the moment and got her phone number while she was still giddy with relief and before she had a chance to question whether it was a good idea to give her number to a complete stranger with gang tattoos on every visible part of his body.

They had been dating, casually at first and then exclusively, for almost a year the first time he hit her. That time was mostly his fault, Oscar was willing to admit. They had been at his *compadre's* house all day for a barbecue, watching sports on his big-screen TV and partying on the patio. Maybe he got too much sun. Maybe he drank a few too many beers. Maybe he was a little too buzzed to drive home. Still, Lorena didn't have to embarrass him in front of his friends by trying to get his keys away from him with everybody watching. It was just a slap. It wasn't like he had punched her with his fist. Not that time anyway.

He apologized the next day, but she was a cold, unforgiving bitch about it and kept on bringing it up every time they argued about anything. That was on her, not him.

As Oscar saw it, he and Lorena had a passionate relationship. Sure, they argued and fought a lot, but they always made up, and their love-making after a fight was always hot and wild. There had only been a few times, three or four maybe, when he had hit her hard enough to leave a mark. He hadn't meant to, but she just wouldn't shut up and get out of his face. What was he supposed to do? This last time, though, had been different. He knew he had lost control. It was the blood. He realized that now. He wasn't prepared for the sight of bright red blood streaming from her busted lip. It had made him go crazy, so crazy that he couldn't remember most of what happened that night.

****

"Goodbye, Oscar." Lorena pulled her handbag over her shoulder and turned away. Oscar caught up with her before she had taken three steps. He grabbed her arm above the elbow, spun her around to face him. She kept her face turned, avoiding eye contact. There were tears in her eyes, but her jaw was clenched and her expression cold and unwavering.

"Where do you think you're going?" He kept his voice calm, like the conversation was as light and natural as picking a restaurant for dinner. When she didn't answer, didn't even look at him, his tone changed. "Get back over here. I'm not done talking to you yet."

"Yes, you are done. And I'm done too. Now, let go of my arm. I'm leaving." She jerked her arm to free it from his grip. He let go.

The first punch, a right cross to the nose with nothing held back, sent the blood flying in a stunning red spray. Before she could speak or even scream, he hit her again with a left to the mouth. More blood flying, and still more blood flowing down from her broken nose and mouth. He leaned in, inhaled the coppery scent with eyes closed in ecstasy, and licked the blood languorously from her face while she screamed. He drew back to hit her again. And again.

The next thing Oscar remembered, he was standing over Lorena's crumpled body, which lay still on the ground. For a moment, he was confused. He didn't remember how she had got there and why he was out of breath, his body humming with adrenalin. Then he looked down at his bloodied knuckles, and a low moan rose up in his throat.

He looked for signs of life – the slightest movement, breath bubbling out of the blood in her nose and mouth, or the rise of her chest. There was nothing but the buzzing of a fly that landed in the blood dripping from her nose. He watched her for several minutes but didn't bend down to check her more closely. He was afraid to touch her, afraid to feel her skin cooling, to feel the absence of a pulse. Instead, he picked up her phone where it had fallen from her hand and put it in his pocket, then kicked the dirt around to hide his footprints.

He looked around to be sure no one was nearby, then got in his truck and sped away.

Al DeLeon watched the tail lights fade into the distance. He moved closer to the girl lying on the ground. She looked so small and broken. He looked down on her for a long time. He wanted nothing more than to wipe the blood from her face and lift her off the hard gravel and take her somewhere safe, but he could only hover ineffectually over her and weep.

****

Oscar was packing clothes into a duffle bag the first time the phone rang. He glanced at the screen, saw an unfamiliar number, and ignored it. When it rang a second time from the same number a few minutes later, he picked it up and answered, "Yeah?" in an irritated growl.

"Oscar, it's me."

It was Lorena's voice on the other end of the line, unmistakably. The shock of it, like a message from beyond the grave, stunned him to silence. He gaped, his mouth moving like a fish only just scooped up to the surface in a net. Finally, he was able to force out a few strangled words.

"Lorena? Baby, is it really you? Where are you?" *I'm dead. You killed me, and I've come back for you.* The words were instantly there in his head, in her voice. He waited for her to say them.

"I'm in the hospital. Where did you think I would be, the morgue?"

Oscar choked. He had to take several breaths to quiet his thumping heart and summon what he hoped was a natural voice, filled with remorse.

"Oh my God, Baby, I'm so sorry. I don't know what happened. I never meant to do anything to hurt you. I was so angry and hurt when you tried to leave, and then when you fell and hit your head, well I was just so scared and freaked out, you know? I just ran. It was instinct. I couldn't help it. I'm so sorry. I love you so much! You don't know how good it is to hear your voice. Tell me which hospital you're in, and I'll be right there."

Oscar sobbed noisily into the phone and waited.

"I'm in Good Samaritan, but don't come here. That's why I'm calling you, to warn you. The hospital called the cops and they're going to be here soon. If they catch you here, they'll arrest you for sure."

"What are you going to tell them?"

"Don't worry, I'm not going to tell them what you did. I'm just going to say that I can't remember anything."

"Baby, I love you so much. I'll make this up to you, I swear."

There was a pause. Oscar could hear Lorena crying softly. There was a deep intake of breath, and finally she spoke. "I want to believe you, Oscar. I'm just really confused right now. You hurt me really bad, and then you just left me there. I could have died."

He started to speak, but she spoke over him, talking faster now. "I'm not ready to see you yet, okay? I'm sorry. I need time. I..., I need to figure some things out. I'm only calling because I don't want you to go to prison. Please, just stay away from me for a while. I have to go now."

The line went dead. Oscar looked at the blank phone screen for several minutes before picking up his keys and walking out the door.

23

Encounters

Rich reached across the seat and turned the ringer off. His phone had been ringing steadily, but he hadn't bothered to look at it to see who was calling him. Right now, he didn't care. After the scene at the hospital with Bobby, he had been pretty well spooked. He had practically run from Bobby's room and didn't remember how he got from there to his car. In the hospital parking lot, he thought he sensed the return of the presence, the old woman Bobby said was a killer. That was probably just his mind playing tricks on him, though, because now that he was in his car and speeding down the highway, he didn't feel anything out of the ordinary.

The phone slid off the passenger seat and onto the floor as Rich swerved into the left lane to pass a sky-blue Buick with an American flag vanity plate that read "DTRDNME". Rich's distracted mind couldn't resist trying to decipher the plate. *Date Red Name? Dotard Enemy?* It came to him eventually – Don't Tread On Me – but he was no longer interested. He was looking at the sky, which was dark with clouds rising up from the south like a monster wave. He pressed the accelerator, bringing the car's speed close to ninety.

Rich replayed the day's events in his mind. That was quite a story the old veteran had told him. While he had been standing there face-to-face with Bobby, listening to him talk about what happened in Vietnam and about the creatures he called Guardians, it was all pretty weird, but it seemed real, and Bobby had come across as coherent and sincere. Rich had found himself believing his outlandish stories. But then things got out of hand, and the old man no longer sounded rational. He sounded bat-shit crazy, to be honest.

Rich shook his head dismissively. He didn't have time for crazy old hobos and ghost stories right now. Lorena was out there somewhere, probably hurt, or worse, dead. She would have called by now if she could.

That thug Oscar was almost certainly right in the middle of whatever was going on, and Rich was going to get some answers out of him one way or another. His fists tightened on the steering wheel as he thought about the times he had caught Lorena covering up bruises with makeup. She always had an excuse, but Rich wasn't stupid. He hoped Oscar would give him a reason to punch the smirk right off his face.

It was only then that it hit him. "I'm a fucking idiot!" he shouted at the top of his lungs. He pounded his fists against the steering wheel and nearly swerved out of his lane. A horn squawked like an angry bee as a navy blue Prius in the next lane sped up to get away from him. Rich thought about what Lorena's boss had told him. Lonny had said nearly the same thing. *Check the hospitals.* Yet, he had just run out of the hospital like a scared little boy and hadn't stopped to ask the formidable Amelia Finkster if there had been a patient admitted named Lorena Cuevas.

What is Lonny going to think? "He's going to think I'm a selfish dumbass," Rich answered himself. "And he's going to be right." Too late to go back now. He would call as soon as he got home. Maybe Amelia would be gone for the day, and whoever answered the phone would be more willing to give up some information.

It was full dark when Rich reached his apartment. He parked and gathered up his gym bag and backpack before climbing out of the car. The humid, close air hit him immediately. The atmosphere was still, expectant. As he slung his bags over one shoulder, the first drops of rain fell, dotting his face and the hood of the car.

He leaned in through the open car door to look for his phone. Out of the corner of his eye, he saw someone standing unmoving in the rain and rising wind. A couple of yards away, under the flickering light of a lamppost, she stood. Her eyes glowed silver as she stared at him with a look on her pallid face of pure malevolence.

Rich knew in an instant that he was looking into the eyes of the Guardian. Her black, old-fashioned dress and hat blended with the darkness, bringing her powder-white face and gnarled, ropy-tendoned hands into sharp relief. Her yellowed fingernails were long and tapered, like the talons of an owl. As he watched, immobilized with fear, Rich saw the creature raise her hands with her arms outstretched in front of her and open her taloned fingers like the wings of some ghastly night bird. A smile slowly spread across the wrinkled face beneath depthless eyes that shown in their own silvery light like moonlit tunnels to hell.

A gust of wind blew particles of sand to swirl around Rich's head and into his eyes. There was a muffled roar, like a distant, massive swarm of bees, and then the dust storm arrived in full force. Hurricane-velocity winds carried a wall of desert sand, rain, and debris blasting against everything in its path, slamming the car door shut and nearly knocking Rich off his feet. Visibility dropped to a foot or less. There was only darkness, the scent of mud and ozone, and the constant howl of the ravening wind.

Rich pulled the collar of his t-shirt up to cover his nose and mouth. He shielded his eyes and tried to penetrate the stinging cloud of dirt to find his way to his apartment before she could catch up with him, but he couldn't keep his eyes open, could barely breathe without inhaling dust. He took a single step forward in what he hoped was the right direction.

She was upon him in an instant, erupting through the murk, eyes glowing like two sparks from a smoldering fire. He had no time to react before he felt the gnarled hands and sharp talons close around his throat. The stench of rancid violets mixed with decay overpowered the smell of the storm and assaulted his nostrils as he struggled for air. He grabbed the skeletal wrists and pulled with all of his strength to free his throat from her grasp, but to no effect. Her grip held fast, and his efforts to pry away even one of the bony fingers from his neck were like trying to break through stone.

Rich tried to think through his panic. He was an athlete. He had been on the varsity wresting team in high school. He was trained to break free from what seemed like unbreakable holds. He could do this. He had to try. He's fighting an old lady, for fuck's sake.

Rich twisted his body and kicked out, aiming at his assailant's groin, but his legs and feet went through the Guardian's body as if it were nothing but a film projection. With his last burst of strength, he lunged forward to head-butt her, but his head met no resistance and seemed to move right through the ancient parchment face. The unblinking silver eyes flickered out, but only briefly before returning, inches from his face.

Deprived of air, Rich felt his cheeks redden and grow hot and his eyes bulge from his face. Pinpoint black spots grew and expanded across his field of vision. He began to drift away into darkness, his hands falling to his sides. He thought he heard voices in the wind, the cawing of a thousand crows, and the spots before his eyes took on the shapes of black winds, beating, moving closer, blotting out all light.

Just as the blackness enveloped the last of his sight, he felt a sharp slap across one cheek and then the other. Through the fog of his oxygen-starved brain, he heard a familiar voice.

"Richie, you idiot, what are you doing? Stop that right now!" Another slap. "Hey, did you hear me? I said stop it! What is the matter with you? Oh my God, don't you dare fall on me. Richie! Snap out of it!"

****

When he regained consciousness, Rich was back in his car, slumped across the passenger seat. Sitting next to him and looking anxiously out each of the car windows in turn, was Lonny. Outside, the winds had died down, and the blowing dust had been replaced by torrents of rain, washing away the mud and broken tree branches to choke the storm drains and build up in sodden heaps in the low places of the asphalt lot.

Rich attempted to speak but managed only a strained croak. Lonny whirled around at the sound and looked at him with a mixture of fear and relief on his face. He leaned over Rich and held his face in both of his hands. Rich felt Lonny's hands trembling against his cheeks. This small detail gave him assurance that he wasn't dreaming. Lonny, against all odds, was really there. Tears of relief welled in his eyes.

In a whisper, Lonny said, "Richie, don't talk, okay? Just squeeze my hand if you understand me." Lonny felt a squeeze. "Okay, good, give me another squeeze if you're feeling okay, or, maybe not okay, but better than you were… not dying." He felt another squeeze. Rich opened his mouth as if to try to speak, but Lonny quickly put a finger to his lips. "Shh, don't talk, I said. I need you to listen to me."

Lonny stole another anxious glance out the car windshield. "There's something out there," he whispered. "I felt it, but I couldn't see anything. I know this is going to sound crazy, but I swear, someone or something very strong was trying to strangle you. I thought you were just having some kind of a fit at first. All I could see was you gagging and turning purple. I couldn't see whoever had a hold of you. I couldn't see much of anything because of the dust storm, but then I felt him there in between us when I tried to go to you. You're going to think I've lost my mind or that I'm making some kind of sick joke, but I've never been more serious in my life. Richie, I think the Invisible Man just tried to kill you."

"Woman," Rich croaked.

"What? How do you know it's a woman? Actually, never mind, I don't care about its chromosomes. Whatever it is, it had you by the neck, Richie. I could feel the hands. I could smell its breath. I tried to push it away, but it was so strong. I don't know how I did it, but I managed to get the car door open and shove you in, and then whatever it was just let go. I've been sitting here for about twenty minutes now waiting for you to wake up and wondering if that thing is still out there waiting too." Lonny shot another nervous glance out the windshield.

Rich struggled to push himself up in the seat. He massaged his throat and looked out the window toward the lamppost where the Guardian had first appeared. The power must have gone out because of the storm. No light penetrated the driving rain. Rich peered through the darkness to catch a glimpse of glowing silver eyes, but the parking lot was in total darkness. They could be anywhere from just outside their apartment to the surface of the moon.

Rich reached across Lonny and switched on the headlights. Lonny looked alarmed and started to protest, but Rich spoke first. "I think she's gone," he said. The twin beams illuminated a few yards in front of the car, revealing a line of parked cars. The rain had diminished momentarily, and he could see that the space beneath the lamppost was unoccupied, except by a ragged patio umbrella that had been blown away by the storm to rest against its base.

"There's a water bottle in my gym bag. Could you please…?"

Rich took a few careful sips of water and cleared his throat. When he spoke again, his voice was stronger, and he turned to Lonny with a genuine smile. "Lonny, I don't know what you're doing here when you're supposed to be in Columbia right now, but I've never been so happy to see anybody in my whole life."

Lonny returned the smile but fought against it and tried to look stern.

"Well, if you had answered your phone the first five or six times I tried to call you, you would know that I decided to catch an earlier flight home. I've been thinking about what you said about Lorena going missing, and I was worried about her, and about you. I didn't want you flying off the handle and doing something impulsive. When you stopped answering your phone, I knew I had better get back here right away."

He leaned in and gave Rich an affectionate peck on the forehead. "We can talk about all that later. Believe me, I have plenty of questions. Like, for example, why you don't seem all that surprised about being jumped in a parking lot by a ghost on steroids. But, don't you think we should focus on what we should do right now?" Lonny realized he had been speaking in a normal tone of voice and glanced toward the windows again before resuming in a whisper.

"Do you think it's safe to get out of the car now, or should we get out of here and drive to a public place somewhere, like Taco Bowl?"

"Taco Bowl?"

"I don't know! It's just the first place that popped into my head. Not Taco Bowl, then. Somewhere else. Anywhere, as long as it's somewhere with a lot of people around."

"She would just follow me there too," Rich answered resignedly. "She's been following me all day, although I didn't really believe it until she tried to choke the life out of me just now. Let's just go home. It's as safe as anywhere, and I need some aspirin."

Unseen, Minerva watched as the smaller man helped her intended target from the vehicle and up the rain-swept stairs to the apartment. Anger and vengeance were familiar sensations for her, but she wasn't used to feeling frustrated. For a mortal to interfere just as she was fulfilling her mission was unheard of. Momentarily caught off guard, Minerva stood by, silent and unmoving, as she considered her next move in what had become a thoroughly irritating game of cat and mouse.

24

Behind Closed Doors

The wedding between Augustus Short and Minerva Latham was as practical, expedient, and devoid of romance as the subsequent marriage proved to be. The ceremony took place at the church within a week of Augustus's abrupt proposal and was witnessed by the deacon and a woman who swept and dusted the sanctuary on Mondays and Thursdays. There were no other attendants. No guests were seated in the pews to dab their eyes as the vows were recited. No misty-eyed well-wishers threw rice at the departing couple after the indifferent minister pronounced the couple husband and wife and they performed the customary and passionless kiss.

After a painfully awkward wedding night in the large mahogany bed where Augustus had acted out his fantasies with his spectral lover, the newlyweds decided by mutual assent to occupy separate bedrooms. Augustus graciously relinquished the master bedroom to his new bride. After all, the memories associated with the room only brought him pain. He moved his clothing and toiletries to the spare bedroom on his second day as a married man and vowed to put the past, and his own feelings and desires, behind him for his own good and for the good of his business.

The initial reaction of Augustus's business associates, customers, employees, fellow church members, and casual acquaintances to his marriage was generally one of astonishment. There had been no courtship, not unless it had been conducted with great secrecy, and Augustus Short had seemed on track to be a lifelong bachelor, married only to his business. There was the usual talk that the bride might be in a family way. Farmers' wives marked their calendars with the earliest date that a legitimate child of the Short union could come into the world and waited with fiendish anticipation for a tell-tale bump showing through the new Mrs. Short's drab skirts.

The "ladies' unmentionables" incident, as it was referred to in the local gossip, led to further suspicion that this was a marriage of convenience, entered into to distract the public from learning about Mr. Short's possible sordid proclivities. Whether this was the case, and it very likely was, the good townspeople waited in vain for evidence validating their suspicions.

The Shorts conducted themselves publicly as a respectable and cordial, if not in any way overtly affectionate, married couple. Mr. Short continued to run his business as ever, and Mrs. Short continued in her role as his receptionist and bookkeeper. They attended church together on Sundays, and Mrs. Short attended Wednesday evening services alone while her husband remained at home. The couple was seen at a local restaurant a couple of times a month, at which time they engaged in quiet conversation as they ate their meals.

The dates on the farmers' wives' calendars came and went without the arrival of a new member of the Short family, putting a disappointing end to the premarital pregnancy scandal.

For a while, the private life of the Shorts was aligned with their public life in its simple routines and domestic tranquility. Minerva Short adjusted quickly to wedded life and her amicable, if essentially loveless, marriage. She viewed her husband as a godly Christian man and was content to serve as his companion, cook, and housekeeper, as she had once considered serving the Church as a nun. The absence of physical intimacy in their relationship was not a source of dissatisfaction, either physical or emotional, for Minerva, who looked upon the sexual act as rather messy and undignified, its sole purpose being procreation, an outcome which she had no desire to achieve. After the death of her baby sisters and her mother's suicide, she had vowed never to place herself in the position to love and lose a child of her own.

On the surface, Augustus appeared equally content with his changed lifestyle. He was cheerful at the office and would greet his employees with even more amiable interest in their work and family lives than before his marriage. He referred to his receptionist as "My Dear" now instead of "Miss Latham". About town, he walked a little straighter and looked more polished in his well-brushed suits, neatly knotted ties, and carefully shined shoes. He always had a smile and a pleasant word for acquaintances and strangers alike as he pursued his daily activities. The farmers' wives commented approvingly that he seemed to be putting on a bit of weight. As more than one observer noted, marriage seemed to agree with Augustus Short.

The private world of Augustus's inner self told a very different story. It started with a vague wistfulness when he would walk by a woman with red hair or see a stylish ladies' hat in a shop window. He found himself reading advertisements in the newspaper for corsets and other ladies' foundations, and on one occasion clipped one such ad and hid it in his wallet, only to take it out again and burn it a few days later. Augustus quickly and firmly dismissed these isolated incidents from his mind, sometimes with the help of a swallow or two of bourbon from the crystal decanter he kept in his home study.

By unspoken agreement, Augustus rarely entered his wife's bedroom for any reason, but one Wednesday evening while Minerva was away at church, he went in the room to look for a particular necktie he had been unable to find in his own room despite a thorough search. He tried the wardrobe first, checking between and underneath the coats, skirts, shirtwaists, and evening dresses hanging there, but the tie was not among them. He turned to the cherry wood highboy and opened a drawer at random. What he found banished thoughts of his necktie completely from his mind.

Augustus reached into the drawer and with the utmost care removed a single silk stocking. He held it up in the lamp light and gazed at it unmoving for several minutes before gently and reverently rubbing the soft and delicate fabric against his cheek. He closed his eyes and sighed deeply. Without conscious thought, he slipped the stocking, along with its mate, from the drawer and into his pocket. He walked out of the room and closed the door behind him.

The following Wednesday evening, with Minerva again safely out of the house, Augustus returned to the highboy in her room, this time with no missing necktie to justify his intrusion into his wife's private domain, and removed a garter belt. He chose an older one that had been pushed to the back of a drawer, as a precaution against her noticing its absence. When he returned to his own room, he placed the garter in his own chest of drawers, underneath his neatly folded winter long underwear. The stockings were already concealed in the same drawer.

For the next week, Augustus visited his borrowed treasures nightly, stealthily opening the drawer and inserting his hand to caress them without risking removing them from their place of concealment. To steady his shaking hands afterward, he helped himself to a small glass of bourbon from a crystal decanter, a wedding gift which formerly had been displayed on a shelf in the study and rarely touched except by the occasional swish of a feather duster. Augustus had removed it shortly after taking the stockings and installed it on his bedside table.

On many restless nights, when he would lie awake and alone in his bed imagining the feel of silk against his skin, he would reach for the decanter and take a swallow without bothering to use the glass.

The days and nights leading up to the next Wednesday crawled by at a snail's pace. When the day finally arrived, the employees of Short's Sure observed that their boss seemed preoccupied and moody throughout the workday, and they wondered if he might be coming down with a minor illness or had eaten something that disagreed with his digestion and was making him testy.

Minerva also noticed her husband's departure from his usual cheerful and sociable demeanor. She offered to stay home from church that evening and make him a bland dinner of beef tongue and boiled potato to help settle his stomach. Augustus politely but vigorously declined her kind offer and insisted that she go to church as usual. And so, with some reluctance, Minerva set out on foot with her Bible cradled in the crook of her elbow to meet up with her nearest neighbor Mrs. Fletcher to walk the short distance to the church together.

Augustus watched through the kitchen window as his wife's tall, erect figure strode purposefully down the paved walkway toward the neighbor's house. When she had passed beyond his line of vision, Augustus let the curtain fall back into place. He paused only briefly, waging a mental battle that was quickly fought and won, then went directly to his bedroom and shut himself in, latching the door behind him.

25

Wednesdays

Minerva traced the change in her husband's behavior back to that first Wednesday evening when he had complained of an upset stomach. He practically shoved her out the door when she offered to stay home from church and care for him. Later, when she returned and knocked on his bedroom door to ask how he was feeling, there had been a considerable delay before Augustus opened the door a crack and poked his head out just long enough to say he was much better now and would be going straight to bed. In the brief seconds before he closed and latched the door, Minerva saw that his face was flushed and sweating, and that he was wearing only his dressing gown.

At first, Minerva reckoned that Augustus's strange behavior seemed to be confined to Wednesdays. He maintained his accustomed routines the rest of the week, both at the office and at home, and spoke to her with his usual polite indifference. But each week when Wednesday evening came around, he grew restless and agitated, and Minerva caught him stealing frequent glances at the carriage clock on the mantle. The first time she noticed this, she casually asked her husband if he was expecting something, perhaps a package or a late visitor. He had looked at her with suspicious eyes.

"Of course not! Whatever do you mean by saying something like that?" he said sharply, not quite making eye contact. He had suggested then that perhaps she should leave for church early so that he could have some time alone and away from her silly notions.

Minerva soon came to the realization that there was a common theme in Augustus's odd behavior on Wednesday evenings: his eagerness for her to leave the house. One week, when she was suffering from a cold in her head and a low fever, he had been outraged when she told him she was staying home from church to rest. He had raised his voice in anger and accused her of putting her own comfort before her duty to God. Chastened by his words, she had bundled up as best she could and walked to church as usual. She had been in such a state when she arrived there, coughing and alternating between chills and sweats, that the deacon felt sorry for her and gave her a ride home. He must have expressed concern to the pastor because the next day, Reverend Whitaker paid a visit to Mr. Short for the sole purpose of reminding him of his Christian duty toward his wife's health and well-being.

That same day, the day which Augustus remembered thereafter as the day he was humiliated and unfairly shamed by the Reverend's admonishment, marked the point at which his drinking started in earnest. The crystal decanter of bourbon was supplemented by bottles of gin, secreted in cabinets throughout the house. Augustus began drinking wine with dinner, something he had done in the past only on holidays or other special occasions. Soon, he was drinking a glass of wine before dinner, and then two glasses. Before long, he was drinking a bottle of wine every evening, while Minerva looked on with silent disapproval.

Minerva consumed wine only as a sacrament taken as the blood of Christ in holy communion. She viewed intemperance as akin to gluttony, one of the seven deadly sins. She watched her husband's rapid descent into dipsomania with a mixture of disapproval and disgust, but held her tongue as a devoted wife should. But when she discovered half-empty gin bottles – not one but three: in a high kitchen cupboard, under the living room sofa, and in the garden tool shed – she decided she could hold her tongue no longer. With the evidence clutched in hands trembling with righteous anger, she confronted Augustus one morning the moment he opened his bedroom door.

"What is this?" she asked, thrusting the sloshing bottles in her husband's face.

Augustus was momentarily taken aback. He stood staring at the bottles in Minerva's hands as though he had never seen anything like them and wasn't quite sure what they were.

"Well?" Minerva persisted. "Are you going to stand there gawking, or are you going to tell me how a respected business man and a Christian has sunk to hiding bottles of liquor from his own wife?"

Without a word, Augustus drew back his right arm and slapped Minerva across the face with such force that the bottles flew from her hands and shattered on the floor. Minerva stumbled back and braced herself against the wall to keep from falling. Bits of glass dotted her skirt, which reeked of gin as the liquid soaked through the fabric.

Augustus looked her up and down, expressionless. In a calm tone, he said, "You had best change your clothes before going to the office. I'll wait for you, but don't be long." Pausing to make sure his own clothes were untouched, he brushed past his wife and walked toward the kitchen.

Augustus's behavior changed following this incident, but not in the ways Minerva had hoped. He no longer bothered to conceal his liquor bottles, but set them out on the kitchen counter and drank openly from them as he pleased. He stopped waiting for Wednesday evenings to retreat to his room after dinner, and began spending most of his free time behind his latched bedroom door. Conversation between husband and wife was much as usual, which is to say shallow, stilted, and infinitely polite. The incident of the gin bottles was never mentioned again.

Years went by, and the changes in the Shorts' domestic life were gradual and imperceptible to the outside world, but unmistakable for Minerva. There were other incidents of physical violence, which always coincided with Augustus drinking to intoxication. Once his judgment was sufficiently dulled by alcohol, he would react aggressively to the slightest perceived criticism or disrespect from her.

It started with a slap or a push. Once, he shoved her so hard that she fell against a table and suffered a lump on her head, which she concealed under her hat until it subsided. Another time, he choked her and left bruises on her throat. She hid them under a scarf.

Minerva dealt with her pain and confusion the only way she knew how, through constant prayer and penitence. She begged God and the saints to show her the path to help her troubled husband return to the light, and she asked forgiveness for her failings as a wife. Each time she walked out of the church sanctuary, she felt a renewed hope and courage that through faith, all would once again be well.

And then one day, while Augustus was out of town for a business meeting in Boston, she decided that a thorough housecleaning would brighten the atmosphere and cheer him on his return. She dusted the books and knickknacks, beat the rugs, wiped down the walls, aired the curtains and linens, and scrubbed the floors from one end of the house to the other. All except Augustus's room.

She stood outside the door to the room with her duster and broom in hand and pondered. Should she take the chance of angering him? Surely, the room must be very dusty, as he never let anyone in to clean it. Finally, after several minutes' hesitation, she tried the door handle. It was unlocked. Taking this as a sign, she went in. What she found there sent her stumbling back into the hallway, all thoughts of dust forgotten.

26

Gone

On the way to the hospital, Oscar called his niece who worked there as a certified nurse assistant and wheedled her into looking up Lorena's room number for him. Upon arrival, he bypassed the front desk and the on-floor nurses' station and went straight to her room. He paused briefly to make sure no one was looking in his direction, then quickly opened the door, slipped inside, and quietly pulled the door shut behind him.

Fortunately, Lorena was asleep. That would save Oscar some time and trouble. He was in a hurry, but he took a moment to lean over the sleeping girl and kiss her gently on the forehead. He looked down on her and watched the steady rise and fall of her chest as she breathed softly in her sleep. Then he turned to study the machines hooked up to her body by various cuffs, IV's, and sensors. He looked for off switches and shut off each one in turn. He held his breath for a moment, fearing he might have missed something and that an alarm would sound, bringing doctors and nurses running in to check their patient.

The room was silent without the constant murmurs and beeps of the machines, and the silence remained unbroken. Carefully, Oscar removed the tube that had been sending oxygen into Lorena's nose and wrapped it around her neck. As he grabbed the ends of the tubing and pulled them tight, Lorena's eyes opened wide and looked straight into Oscar's. She struggled to speak, but her airway was cut off and she could only gape and stare with terror and disbelief in her eyes.

"I'm sorry, *mi hija*. I do love you. But, you see, I can't go back to prison. I know you said you weren't going to tell the cops what happened, but how can I take that chance? Cops can be very persuasive, and let's be honest, you have a habit of talking too much."

Lorena made a gagging sound. Her tongue thrust out through her open mouth. Her eyes bulged and streaked with red as blood vessels ruptured under pressure. Oscar maintained his grip on the tubing, and shook his head sadly.

"No, *mi amor,* this is just what I have to do. Try and forgive me."

Oscar gave the tubing a final tug and leaned in to be sure Lorena was no longer breathing. Her eyes were still staring accusingly toward him but no breath passed through her lips. A tear rolled down Oscar's cheek as he pulled up the sheet to cover her face.

Moving quickly now, Oscar went to the door and carefully stuck out his head to make sure no one was approaching. He then ducked out into the hallway and strode briskly toward the elevators. He punched the down button and entered the elevator that arrived moments later.

As the doors shut, and Oscar began his descent to the lobby, a second elevator arrived at the floor he had just departed from. Two police officers stepped out and approached the nurses' station.

"Excuse me, nurse. We are here to speak to a Miss Lorena Cuevas. Are you able to take us to her now?"

"Certainly, officers. My name is Monique Green." She smiled and came out from behind the nurses' station desk. "I was on duty when Miss Cuevas arrived. She wasn't in any shape to talk to anybody for a while, but I think she's ready now. Right this way."

In the parking lot, Oscar climbed into his truck and stripped off his leather gloves. He put his face in his hands and sobbed once, long and low. He sat up straight and savagely wiped away the tears that had trickled down his cheeks, then started the engine.

****

"Is she in here?" Lonny stepped in front of Rich as they entered the apartment and attempted to shield the much larger man with his body. He flicked the light switch, but the entry way remained dark. The power was still out from the storm.

"No, I don't think so." Rich sidestepped around Lonny and felt his way toward the kitchen, opening drawers and fumbling through them. "At least I can't see her or feel her or smell her. I can't really be sure, though. I guess if she attacks me again, we'll know."

"Is this funny to you? My God, Richie, you almost died out there, and it might not be over, and I don't know what to do! It's not like we can call the police. 'So, officer, I can't really give you a description of the assailant because he's, or she's, invisible. But, don't worry, my boyfriend here can tell you what she looks like because he can see her even though nobody else can. He thinks she's a ghost.' Yeah, that's going to go over just great."

"Lonny, would you please stop? Let's just sit down and try to think this through, okay? Here, I found a flashlight and some candles. Could you please take one and go get me a couple of aspirin? They're in the bathroom medicine cabinet."

"Yes, of course, let me get that for you right now. I'm sorry. I'm scared to death, and I forgot all about the fact that you just got attacked. Give me the lavender-scented candle. It's supposed to be calming."

The flickering candle flame moved down the hallway, along with the sound of Lonny's voice as he kept up a nervous chatter.

"You're right, we need to calmly talk this through and try to come up with a reasonable explanation and figure out what to do. Obviously, Lorena isn't here either, and we still need to find her. I'm ashamed to admit I forgot all about her when whatever that was happened just now in the parking lot. Did you find out anything today?"

There was no answer. The dark apartment suddenly felt unnaturally quiet, and the darkness seemed denser and blacker than it had been before Lonny stepped into the bathroom. His reflection in the mirror over the sink looked pale and ghastly in the candlelight. He thought he saw something moving behind him, silent and stealthy.

"Richie?" He spun around, and the candle blew out. Something brushed against his leg. He kicked out, and his ankle was punctured by teeth, sharp as needles. He screamed.

In the kitchen, Rich clicked on the flashlight. A sickly yellow light shone briefly, then sputtered out. Rich shook the flashlight, and the light reappeared, wan but steady. He aimed the beam at the cabinets and sink and poured himself a glass of water. As the cool liquid flowed down his inflamed throat, he felt a wave of exhaustion wash over him. It had been the longest and strangest day of his life.

His head pounded. He wished Lonny would hurry up with the Tylenol. Why was he taking so long? It struck him then that he could no longer hear Lonny's voice. He had been chattering away like a magpie before, and then he just wasn't. Rich reached for the flashlight. At the same instant, a scream broke the silence, and Rich dropped both the flashlight and the glass.

The flashlight rolled across the kitchen tile, briefly illuminating the tiny shards of glass, like ice crystals floating in miniature pools of water, scattered across the floor. It collided with a table leg and the light went out, plunging the room into full darkness. From the distant bathroom, the screaming had stopped abruptly.

"Lonny? What happened? Are you okay?" Silence, except for the crunch of glass beneath his shoes as he treaded slowly, careful not to slip in the puddles of water, in the direction of where the flashlight had landed. He knelt on his hands and knees and felt around on the tile floor with both hands. He stubbed a finger on a table leg and cursed softly, but continued searching for the metal casing of the flashlight.

Instead of the smooth cylindrical shape he was expecting, his hand encountered something soft. It felt like a shoe. As he reached to explore the object further, it was quickly pulled away from his grasp.

Rich drew back instinctively and started to rise up, but his head smacked hard against the underside of the table and sent him back down to the floor. He flailed around on the wet tile and tried to scuttle backward. His hand brushed against the flashlight at last. He grabbed it and shook it. A weak light sputtered to life. He aimed the flickering beam toward where he had felt the shoe. Two glowing eyes looked back at him.

With a parting hiss, Effie picked up the slipper and scampered away toward the living room.

Rich sat up and rubbed the lump on his head. "Damn cat," he said. "Stupid thing nearly gave me a heart attack." His heart was pounding in his chest. He felt an irrational urge to giggle, but then remembered Lonny and the scream.

He leaped up, sliding and nearly falling down again on the slippery floor, and raced to the bathroom. The door was closed, but the knob turned in his hand, and he opened it quickly. There was a stifled shriek from somewhere in the room, but at first glance, Rich could see nothing by the thin beam of light except an extinguished candle lying on the floor next to two small drops of blood.

"Lonny!" he shouted. "Where are you?"

A figure moved behind the shower curtain. Fingers appeared around the side of the curtain and drew it back just enough to reveal a pale and frightened face.

"Lonny! What are you doing in there? What happened? Why is there blood on the floor?"

"I saw something, Richie! It was behind me in the mirror, and then something grabbed me by the ankle and bit me. When you burst in here right now, I thought it was back."

"Hey, come out of there. Come here. It's going to be okay." Rich reached out and took Lonny's hand and helped him out of the tub. He pulled him into a gentle embrace. At that moment, the electricity came back on, and the hall lamp cast a warm pool of light into the room.

"But, what about the thing that bit me? It's out there somewhere!" Lonny whispered, his face pressed against Rich's chest.

"I'm pretty sure that was Effie," Rich said. "Come on. Enough of this. We're both exhausted and strung out and jumping at our own shadows. Let's just go sit down for a while, okay. We'll figure this out together. Between your brains and my brawn, we're unstoppable, right?"

"I hate that cat," Lonny replied, but he gave Rich an extra squeeze as they walked hand-in-hand to the living room. They sat together on the couch, arms wrapped around each other, and rocked back and forth in silence as the night gradually gave way to dawn.

****

The Guardian had not returned, and eventually Rich and Lonny made their way to bed and slept fitfully until the morning sunlight shined through the window blinds and onto their faces. They spoke little until they had both showered and were seated at the kitchen table with mugs of coffee and plates of egg white omelets with diced peppers and mushrooms in front of them.

"This is good," Lonny said, looking up from his plate with a smile. "I missed your cooking."

"I'm flattered, but I have a feeling you are missing your mother's famous *arepa con quesito* right now way more than you ever missed my cooking."

"Both have a place in my heart. But, you're right, it nearly killed me to walk out of Mama's kitchen to fly home. The smell alone...my God, she's like a siren of hungry Columbians. People walk by the house and find an excuse to come to the door just to get a whiff of her cooking."

Rich chuckled. "I'm glad you made the sacrifice. Like I said last night, I have never been so happy to see anyone as I was to see you show up out of the blue like that. And just in the nick of time too."

"Sitting here now, talking and eating breakfast like any other day, none of what happened last night seems real. It's like a crazy dream. Maybe it was a dream. I've heard of people who are really close sharing dreams, or even delusions. Maybe we're both delusional."

"No, I don't think so. I didn't have a chance to tell you, but I met this homeless guy, Bobby, yesterday, and he told me all about these things. He calls them Guardians. He told me one was following me. He got really freaked out about it – enough to get himself hit by a car."

"Hit by a car?" Lonny interrupted. "Richie, tell me you didn't hit some poor homeless man with your car."

"No! No, of course not. Just listen, okay. I'll get to the part about him getting hit by the car. Anyway, I would have brushed off what he said as just drugs talking or schizophrenia or something, except that I had been feeling like someone was following me right before he told me. Like, really feeling it. It started when I was at Los Sombreros, looking for Lorena. I figured it was just my imagination but then this guy – Bobby – sees me and starts flipping out, yelling, 'She's following you!'

"I tried to blow it off as just a crazy coincidence – I know I can be kind of gullible – but then then later, at the hospital..."

"Hospital? You went to the hospital? Did you ask about Lorena? Was she there?"

"Yes. And no. I don't know." Rich waved a hand in front of him as if to ward off the subject. He was too tired and too ashamed to explain that he had gone to the hospital but forgot to look for Lorena there. "Okay, so remember I told you about what happened to Bobby, right? He got hit by a car, and I went to see how he was doing later, and..."

Rich's phone chimed. He glanced at the screen and answered. "Hey, James, what's up?"

"Have you been following the news?"

"No, not this morning. I had a pretty wild night last night. Why, what's going on?"

"Turn on the TV, Channel 12. They're still running the story right now. I'll hold on."

Rich picked up the remote from the living room coffee table and found the right channel. A young woman with a microphone in her hand posed picturesquely in front of the entrance to the county hospital. She had been reporting the story before the TV clicked on, and Rich caught her in mid-sentence: "...are shocked by the brazenness of this crime, occurring right under the noses of hospital personnel. Police are asking anyone who knows the victim or has any information that might help get this dangerous killer off the streets, to call the number on your screen. Again, police have identified the victim as Lorena Cuevas, age twenty-two, of Phoenix..."

Rich threw down the remote and grabbed his car keys. He pushed his feet into a pair of flip-flops and ran out the door. Lonny ran after him, shouting for him to slow down. Inside the apartment, Rich's phone lay forgotten on the kitchen counter.

"Rich? Hello? Rich, are you there?"

27

Revelations

Augustus's room was indeed very dirty, quite shockingly so from Minerva's perspective. The bed linens were in a heap on top of the bed, and there were piles of clothing strewn about on the floor. There was a thick layer of dust on top of the bureau and nightstand, and grime on the windowsill. Empty bottles were tossed carelessly in the corner. The atmosphere of the room was stale and stifling with the window closed, and there was a pervasive odor of sweat and must.

Minerva stood in the open doorway and clucked her tongue at the mess spread out before her. "This is going to be harder work than I thought," she said to herself. "Well, first things first. Let's get some fresh air in here."

She pulled back the curtains and opened the window, letting in sunlight and a gentle breeze. She turned to survey the room with her hands on her hips and decided to start with the piles of clothing and bed linens. It would all need to be laundered, but first she would sort through the piles and strip the bed, then gather everything up and carry it out of the room to clear the way for dusting and sweeping.

She carried the first armload out and dropped it on the floor in the hallway, then returned and whisked the duvet off of the bed with a snap. Something small and brightly colored flew up with the duvet into the air and drifted toward the floor. A gust of wind through the open window blew it under the bed.

Minerva knelt down to retrieve whatever it was. Peering into the dark, narrow space between the underside of the bed and the dusty floor, she spotted a red piece of cloth, along with several other items in a heap near the head of the bed. She reached under and pulled the items toward her, then deposited everything onto the mattress.

At first, Minerva's brain refused to acknowledge what she was seeing. She picked up the red cloth and spread it out in front of her. It was a silk scarf. Its pattern seemed familiar. At first, she couldn't place it, but the sight of the scarf filled her with a flood of emotion: happiness mixed with longing, and an almost overwhelming sense of loss. Finally, a memory pierced through the fog in her head.

It had been nearly a lifetime ago, when she was a small child, before Sally and Esther were born. The family was on a seaside holiday, and she was making a sand castle while her mother sat nearby reading a book. Minerva didn't recall where her father and older sisters were, probably walking along the beach, looking for seashells or bathing in the warm, salty water. But she remembered the scarf.

It was a windy day, and Mother had anchored the corners of her beach blanket with stones that Minerva had collected for her along the shoreline. Mother was wearing a floppy straw hat to keep the sun off her face, and she had tied the red scarf around it and under her chin to keep the hat from flying off. Minerva remembered calling to her to look at the castle she had built in the wet sand. "Hurry, Mother, look before the sea washes it away!"

She remembered Mother's smile and the ends of the scarf swirling around her face like scarlet flames in the breeze.

After her mother died, Minerva kept the scarf to remind her that there had been happy times before the tragedy that so suddenly had struck down three members of her family. For many years, the scarf had lain neatly folded and eventually forgotten in a drawer in a chest in Minerva's bedroom. She couldn't fathom what it could be doing here now, tucked into Augustus's bed.

Minerva turned her attention to the other items now scattered across the bed. There was an old corset and a garter belt, which she recognized as her own, and a single silk stocking. The tip of a second stocking peeked out from under a pillow. With a shaking hand, Minerva lifted the pillow out of the way. Underneath was a pile of photographs affixed to stiff cream note cards, like picture postcards, well-worn and dingy along the edges. She scooped them up to look at them.

Each card contained a photograph of one or more men. All were nude. In some, the men appeared to be engaged in wrestling or other sports. In others, the nature of the men's interactions with each other was all too clear. Minerva looked briefly upon an image of two men, one kneeling before the other, his mouth encircling the standing man's erect phallus. Minerva dropped the cards onto the bed with a gasp and quickly pulled the pillow back over them. Trembling uncontrollably, she gathered up the lingerie and pushed it back under the bed.

With her mother's red scarf still twisted around her hand, she threw the duvet back on the bed, along with the pile of linens from the hallway. She grabbed her broom and duster, and retreated from the room, slamming the door shut behind her. She dropped to the floor in a near faint and sat there shivering and sobbing until the hallway began to darken with the setting sun.

By the time Augustus returned the following day from his business trip, Minerva had decided that, at least for the present, she would not mention what she had discovered. She needed time to recover and to think about what she should do. Should she go to Reverend Whitaker? Should she confront Augustus? Should she pack her belongings and leave, perhaps go to one of her elder sisters' homes and beg to be taken in? But what would she say to them? Surely, she couldn't tell them the truth. It sickened her to imagine describing to anyone what she had seen. No, at least for now, she would say nothing and pretend she had never entered that room.

Minerva didn't think about the red scarf again until the moment she saw Augustus striding up the front walk toward the door. Too late to try to slip it back into his room. In her initial shock, she had returned the scarf to its rightful place in her bureau drawer without giving it a second thought. Now, she pictured her husband finding it missing from his bed and demanding an explanation. Fear rose up inside her like a rush of cold water, but then she came to the realization that it would be even more difficult for Augustus to explain the scarf's presence in his room than it would be for her to explain its absence.

Squaring her shoulders and settling a pleasant expression on her face, Minerva opened the door and welcomed her husband home.

After dinner, Augustus retired to his room. Minerva watched from a distance as he entered the room and shut the door behind him. She realized that she was holding her breath. She mentally reassured herself that it was highly unlikely that Augustus would admit to the stolen and shameful items in his possession. Calmed by this logic, she stopped watching the bedroom door and returned to the kitchen to begin washing up.

Minerva was leaning over the basin of dishwater, scrubbing the grease from a china plate, when she was grabbed suddenly from behind and spun roughly around to face a red-faced and furious Augustus. The plate flew from her hand and shattered on the floor.

Before she could speak, he seized her by the shoulders and shook her violently. "What were you doing in my room?" he shrieked, punctuating every word with another shake. "Answer me! What gives you the right to snoop in my private space? What were you looking for, eh? What did you see?"

Minerva was too shocked to speak. When she failed to answer right away, he slapped her across one side of the face and then the other. "Say something, woman!"

"I...I don't know what you mean, Augustus," Minerva replied. Her cheeks stung, and her voice sounded strange in her own ears, like an echo from the bottom of a canyon. "I haven't been in your room. What makes you think I went in there? Was something out of place?"

She watched his face closely for a reaction and was rewarded with a slight twitch of one eye and a brief hesitation, no more than a second or two, while he looked searchingly at her face before shoving her back against the counter.

"The window is open," he said calmly, his soft tone in stark contrast with the fire in his eyes.

"The window? Well, you must have opened it yourself before you left for your business meeting and forgot to close it again."

"I never open that window. You were in there, so don't lie to me!" Augustus advanced on his wife, who tried to sidle around him to create a path of escape, but he grabbed her by the hair and leaned in so close to her face that her ears rang with his shout. "What did you see?"

In that moment, seeing her husband's raging face, feeling the spray of the spittle that flew from his lips while he screamed at her, something changed inside of Minerva. Despite the pain in her scalp where Augustus still held her by the hair, she stood up to her full height and looked him straight in the eye.

"I saw exactly what you think I saw," she said coolly. "I know why you married me, Augustus Short. Maybe I have always known but was too ashamed to face the truth. I have prayed every day on my knees for guidance, so that I could be the wife you needed. I was never so naïve as to think you could love me, but I was determined to save you. For all these years, I have felt worthless and guilty for failing you as a wife. But today I realized that the shame isn't mine to own. It's yours."

Minerva reached back and unclenched Augustus's fingers from her hair. She took a step forward, and Augustus took an involuntary step back. She smoothed down her hair and straightened her apron as he stood frozen in place and stunned to silence.

"This is your home," she continued. Her voice was stronger now, firm and confident. "I understand that, and you can do as you please in it. If you choose to engage in your vile fantasies behind closed doors, I have no power to stop you. You will answer to God, not to me, for your sins. With that being understood, I need for you to heed what I'm about to say. If I ever see any further evidence of your debauchery, whether it be liquor bottles strewn about the house, or personal items missing from my room..."

At this, Augustus opened his mouth to speak, but Minerva put up a hand to silence him and continued. "...I will consider it my Christian duty to bring your behavior to Reverend Whitaker's attention. Further, and I say this in full consciousness of the consequences, if you ever lay a hand on me again, I will kill you."

28

Revenge

"Richie! Slow down before you get us both killed! Where are we going anyway?" Lonny gripped the arm rests with white-knuckled intensity as the car tore down the freeway, swerving between lanes to pass other vehicles as if they were stationary.

Rich blinked back tears and pressed the accelerator. "I know who did this to Lorena. I'm going to go find that fucking gangster piece of shit and tear him apart."

"Oscar? You think Oscar did this?"

"Who else? He's beat her up before. She would never admit it, but I've seen the bruises. Whenever I tried saying anything to her about it, she would just get mad and tell me I was imagining things and should just mind my own business. I shouldn't have backed down. I should have done something about him a long time ago, but I let her talk me out of it. That's on me. But now, he's going to pay for what he did. At least I can do that much for her."

"Richie, listen to me. You're getting way ahead of yourself here. You need to let the police handle this. That's where we should be going – to report what you know to the police, so they can do their job. You're probably right that Oscar did this, but what if you're wrong? Are you going to go beat the man to death and ask questions later?"

"No, I'm going to shoot him."

"What? No! For God's sake, no! No, no, no! You have a gun? Where the hell did you get a gun? Richie, please, pull over. Anywhere. Right now. Let's get off this freeway before you crash into something, and then let's talk about this. If you're sure it was Oscar, why not just call the police and tell them? You can't just shoot somebody!"

Rich took his eyes off the road to look at Lonny, who had his own eyes laser-focused on the windshield as the scenery whizzed by in a blur. "I could have saved Lorena, but I sat on my hands and did nothing, and now she's dead." He spoke softly but with such cold intensity that Lonny forgot about his reckless driving and turned to stare at him, wide-eyed.

"I owe her this," Rich said.

"Richie, you're scaring me. You're upset and you're not thinking clearly. I'm sorry, and you know I love you and I understand how you feel about Lorena, but I'm going to call the police myself. I'm doing it for you." Tears were streaming down Lonny's face now, and his voice shook as he spoke. "I don't want you to go to prison."

Lonny patted his pants pockets and looked around on the car seat. "I think I left my phone back at the apartment. I'm going to have to use yours. Where's your phone?"

Rich said nothing for a moment, then felt his own pockets. "I don't have it. Must have left it behind. I guess calling the police is off the table, then."

"Don't lie to me, goddammit! Where's your fucking phone?"

"I said I left it behind! Do you want to frisk me? Jesus, Lonny. Get a grip." Rich took the next freeway exit and was forced to slow down by the congested downtown traffic.

Once the car was moving at a subsonic speed, Lonny felt his heart rate return to something close to normal. He risked taking his eyes off the road again and began rifling through the contents of the glove compartment and the console behind the cup holder, then felt around under the seat. He twisted around and reached into the back seat, shuffling through debris on the floor. There were a few crumpled papers, discarded receipts, a paper cup, and a couple of empty kombucha bottles. A crumpled paper bag caught his eye, but when he opened it, he found it contained only an old sneaker, a dirty sock, and an empty can of almonds.

He opened his mouth to ask the obvious question, but Rich spoke first.

"It's in the trunk."

"The other shoe?"

"What? No, the gun! You weren't looking for the gun?"

"Yes, of course I was looking for the gun! Richie, this is insane! You're going to get us both killed. Is that what you want?"

Rich didn't take the bait. He steered the car into the same neighborhood he had visited the day before. Only this time, a hulking red Ford pick-up was parked in front of the Urias house. Rich pulled over to the curb several houses away and sat with the engine idling. Across the street, three little girls played hopscotch on a design roughly drawn on the sidewalk in purple chalk. The sound of their tinkling laughter and sing-song rhyme carried in a gentle breeze and broke the surreal silence of the otherwise empty street.

"Halloweena Heckatee, couldn't brew a cup of tea. The only portion she could brew was wishy-washy mousetail stew!"

"So, what now?" Lonny said. "Are you going to casually get out of the car, take your gun out of the trunk, walk up to the front door in broad daylight, and ask for Oscar to please come outside so you can shoot him in front of a bunch of kids? Is that your plan?" Rich remained silent, staring ahead at the parked truck. "Where did you get the gun, Richie?"

"It was my Grandpa's." Rich said in a low voice, without taking his eyes off the truck.

"What, like something he used when he was in the Army?"

"No," Rich hesitated, then sighed and went on. "It's a deer rifle. A Winchester. He used to take me hunting when I was little, so when he passed away, my Grandma gave it to me."

"A deer rifle? Seriously? You're going to take on a thug like Oscar right here in Thug Land, U.S.A in front of God knows how many gangsters on this street, each with a loaded assault rifle on their kitchen table at this very moment, and you're going to do it with a deer rifle. I swear to you, Richie, if you try to get out of this car, I am going to wrestle you to the ground and scream at the top of my lungs for someone to call for an ambulance. I am not kidding."

"Shh…" Rich said. "Here he comes."

Oscar came out of the house carrying a large duffle bag over his shoulder and gripping a couple of filled plastic grocery bags in his left hand. His right arm hung at his side within easy reach of an evil-looking, black metal pistol shoved into the waistband of his jeans. His mother watched from the doorway as he loaded his bags into the passenger side of the truck and then walked around to the driver's side. He didn't look back at the house as he climbed into the vehicle, and his mother eventually receded from view and closed the front door.

"It looks like he's skipping town," Rich said. "Do you still think I might be wrong about him killing Lorena?"

"I never said you were wrong. I said you can't take the law into your own hands. So, what now? Are you ready to call the police? I already memorized the license plate number. If we hurry and stop at the closest convenience store or gas station, we can call and tell them where he is before he has a chance to get very far."

"By the time we get the police to take us seriously, then have us talk to whoever is working Lorena's case, then actually send someone out to investigate, Oscar will be across the border. He probably has a buttload of places he could go in Mexico and stay with family or friends until things blow over. He could hole up down there for years. I need to stop him now, before he gets away."

Rich watched the truck pull away from the curb. He waited until it turned the corner, then followed it out of the neighborhood and toward the freeway.

****

Something was wrong. Minerva could feel it, or rather, she could no longer feel it. Her connection with the injured girl in the hospital had snuffed out like a candle in a draft. She closed her eyes and willed the darkness to speak to her, to guide her as it always did to find those in need of the swift justice she dealt. Concentrating, searching, she could feel the presence of the muscular young man, distant now and moving. He was no longer at the apartment where she had been impeded by the sudden appearance of his companion. She regretted now that she had left him unattended because clearly something had happened in her absence. The girl's essence, the life force that anchored Minerva to this place and time, was gone.

Minerva focused her mind and slowly opened her eyes. She stood in the hospital room and looked down on the bed where she had last seen Lorena. The bed was now unoccupied, but the room was far from empty. A uniformed police officer took notes as two men in suits spoke with a nurse who dabbed her face with a wad of tissues as she answered their questions. A gray-haired doctor with worry lines on his forehead stood at her side and patted her on the shoulder. A man with a camera moved around the room, snapping pictures of everything from floor to ceiling while noisily chewing a large wad of gum. Another man peered through thick, smudged eyeglass lenses as he carefully labeled small plastic bags. Minerva observed that one of the bags contained a knotted length of plastic tubing that had been cut in two.

"No, Officer, she didn't give me a name, but whoever he is, I'm sure she was afraid of him." Minerva moved closer to listen to what the nurse was saying. "That's why she didn't want to talk to the police. I see it all the time – a woman ends up in the hospital with broken bones and internal bleeding and you name it, but she still doesn't want to point the finger at the man who put her there. It's fear, detective, plain and simple. Fear of being alone, no way to support herself or her kids, no where to go. But most of all, it's fear that he's going to make her pay for putting him in jail. Because most of the time, when a man gets locked up, sooner or later, he gets out again. And he will have had all that time to get good and pissed at the woman who put him there and to think up all the ways he's going to punish her for it."

The nurse paused to blow her nose into the tissues. When she spoke again, her voice quavered with emotion. "Miss Cuevas was scared, and it was me who talked her into being willing to speak to the police. I don't know how he found out or even if he found out she was going to speak up, but she was right to be afraid of him. Now she's dead, and I can't help feeling like it was my fault for pushing her too hard." She put her hands over her face and began to cry. The kindly doctor moved closer and put his arm around her.

As the nurse sobbed quietly and rested her head on the doctor's shoulder, Minerva turned away. "Enough," she said aloud, although none of the room's occupants heard her. "This has gone on long enough. I was too late to save you, my dear, and for that I am so very sorry. I can assure you, though, that he will never hurt anyone else. I will see to that."

Minerva closed her eyes.

29

Redhead

For nearly ten years following Minerva's discovery of her mother's red scarf, after her warning as Augustus held her by the hair in the kitchen with broken china at their feet, peace reigned in the Short household. It was not the comfortable and serene peace that comes with a long marriage between lovers and friends. The silence in the home was not the silence of two kindred souls, confident in their connection and content to sit quietly together and read by the fireside. It was a peace born of fear, held tenuously in place, like a rickety gate against a powerful wind, by their mutual need to maintain a respectable image with the farmers and the farmers' wives and the employees of Short's Sure and the congregation of Reverend Whitaker's church. It was a silence born of a mutual animosity so alive and so close to the surface that a single word or phrase ("Would you be so kind as to pass the salt?") threatened to spark an explosion of shouting and violence.

Minerva's life had changed relatively little since the incident in the kitchen, with the significant exception of the cessation of physical abuse from her husband. Something in her eyes or the tone of her voice on that fateful day a decade ago must have left an indelible mark on Augustus's prudence, if not his conscience. He wasn't any more attentive or affectionate, or even particularly polite, toward his wife, but he was wary. The secret she held had the power to ruin him utterly, so he participated in their mockery of a marriage to preserve his social standing, and Minerva continued to play her part as his devoted wife.

Little did Minerva know that Augustus harbored a seething pot of resentment and frustration in his gut which with each passing day rose higher and higher until he could almost taste it, like bitter gall on his tongue. From her perspective, his silence and his long periods of time spent locked in his room, had become commonplace. She far preferred this behavior over his alcohol-fueled rampages, when he would say hateful, wounding things and break anything in his path, especially objects of sentimental value to her. On one occasion, he had shattered a china tea pot that had been her mother's. The smirk on his face left no doubt that the object of his ire had been chosen deliberately to cause her the most pain. These episodes became more frequent, but gradually so over the years, and by the time his drunkenness was a daily occurrence, Minerva could barely remember the time in their lives when he had been sober.

On the day of Augustus's sixty-fifth birthday, Minerva was not concerned when he failed to come home to the birthday dinner and cake she had prepared for him. He had commented that morning that he might be held up after hours at the office conducting an inventory. (Minerva had retired from her secretarial role with Short's Sure several years back.) Knowing he was likely to return home late, she made a savory stew with beef and vegetables that could easily be reheated and served with bread rolls and cheese. The sugar-glazed lemon poppyseed cake would keep until his arrival, no matter how late he proved to be.

So, as the sunlight faded and was replaced by gaslights and the rising moon, Minerva was not surprised to find her husband still absent. She was very much surprised, however, when he finally came home at close to midnight, not because of the hour, but because he did not come home alone.

Roused from a light slumber by the sound of someone fumbling at the front door latch, Minerva rose, put on her flannel dressing gown, and pulled back the curtain just enough to peer out and see two figures standing on the front porch, swaying drunkenly and talking in a loud whisper. One attempted to fit a key into the lock, while the second figure, equal in size to the first, showed itself to be a woman by uttering a sharp, feminine giggle. She moved briefly into a thin ray of light from the street lamp, and Minerva could see red hair lying in loose waves around her shoulders. She wore a shabby cloth coat with a fur collar that failed to cover a pair of pale freckled breasts rising above the low neckline of her dress. Even in the dim light, Minerva could see that the woman was no longer young and had attempted to conceal the fact with an excess of makeup.

As Minerva watched, the woman put her arm through Augustus's and snuggled against his shoulder. Her face was turned toward the window, and her gaze seemed to meet Minerva's through the narrow gap in the curtain. Minerva stifled a gasp and took an involuntary step back, even though she knew that the glass was opaque as viewed from the lighted street into the darkened room. The woman couldn't have seen her standing there, watching. Could she?

With the fingers of both hands pressed to her lips, she turned uncertainly toward the bedroom door, then away again, uncertain of what to do. She heard the front door open and close again as quietly as its squeaky hinges allowed. Muffled whispering and another high-pitched giggle moved along the corridor leading to the bedrooms. Minerva darted toward the door, but instead of going out to confront her husband, she carefully turned the key in the latch, locking herself in. She leaned against the door to steady herself and sobbed softly. Through the wall, she heard the latch turn on Augustus's bedroom door.

Minerva spent the remainder of the night lying in her bed and staring up at the ceiling with pillows pressed against her ears to muffle any sound that might carry from the bedroom across the hall. In the predawn hours of morning, she dozed off and dreamed of dying.

In the first dream, she drowned slowly and languidly in a deep well while the glow of a full moon danced and distorted and finally receded from view as her head slipped under the water. She sunk ever deeper, arms floating up and away from her body, and bubbles of air rose like helium balloons from her open mouth toward the surface.

In the next dream, she suffocated in a room filled with smoke and flame from which there was no escape. Ashes flew around her and brushed against her skin, and they made a sound like the wings of birds. She opened her mouth wide and wider, impossibly wide and pulled the smoke and ashes into her lungs until it filled her, and there was nothing else in the world.

In another dream, the most frightening dream of all, she lay on her back in utter darkness and silence, unable to move her arms and legs or rise up because she was confined to a tight space, no more than a few inches on all sides. Her fingernails scratched uselessly at wooden slats beneath her body until her fingertips stung from a dozen splinters. She inhaled the stale air and smelled the unmistakable scent of damp soil. Something small and slimy wriggled through her hair and slipped into her ear canal.

She was awakened, sweating despite the chill in the air, by a ray of sunlight shining through the crack in the curtains and by the sound of Augustus whistling and clanging dishes around in the kitchen. She sat up instantly, her first thoughts, born of many years of marriage, to make breakfast for her husband and prepare his lunch and thermos of coffee to take to the office. Her bed linens lay in a heap on the floor, where she had kicked them off during the night. As she swung her legs over the side of the bed and reached for her dressing gown, she remembered.

Sitting quietly on the side of her bed, Minerva waited for her husband to leave. By the small clock on her bedside table, no more than twenty minutes passed, but the minute hands seemed not to move at all, and more than once, Minerva picked up the clock and held it to her ear to verify it was still ticking. When the front door finally swung shut and Augustus's shoes clacked down the walk and away from the house, she rose and crept tentatively out of her room.

The door to Augustus's room was shut and locked as usual. Minerva knocked lightly on the door, half expecting a female voice to answer in response, but was greeted by nothing but silence. She kneeled and tried unsuccessfully to look through the key hole, then put her ear to the crack in the door. The only sound was her own anxious breathing. She knocked again, boldly this time, and called out, "Is anyone in there?" The caw of a distant crow was all she heard.

Minerva walked slowly through the house, looking for signs of the whore (for a whore she surely must be) her husband had brought home with him. Nothing was out of place in the entry way, the front sitting room, or the corridor leading to the bedrooms. In the kitchen dust-bin, she found an empty wine bottle, but that was hardly unusual. She noticed that there were no dirty dishes from Augustus's breakfast. He must have washed them himself and put them away. That was very un-usual, but it didn't help her to quell the rising suspicion that she had dreamt the whole sordid incident of the red-haired floozy.

She was turning to leave the kitchen when another crow's caw, much closer and louder than the other, startled her and caused her to turn toward the door that led to the back garden where the bird call seemed to have originated. Her gaze fell first on the window, through which she could see a single bird with shiny black feathers and dark in-telligent eyes, perched on the garden fence. It was soon joined by a sec-ond crow, then another.

As she traversed the room to take a closer look, she glanced down and noticed a scattering of rich garden soil on the floor, leading in from the garden. A pair of old boots Minerva recognized as her husband's were placed against the wall next to the door. More of the still-damp soil clung to their soles.

"Now, why on Earth…?" Minerva muttered. She stepped around the boots and soil to the window and looked out on the garden. At least a dozen crows filled the small garden, some perched on the fence and the branches of a crabapple tree, others carpeting the ground and glis-tening in the morning sunlight like so many polished onyx stones. The birds hopped lightly over a patch of freshly turned earth, their curious eyes and active beaks seeking out worms and insects newly brought to the surface. Minerva watched them with a furrowed brow for several minutes before shrugging her shoulders and turning away to ponder the soil on the floor of the otherwise spotless kitchen.

"Have you been gardening?" Minerva broke the silence over dinner that evening and watched her husband's face closely for a reaction. He looked up from his plate of leftover stew and returned her gaze for a long moment before answering. Was that a twitch in his right eye? Minerva wasn't sure.

"If you call ridding the garden of an infestation of moles 'gardening', then yes," Augustus replied smoothly. "I noticed several holes out there a week or so ago and decided to take action. I think I got all of the nasty little rodents, but time will tell. I might have missed a few." He looked down at his plate and continued eating without another word. Minerva was tempted to ask what led him to undertake the project of exterminating moles at the crack of dawn on a work day, but she held her tongue, still uncertain about how much of what she had seen and heard last night was real and how much was just another dream in a night that had hosted a suite of nightmares. The rest of the meal was eaten in silence.

For weeks after Augustus's birthday, Minerva noticed a marked change in his mood and behavior. Before, he had been sullen, irritable, and closed, speaking to her only with a sarcastic formality when sober and a raw hatred when drunk. Now, he smiled and hummed a cheerful tune as he went about his daily routine, and his behavior toward her was like it had been many years ago before the abuse began. He wasn't affectionate or loving certainly, but he spoke kindly to her and looked at her without the smoldering malice she had grown used to seeing in his eyes. He even cut down on his drinking.

The passage of time had gone far toward convincing Minerva that the "red-haired floozy" had been nothing more than an especially vivid dream. Still, she thought, if the woman had been real, maybe it was worth it for him to have dalliances with whores if it made him so much easier to live with. She was ashamed of herself for having such a wicked thought the moment it arose, and she dismissed it firmly from her mind. Still, the idea that a sinful Augustus was preferable to a chaste one wedged itself there, and it lurked always just beyond the edge of her consciousness.

One evening, Augustus came home from work in an unusually cheerful mood and bearing an armload of groceries. When he announced that he intended to make a special dinner for the two of them, Minerva was speechless. She allowed herself to be shooed out of the kitchen, as Augustus declared he wanted the meal to be a surprise. She waited on the sofa in the sitting room with a book on her lap and an embroidery hoop at her side, but she attended to neither as the sound of her husband humming "Nearer, my God, to Thee" drifted in from the kitchen. Her mind was in turmoil, caught between hope and suspicion. She said an internal prayer, asking for forgiveness for her doubts and thanking God for the miracle of Augustus's changed ways, adding, because she couldn't help thinking of the red-haired floozy, that she was grateful regardless of what triggered the change. The Lord works in mysterious ways indeed.

The dinner Augustus prepared was simple – fish fillets, boiled potatoes, and string beans – but Minerva was surprised at how flavorful it was. She found herself relaxing more and more as she ate her meal and drank the milky coffee Augustus had served with it. Augustus talked about the events of the day at Short's Sure, and Minerva listened and asked questions to keep the pleasant conversation flowing. She began to feel very drowsy and wooly-headed. An incessant buzzing in her ears grew louder and threatened to drown out her husband's words. She struggled to stay attentive but could barely keep her heavy eyelids open.

"I'm sss…, so ssorry, Augustus. I don't know what's come over me. I'm just so tired…" The room began to spin. Augustus's face came into view, then doubled and warped like heat rising from stone. He was saying something, but Minerva couldn't make out the words. She felt herself slumping to the side and tumbling from her chair, but she never felt herself hit the floor.

30

All in her Head

Minerva awoke with a pounding headache and with sunlight streaming through the window and onto her face. She was in her bed but fully dressed except for her shoes. She sat up slowly, clutching her head and gasping at the pain. She couldn't remember going to bed last night. She struggled to clear her muddled thoughts, but all she could recall after sitting down to dinner with Augustus the night before were flashes of indistinct sounds and images: her husband's voice speaking to her in words she couldn't understand, herself sliding down from her chair to the cold floor and looking up at the ceiling, Augustus's face swimming in and out of view as he reached for her. She concentrated, shook her head, massaged her temples to ease the tension, but nothing helped. That was all she could remember.

Gingerly, Minerva arose from the bed and pushed her feet into a pair of slippers. She took careful steps across the room until she was confident she could walk without becoming dizzy and falling again into unconsciousness. She made her way toward the sitting room. The carriage clock on the mantle indicated it was approaching noon. She had never slept through the entire morning in her life, even when in the depths of grief over the deaths of her mother and sisters. The idea of losing half a day was so disorienting that Minerva stood staring at the clock for several minutes before she could believe what she was seeing.

Even though Augustus was almost certainly at the office at this time of day, Minerva went to his bedroom door and knocked. When there was no response from within the room, she tried the door knob and found the door to be latched as usual. "Augustus?" she called out, just to be sure. Still no response. Standing in the corridor, still rubbing her temples with her head down and her eyes nearly closed, Minerva caught a flash of dark red illuminated by a ray of sunshine that streamed through her own open bedroom door onto the green and tan runner rug that stretched from one end of the corridor to the other. She kneeled to get a closer look, sending another wave of pain through her head.

The dark spot on the rug was small and round, about the size of a dime, and it appeared to have the consistency of grape jelly. She reached out and touched it, and her finger came back stained a deep red. A coppery smell arose from the red blotch and assaulted Minerva's nose. Alarmed and repulsed, she lifted herself from the floor as fast as her stiff hips and popping knees allowed and hurried to the kitchen to wash her hands, then returned to the corridor with a damp rag to sponge the rest of the spot from the rug.

"Did I bump my head?" Minerva wondered. She felt her scalp and down her arms and legs, then looked herself over in the full-length mirror in her bedroom, but could find no scrapes or injuries to account for the blood, and she was quite certain that the spot had been blood. Confused, and with an underlying sense of dread, Minerva walked slowly through her home, looking for any clue to explain the blood spot and what had transpired that left her in bed with an aching head and no recollection of how she got there.

There were no other mysterious spots in the corridor or in the sitting room. As she entered the kitchen, Minerva flashed back on the images of yesterday's dinner: the food and drink, the pleasant conversation, and then the odd echoing of Augustus's voice and herself falling away into oblivion. The kitchen showed no sign of the events she remembered. The chairs were pushed in neatly under the table top, which had been cleared of the food and dishes and wiped clean. The china, silverware, Augustus's wine glass, and her coffee cup and saucer had been washed and put away. A roasting pan and two cast iron pots sat on the counter where they had been placed on a mat to dry after being scrubbed clean.

Augustus's apparent solicitude in putting her to bed and then cleaning up the kitchen after whatever had happened last night touched Minerva's heart. Surely, the changes she had begun to see in him and had been afraid to believe in, were true. She bowed her head and said a prayer of thanks, asking also for guidance and strength to deal with whatever was happening to her mind and body. Since the red-haired floozy incident, she had begun to doubt her own senses, and now she wondered if her body too was betraying her.

As she lifted her head from prayer and opened her eyes, Minerva's gaze landed on the door to the garden. A tiny red smear just above the knob stood out in sharp contrast with the whitewashed door. She moved closer and bent down to inspect the smear. It looked and smelled like blood. She opened the door and found two long red hairs caught in another, larger bloody smear on the inside of the door frame. She stared at the two hairs, now floating up like scarlet ribbons around a May pole in the gentle breeze coming in from the garden. A scream started somewhere in the pit of her stomach and surged up through her body and into her throat. She put her hands over her mouth to force the scream back down. Only a soft whimper escaped from her trembling lips.

Whatever was happening would need to be dealt with, Minerva chided herself, and hysterics were not going to help.

A sudden caw from just beyond the garden door made Minerva jump and utter an involuntary yelp. Careful to avoid the blood and hair, she opened the door wider and looked out into the garden, where a dozen or more crows were again littered across the ground and perched on the fence and in the tree. Several of the crows were busy in a patch of newly turned earth, near to the other patch where Augustus had been digging up mole tunnels. A few of the crows looked her way and flapped their wings aggressively but quickly returned to scratching and pecking in the soil, unafraid of the trembling human who stood in the doorway watching them.

"Minerva, dear, I'm home!" Augustus's voice was followed close behind by the sound of the front door shutting. In a state of near panic that she couldn't have explained to herself or anyone else, Minerva retreated quickly from the kitchen to greet her husband, leaving the garden door slightly ajar.

She met up with her husband in the entry way as he was taking off his hat and coat and placing them on the coat rack. "It's such a relief to see you up and around," he said with a warm smile. "You gave me quite a scare last night. How are you feeling?"

Augustus's face wore an expression of such concern, and he touched her arm with such tenderness as he led her to a chair in the sitting room, that Minerva felt tears welling up in her eyes.

"I feel fine, other than an ache in my head. What happened, Augustus?"

"What do you remember?" he asked gently, but his eyes looked into hers with a piercing intensity.

"I remember sitting at the table, enjoying the lovely meal you prepared." Minerva smiled at her husband. "Then I think I must have fallen. The next thing I knew, I was waking up in my bed, having slept through the entire morning. I only just now came out of my room."

"You must have had a dizzy spell of some kind," he said. "You were sitting at the table talking – about strawberries, wasn't it? How you hope they are as good this year as last. Then all at once you became very quiet, staring ahead of you at nothing. And then you just toppled out of your chair. It happened too fast for me to catch you before you reached the floor, and I think you must have hit your head on the table leg on the way down because when I got to you, you were quite senseless. I tried to revive you with smelling salts, but in the end, all I could do was put you to bed. I checked in on you this morning, and you seemed to be resting peacefully, so I decided not to call in the doctor until you had a chance to wake up on your own. I came home early as you see, hoping to find you fully recovered. I hope you can tell me that you are."

Minerva hesitated at a sudden, barely perceptible shift in Augustus's tone and the steely, searching look in his eyes. "*Is this all in my head?*" she thought. She opened her mouth to speak, but Augustus had looked away and didn't notice. He resumed speaking.

"I have to say that I've been rather concerned about you lately, Minerva dear. This fainting spell is certainly the most alarming incident that has happened, but it isn't the first. You get such a lost and dreamy expression on your face sometimes, and when I speak to you, it's as if you can't hear me. I've found myself wondering where your mind has gone. You seem to become confused at times and ask the strangest questions. For example, you asked me once if I knew why there were crows in the garden, and just the other day, you asked me where my boots were so that you could clean them, but you had already cleaned them that very morning."

"I...I don't remember that." Minerva began to tremble so violently that she sat on her hands to keep her husband from noticing. Could it be true? Was she losing her mind? Was some form of brain fever causing her to imagine things, like the red-haired floozy, the blood on the floor and on the garden door, the red hairs? Minerva had to physically stop herself from shaking her head as her husband continued to watch her with his penetrating stare.

"Well, you see, that's just what I mean. The incident with the boots was only two or three days ago, and yet you've already forgotten." Augustus chuckled, and he patted Minerva's knee affectionately. "Oh, now, don't look so worried. I'm sure you'll be just fine. I didn't mean to upset you. If you would like for me to give Dr. Sanders a call, I'm sure he would be glad to come examine you and give you something for your aching head..."

"No, no," Minerva broke in quickly. "I'm quite alright. The rest did me good. Maybe I was overtired last night, or maybe it was the coffee."

"What do you mean, maybe it was the coffee?" Augustus's voice resumed its cold intensity, and his grip on Minerva's knee tightened.

"What? Oh, nothing really." She found herself growing frightened and confused, like a lost child confronted by a police officer in the street. "I just mean that I'm not used to drinking coffee so late in the evening, and it might have made me a bit dizzy. It was very good coffee, and I was enjoying it so much." Minerva held her breath awaiting her husband's reaction, and only let it out in a slow, silent sigh when he let go of her knee and appeared to relax.

"Well, never mind. You just take it easy tonight. There is some left-over chicken and potatoes for our dinner tonight, so no need to trouble yourself." Augustus rose up and strode toward the kitchen with his lunch pail and coffee jug.

Minerva closed her eyes and took several deep breaths to steady her nerves. In the background, she heard the unmistakable sound of the garden door closing. Only after she heard Augustus come out of the kitchen and walk down the corridor to his room, did she dare to creep into the kitchen to look for the bloody smear and hairs on the garden door. They were gone. Had they ever been there at all? Minerva leaned heavily against the door and looked out into the garden, where the last of the crows flew up and away over the back fence. And then there was nothing left, not a distant cawing or a rustle of wings, or any sign that the birds had ever existed at all outside of her own imagination.

****

There were other incidents over the ensuing months: episodes of dizziness, forgetfulness, and awakening with a headache and a blank spot where the memory of the past several hours should be. Minerva covered up what happened each time as though her life depended on it. She acted as if everything was normal and never mentioned the incidents to Augustus, who seemed to conspire with her in pretending she wasn't slipping away into dementia or madness.

There were other signs as well. She had vivid dreams of people in the house, laughing and singing and then suddenly falling silent, sometime with a final muffled scream or the thud of a heavy weight hitting the floor. Once, she found a piece of torn fingernail on the rug – a woman's garishly lacquered nail. She was afraid to show it to Augustus, so she hid it in a drawer, but when she went back later to look for it, it was gone.

And then there were the crows. Minerva began to fear looking into the back garden because they were always there, sometimes only one or two, sometimes in great numbers, but always watching her with beady, black eyes that conveyed an ancient and merciless intelligence. She felt they were drawing her in, luring her to the patches of naked earth that never seemed to settle or produce plant life. Minerva was curious about those patches and she longed to kneel on the ground and plunge her hands into the dark, rich soil, seeking whatever mysteries were hidden there, but she held back, repulsed and afraid.

She told herself that it was the crows that she feared, although even that sounded mad. After all, they were only birds, and very common in the area, so there was no rational reason to fear them or to impose human thought or intention on their tiny brains. What she truly feared, and what she fought with all her mental and physical strength to suppress, was that she wasn't mad at all, that everything she thought she saw and heard and everything she felt was real, and that she was living with a monster.

31

Garden

Augustus hummed a tune as he stirred the sleeping powders into his wife's cup of coffee. He had heard the tune at a piano bar downtown a couple of weeks ago, and he couldn't get it out of his head. The pianist had been first rate, much too good for the seedy establishment where the drunken, raucous laughter and voices raised in anger over card games played by dim lamplight threatened to drown out the music altogether. Augustus was careful not to visit the same bars and dance halls more than once so as not to be recognized, but he was tempted to break his rule just this once and go back to hear that piano music again. It was that good.

"Here you are, my dear." Augustus smiled down at Minerva as he handed her the coffee mug. "There's nothing quite like a nice hot cup of coffee on a chilly autumn night, don't you agree?"

"Thank you, Augustus. It used to be that if I drank coffee too late into the evening, I would have trouble sleeping, but somehow I never have that problem with your coffee. It's so relaxing that I drift right off to sleep like a baby." Minerva took a small sip. "Augustus, if it isn't too much trouble, would you mind bringing me some of those ginger biscuits from the kitchen? I seem to have a sweet tooth tonight, and they would be perfect with your excellent coffee."

Minerva watched Augustus leave the room. As soon as he was out of sight, she got up and tipped half her coffee into a potted plant, then settled back into her chair. Augustus returned with the biscuits, and the couple engaged in pleasant conversation until Minerva began to yawn, and her eyelids fluttered as if they were too heavy to stay open. Through half-shuttered eyes, she stole a glance at her husband, who was watching her with an expression of such raw eagerness that she nearly gave herself away with a sharp intake of breath. She quickly turned the gasp into another yawn and pulled herself up in her chair. "I'm sorry, Augustus," she said. "I really must be getting to bed. I can't keep my eyes open another minute."

"Of course, of course, my dear! You go ahead and get your beauty sleep. I'll just be up a bit longer reading. Good night!" The smile on his face reminded Minerva of a snake she had encountered one time in the garden moments before it leapt on a mouse in the tall border grass and swallowed it whole. "Pleasant dreams!" he called after her as she made her way down the corridor to her bedroom.

Once the door clicked shut behind her and she turned the key in the lock, Minerva breathed a sigh of relief. Gone were the sleepy eyes and yawns. The expression on Minerva's face was wide awake and determined. She stood up to her full height and ran steady fingers through her graying hair. She poured water into the basin and splashed some onto her face, then patted it dry. She removed the pins from her hair and brushed it out but did not get undressed. She turned down the bedside lamp until its meager glow could not be seen by anyone passing by her door. The room was chilly, even with a small fire lit in the bedroom fireplace, so she added a few sticks to the fire and, taking the duvet from the bed, settled herself with it in the armchair nearest the door.

Almost immediately, Minerva heard the sound of footsteps in the corridor, followed by the quiet opening and shutting of Augustus's bedroom door. This was unexpected and dealt a decisive blow to Minerva's confidence. Could it be that he was only retreating to his room for the night, as he had done nearly every night for the duration of their marriage? Had the sinister plot she had been so certain was playing out two or more times a month while she lay drugged and insensible in her bed been nothing more than a product of her overactive imagination? Had she become paranoid? Was this yet another sign that she was going mad? Minerva gnawed on a cuticle and stared at the outline of her bedroom door, barely discernible from the surrounding wall in the dim firelight.

A clock on the bedside table ticked away the minutes as Minerva kept up her vigil. A quarter of an hour passed, then half an hour. Minerva was starting to doze in her chair when she heard the unmistakable sound of Augustus's door softly opening and closing. Instantly, she was fully awake and straining her senses to hear every sound and see even a shadow or flash of light under the door. She did not have long to wait before footsteps passed again down the corridor toward the front of the house, followed by the careful opening and shutting of the front door.

Minerva jumped up and ran to her window. Looking through a tiny crack in the curtain, she could see her husband strolling down the sidewalk in the direction of downtown. He swung his cane jauntily as he walked, and Minerva thought she could hear a whistled tune, growing fainter as his figure moved farther down the road and blended with the darkness of the moonless night.

When Augustus had passed out of sight, Minerva moved away from the window and paced the room. That her husband had been drugging her coffee so that he could slip out at night had been confirmed, but this validation gave her little solace. She could let go of her fear of going insane, true, but what reality would replace that fear? Where was Augustus going, and what was he doing that required such extreme measures to protect his secrets? Minerva thought of the blood stains and the red hair and lacquered fingernail that had disappeared soon after she discovered them. Those too had been real.

Piercing the silence of the night, the caw of a single crow startled Minerva from her musings. A mental image arose unbidden and unwelcome of a naked patch of earth in the garden that remains fresh through sunshine and rain. A place where the soil is dark and rich, but nothing ever grows.

"No!" Minerva shut her eyes tight and shook her head to dispel the image. She pressed her hands against her ears to muffle the crow's accusations. "No! It's nothing like that. He's seeing another woman, I'm sure of that now, but that's all it is. I really did see the red-haired floozy – I didn't imagine her – and that's probably who he's still consorting with behind my back." As if in reply, the crow cawed a second time.

Trembling beneath the duvet still clutched around her shoulders, Minerva walked unsteadily from her room, compelled toward the kitchen and its view of the back garden like a somnambulist caught in a nightmare. From the dark kitchen window, the garden appeared equally dark without the aid of moonlight. Still acting as if by some will other than her own, Minerva lit a kerosene lantern and carried it out into the garden. Its rays fell immediately upon the bare patch of earth and caught the shining eyes of a crow. It seemed to be staring directly and deliberately at Minerva's face. It waited, fearless in the presence of the human, until she took a tentative step toward it, then flapped its ebony wings and lifted into the air, trailing bits of soil from its talons as it disappeared into the night.

As she approached the place where the crow had been, Minerva's lantern reflected something sparkling amidst the dirt and drifting leaves. Minerva held the lantern directly over the spot and froze, uncomprehending of the tableau laid out below in the disturbed earth. She began to sweat despite the cool night air, and her vision filled with dark spots, harbingers of a fainting spell. She widened her stance to stay upright but her knees gave way and she found herself kneeling on the ground, still clutching the lantern that was all that came between her and being left alone in the dark with the hideous thing the bird had uncovered.

The crow and its fellows had been very busy, or perhaps they had been assisted in their efforts by a wandering cat or other nocturnal creature. Several small holes had been scratched into the earth, spaced several inches apart. One hole revealed a row of white bone buttons on pin-striped silk. A few of the buttons had been pulled free and removed, no doubt by the crows. Others hung on loose threads.

Another hole revealed red meat, gnawed and picked at until the bones beneath shone white by the lamplight. It was a small hole, no more than six inches in diameter. Minerva's mind tried to make sense of it, to explain it away as the carcass of an animal, perhaps the remains of one of Augustus's moles, although it would have had to be the largest mole ever seen in all of New England. The next hole dispelled this fantasy like a puff of smoke and left Minerva paralyzed with horror.

In the hole was the object that had sparkled when Minerva held up her lantern. It was a ring with a large facetted red stone, obviously glass, set in brass. It rested on the middle finger of a woman's left hand which emerged stiffly from the soil at a forty-five-degree angle like a trampled weed. The crow had been working on the finger that bore the ring, tearing at the swollen flesh to get its prize past the knuckle. There was little blood left to drip from the ravaged finger, and the remaining flesh was nearly as pale as the bones showing beneath it.

Compelled beyond reason and terror, Minerva leaned forward and used her bare hands to begin scraping away the soil from the spot directly above the row of buttons. The tip of a nose quickly emerged, followed by the lower half of the face, its carmine lips open around a mouth packed with mud. Whimpering and shaking convulsively now, Minerva continued freeing the woman's face from its shallow grave. She gagged when she uncovered the eyes, which were open, cloudy, and plastered with debris, including an earthworm that sought to nestle itself deeper under the right eyelid. She scraped away more soil from the ears and forehead, then suddenly stopped. She opened her mouth to scream, but the sound stuck in her throat.

Where the woman's hair should have been, a bloody skull was revealed, with patches of raw flesh still clinging to it. Minerva was immediately reminded of stories she had heard of white women being scalped by savages who attacked wagon trains traversing the vast western frontier. But this was not the Wild West, and the savage who did this was no copper-skinned native. She reached out a trembling hand and plucked a long hair that had still been attached to a piece of the shredded flesh remaining on the skull. She wiped it clean against the pin-striped fabric sticking up from the grave and held it up to the lamp-light. The hair was red.

In the distance, Minerva heard a sound that started so low that she barely registered its presence until it had traveled the length of the street and almost to her front door. Someone was whistling a merry tune. The sound was so jarring, so irreverent, so obscene against the backdrop of the woman in the shallow grave, that Minerva initially felt anger at the unknown whistler and pursed her lips in scorn. Then, with a stab of panic, she recognized the tune as the one Augustus had been whistling when he left earlier in the evening.

The sound of a woman singing along to the whistled tune in an off-key, slurred voice, joined in, followed by a peal of laughter. The man's voice – Augustus's voice – murmured something, and the woman giggled and shushed audibly, as though they were two children sneaking in after dark and trying not to wake their parents.

How long she had spent kneeling in the garden, Minerva didn't know. It could have been mere minutes or it could have been several hours. Time and reality were as confused and muddy as the soil beneath her hands.

Jolted from her state of paralysis by the sound of the front door opening, Minerva wrenched herself upright, despite the protest of her arthritic knees. She leaned over the grave and quickly covered up the exposed body with loose earth. She had to force the stiffened hand with the ring back under the soil, and she heard a loud crack as the bones of the forearm snapped.

She grabbed her lantern and the duvet and looked around for a means of escape. If she tried to go back into the house through the kitchen door, she risked being caught. She prayed she had at least shut the door behind her when she entered the garden, but she had been in such a daze, she couldn't be sure. She could try going around the side of the house and reentering through the front door, but she assumed Augustus would have locked the door behind him, and the risk of getting caught was again too high. Minerva tried to steady her breathing and think. Right now, what she needed was a hiding place.

Keeping her lantern low to the ground to avoid shining it through the windows, Minerva looked desperately around her. She spied the tool shed in the far corner of the garden and ran toward it. Tears of relief came to her eyes when she pulled on the handle of the door, and it opened with a barely audible scrape of warped wood against its frame. She rushed inside and closed the door behind her. Working as quickly as her trembling hands allowed, she removed the belt from her skirt and tied it, one end around the inside handle of the door, and the other end to the leg of a heavy work bench. She found an empty crate, which she upturned and sat down on before shutting off the lantern and plunging the small space into darkness.

At first, she was shaking so hard that the crate beneath her squeaked and groaned with her movements. Fearful of making even the slightest sound, she forced herself to take several deep breaths to slow her pounding heartbeat and allow her body to grow still.

How long she waited in the dark, Minerva didn't know, but after what felt like an eternity, she heard the eerie whistling again, only this time it was coming from the garden, so close that she could hear the scratching and thudding of something heavy being dragged and then dropped on the ground. Someone said "Oof!" as the heavy load was released. The whistling had stopped, and Minerva heard Augustus's voice, mere inches from where she sat on the crate with her hands over her mouth to mask the sound of her own breathing.

"It will just be a moment, my dear, while I prepare your bed for you. I'm sure you'll agree it's a lovely view of the garden, and during the day there will be birds singing and plenty of sunshine. You'll have company too and all the time in the world for you ladies to gossip and whisper together. Sleep well, my lovely one."

The whistling resumed, accompanied by the sound of digging in loose soil. Minerva listened in horror and matched the sounds that penetrated the thin shed walls with images in her mind of a woman's body with a slick, bloody streak on the top of her head, red blood in place of red hair, being lowered into a shallow hole and covered with shovelfuls of dirt that were then patted down with a few brisk swings of the shovel.

Minerva held her breath and tried to cower deeper into the darkness as she pictured Augustus returning the shovel to the shed and discovering her hiding place, but several minutes passed in silence, and she decided that he must have dropped the shovel somewhere and gone back inside the house. Still, she remained motionless and waited for several minutes longer before rising from the crate and lying down on the floor with her duvet to wait out the rest of the night.

Once settled on the hard floor in the dark, she gave in to the overpowering emotions brought on by the night's hellish events. She stuffed a corner of the duvet into her mouth to muffle the sound and sobbed her heart out for the poor woman in the grave, for herself and her life forever changed, and even for Augustus. She cried for the man Augustus had been when she was a young woman working as his receptionist, and she cried for whatever sickness or evil had taken hold of him and turned him into the monster she now understood him to be.

There were many hours left until dawn, and no chance of sleep for Minerva, lying alone in the pitch-black darkness, listening to the wind squealing through cracks in the vertical slats that made up the walls of the tiny wooden shed. When her sobs finally subsided, she lay motionless, staring into nothing. The image of the scalped woman with the clouded, dirt-encrusted eyes and the cheap, brass ring on a broken hand, was always there, even when she closed her eyes.

Minerva thought about the bare patch of earth where the woman was buried, and where Augustus had returned tonight, apparently to add another victim to his garden of corpses. The area had been disturbed more than once over many weeks. She had stopped looking when she found the first woman's body, but there could be others. One for every time she had been drugged. How many times was that? Ten? A dozen? Even more? She couldn't be certain. The possibility that Augustus had gone out into the night and committed this abominable act with so many women, then brought them home one-by-one and planted them like so many flowers in the garden, was staggering.

Minerva knew that she would have to do something. She couldn't just keep this a secret, even if the women were ungodly whores who should have known the risk of engaging in sin with wicked men like Augustus. Minerva firmly believed in the absolute dichotomies of virtue and sin, good and evil, right and wrong. According to her faith, there was no room for compromise. And where there was sin, there must be punishment. She told herself that the women had got what they deserved, just as she had got what she deserved when she had failed to protect her baby sisters from coming to harm. Her marriage had been her punishment. Or so she had thought until this night. Now, she wondered if the many years of abuse had been nothing but prelude to her true punishment of forever seeing that woman's ravaged face.

But what about Augustus? He certainly had sinned too. Without a doubt, his vile actions had earned him the strictest punishment that either God or man could mete out. Should she go now and find a constable and turn him in, betraying her own husband for the greater good? Should she confront him herself instead and plead with him to turn himself in, even though it meant risking that she would join the others in the garden to be picked to shreds by the crows? Minerva shifted into a kneeling position and clasped her hands in prayer. She begged for guidance and strength to do whatever was required of her.

When morning came, Minerva waited in the shed until she felt confident that the time for Augustus to leave for work had passed. With a stiff back and much creaking and popping of her knees from lying on the hard wood floor, she untied her belt from the door handle and opened the door just enough to poke her head out and look around. Satisfied that she was alone, she made her way slowly and painfully to the kitchen door, taking great care to avoid looking in the direction of the disturbed patch of earth and the horrors it held just below the surface.

Before entering the house, she peered through the window for any sign of her husband's presence. The countertop was bare, and the cup from Augustus's morning coffee was rinsed and placed upside down on a towel to dry. The lunch pail and flask of coffee that he took with him to the office each day were nowhere in sight. With infinite caution to avoid making even the slightest noise, Minerva opened the door and went inside. She froze like a frightened rabbit when the door squeaked as she closed it behind her.

After several minutes without moving a muscle and hardly daring to breathe, she removed her shoes and tread softly on stocking feet to the front sitting room and through every room and closet until she was certain that she was alone in the house. She checked the latch on the front door to make sure she wouldn't be taken by surprise if Augustus returned unexpectedly, then washed her face and hands and dressed herself in a charcoal wool traveling suit. She arranged her long, gray hair in a tight bun at the nape of her neck and placed a periwinkle blue felt hat on her head, secured with several pins against the blustery wind. She pulled a large carpet bag from under the bed and filled it with clothing, a small pewter jewelry box, toiletries, and her Bible. She picked up the now heavy bag and walked from the room, but quickly turned back and placed the bag on the bed. She opened a drawer, removed her mother's red silk scarf, and stroked it gently before adding it to the bag.

Minerva returned to the kitchen, where she wrapped two apples, a small loaf of bread, and a hunk of hard cheese in a cloth and put the bundle into her handbag. She then stood on a chair to reach a high cabinet and retrieved a tin box that had been shoved into a dark corner at the back of the shelf. She removed the loose bills and coins from the box and added them up before placing them in her handbag: four hundred and sixty-two dollars and seventy-five cents. Minerva had been saving money in the box, first from her earnings at Short's Sure, then from the money Augustus gave her for household expenses, since her wedding day. Deep inside, she had known she needed to prepare for this day, although she could never have imagined an ending as devastating as the reality.

With her handbag held in the crook of her elbow, Minerva pulled on her gloves and picked up the carpet bag. She took a deep breath, lifted her chin, and walked out the front door without a backward glance.

32

Cherry Pie

"The flowers are lovely, Miss Latham." The young pastor looked around with approval at the arrangements of pale pink roses, sweet alyssum, and white daisies on the altar and on the platform bearing the child-sized white coffin. "The Binghams will be very grateful for the care you took in putting them together for their little one."

Minerva looked up at the thin, young man's benevolent face and smiled. "Thank you, Reverend Palmer. It was the least I could do for that poor, dear couple. It's so sad to lose a child at any age, but they are so young themselves, and little Sarah was such a sweet baby." She adjusted the roses in one of the vases and took a step back to observe the effect. "Still, we must remember that God's will must be done. They must content themselves with the other children He blesses them with."

Her back was turned to the Reverend, and she didn't see the troubled expression that showed briefly on his brow as she spoke. He recovered himself in time as she turned back to face him. "Is there anything else you need today, Reverend? I was thinking I might bake a nice cherry pie or two to bring to the funeral luncheon tomorrow. If there's nothing else, I'll just be heading home to get started on my baking."

Nearly five years had passed since the day Minerva walked away from the home she had shared for thirty years with a husband she had hardly known. She had gone straight to the train station and bought a one-way ticket to Lima, Ohio, which she had chosen for no other reason than that she liked the name. Upon arrival in Lima, she had quickly found a small house for rent near an old and somewhat dilapidated Lutheran church. She rented the house in her maiden name.

Minerva, now Miss Latham once again, placed an advertisement in the local newspapers, offering her services as a bookkeeper and accountant. Well before her savings from the tin box ran out, she was making a humble but sufficient income managing the accounts of the Lutheran church and a handful of small businesses. She also found time to volunteer at the church, tidying up after services, making floral arrangements for weddings, baptisms, and funerals, and doing other light work to assist the very young but earnest pastor.

Most of the time, Minerva was content with her new life. Her little house was cozy and comfortable. She had money enough to keep food on the table, supplemented by a small garden of herbs and vegetables, and plenty of fuel for her stove and fireplace. The neighbors were pleasant without being intrusive. For the first time in her life, Minerva answered to no one but herself. No one but herself and God, that is. And therein lay the source of a crushing weight of discontent that descended upon her unexpectedly from time to time and disturbed her sleep with troubled dreams she couldn't remember upon awakening. Minerva was plagued with guilt.

Sometimes weeks would pass without thinking about the choice she had made five years ago to walk out the door and leave her husband and the fallen women of the town to their fate. Then, inevitably, some small thing – seeing a woman with red hair or hearing the harsh cry of crows soaring overhead or feeling the cold, moist soil in her hands as she tended her garden – would jolt her mercilessly back to that night in the shed, mere feet from where Augustus whistled a merry tune as he buried his latest victim.

Always, she ended up with the same questions. What else could she have done? What else *should* she have done? And worst of all, what else had happened since she left – how many more bodies were being picked apart by crows as they moldered in shallow graves while she sat safe and sound before her fireplace knitting a blanket for the christening of a neighbor's new baby?

Minerva had spent many hours kneeling in prayer until her knees grew numb from the pain, seeking forgiveness for her selfish act in running away and begging for guidance as to what she must do to achieve atonement for her sins. But God remained silent, and Minerva would rise painfully to her feet and climb into her lonely bed with a still-troubled heart before drifting into the smothering forgetfulness of sleep.

After she finished with the flowers at the church, Minerva went home and immediately set to work on the pies for little Sarah's funeral luncheon to be held the next day. Her bony but nimble fingers worked the pie crust dough with practiced skill. As she rolled out the dough and cut it to fit the pie pans, she absent-mindedly hummed a tune she once heard in a dark garden through the walls of a dank wooden shed.

Minerva had filled the pie shells with sour cherries steeped in sugar and was about to put the pies in the oven when she heard a brisk tapping sound. Someone was knocking on the front door. She wiped the flour from her hands onto her apron and shuffled in her house slippers to the door, all the while muttering to herself that it was quite late for an unexpected visitor. She was prepared to say as much to whomever was knocking, but when she opened the door, she was momentarily rendered speechless and could do nothing but stand and gape at the man who had broken free from her nightmares to stand nonchalantly on the other side of the threshold.

"Hello, Minerva," Augustus said. His voice was the same as she remembered, the same voice that still haunted her dreams five years later, but his appearance had changed so much that Minerva wondered if she would have recognized him if he passed her in the street. The passage of time had not been kind to Augustus Short. His clothes hung loosely on his frame as though his body had shrunken into itself. His hair, once full, carefully groomed, and nearly black, was now sparse, white, and disheveled. He had dark circles under his eyes and a noticeable twitch in his pale lips.

"May I come in?" he said in the same calm voice, as if his presence at Minerva's door was no more out of the ordinary than a visit from the postman. The question jolted Minerva out of her shock-induced trance, and she opened the door mechanically and stepped back to allow him to enter. In her last moments, she would wonder why she had so quickly and compliantly let the monster in, the same monster she had traveled alone across state lines with nothing but a carpet bag and a few hundred dollars to avoid. The same monster she had hidden from for five years and yet had never really escaped. But she did let him in, and there would be no more running from fate.

Augustus carried a duffel bag in one hand, and he looked around for a place to set it down. He dropped the bag on the floor by an arm chair and sat down without waiting for an invitation. Minerva stood just inside the entryway, wringing her hands against her apron, as if she could will him to turn around and walk back out the door. After a long and awkward silence, she shuffled into the room and perched on the edge of the little sofa facing the arm chair. Her husband looked over at her with his dark, sunken eyes, made darker still by the fading light of the setting sun through window shades not yet drawn closed for the night.

"What are you doing here, Augustus?" Minerva asked with a quiver in her voice. Her own voice echoed in her ears with a dreamlike quality that made her want to pinch herself awake.

"I could ask you the same thing, Minerva," he replied. "I've been looking for you for five years. The whole town looked for you, at least at first. As time went by without a trace of what had become of you, people came to their own conclusions. They tended to be in one or the other of two camps. Some thought you had run off with another man. At your age, most people didn't think that likely. The rest figured you were dead. And some of them thought I was the one who must have killed you."

He stared at her, unblinking, his rheumy eyes deep in the dark hollows of their sockets. "I wonder if you can imagine what it's like to stand accused of murder in the eyes of your friends and neighbors," he said, "to hear them whisper as you pass by, to pull their children across the street to avoid you, as though whatever evil possesses you could slough off and infect them. Do you know what that's like, Minerva? No? I can tell you that it's very bad for business."

Minerva did not answer. She sat rigidly on the edge of the sofa, still wringing her hands and rocking her body ever so slightly forward and back. Augustus studied her face, his own expression masked. When he spoke again, there was a barely perceptible tremor in his voice.

"Why did you leave me?"

Minerva stopped rocking. She shoved her hands beneath her thighs to calm her movements. At last she spoke. "Do you really need to ask me that? I know what you did, Augustus. I know about your perversions and your whores. What's more, I know about those poor women in the garden."

Augustus flinched, and the little color left in his sickly complexion drained away, leaving his face ashen and drawn.

"Did you think you could keep your dirty secrets to yourself by drugging me and then committing your foul acts while I slept just across the hall? And then burying those poor wretched women practically in plain sight in my own garden? How many were there, Augustus? Five? Ten? And how many more since I left you there alone with no one to bear witness to your depravity? Did you really think I wouldn't find out what you were doing? Or were you just waiting for me to give you the excuse to slice off my scalp too and bury me there along with the others?"

Minerva's voice had grown shrill, filled with the rage and shame she had been holding in for so many years. She didn't realize that she had stood up from the sofa. She was towering now over Augustus, who remained sitting quietly in the chair and looking up at her with inscrutable eyes in his sunken and withered face.

"Your scalp wouldn't have worked at all," he said quietly.

"What did you say?" Minerva fought to hold on to the strength of her anger, but his calm voice and piercing gaze threw her off balance.

She felt her confidence ebb away. She broke eye contact and found herself wringing her hands again and twisting her apron into a knot.

"I said your scalp wouldn't do. Wrong color, you know. I've always preferred redheads. If I had been born female, I would have been a redhead." He chuckled mirthlessly without looking away from his wife's face. He never blinked, but tears glistened in the corners of his eyes. "If I had been born female," he continued, "so much would have been different. You and I would never have married, for one thing."

Minerva lifted her head to glance at her husband. She saw him staring back at her and quickly turned away again. "Why did you have to kill them, Augustus?"

Her voice had lost its righteous anger and was subdued, resigned, tired. "I know you never loved me, not from the start. I was nothing more than a prop to give you an air of respectability and to keep prying eyes from finding out your shameful secrets. God forgive me, I hated you for the things you did – the drinking, the violence, the obscene pictures, the women – I thought you were only having affairs, you see." A short laugh on the edge of hysteria burst from her lips.

She swallowed, took a deep breath, and went on. "I thought it was my fault. If I was a better wife, a more attractive, more passionate woman perhaps, you wouldn't need any of that. And so, I carried on and kept up the façade because I was ashamed. But then I found a dead woman in my garden."

Minerva met her husband's gaze, and this time she held it. "I heard you that night as you dug a new hole for the body of the latest woman you murdered. You were singing. I could hear you but you didn't know I was there. You killed a human being with your own hands and you were singing as you disposed of her body.

"You want to know why I left you, Augustus? Knowing what I knew, hearing you singing as you dug that woman's grave, how could I stay? I had to leave. It was my only choice. If I had stayed, your body would have been the next one to be planted there." She was leaning over him now, and tears she didn't feel were dripping from her face. "I've dreamed about it a thousand times – what it would have been like if instead of hiding like a coward, I had taken the shovel from your hands and bashed your brains in with it. And those are my good dreams."

It was Augustus's turn to look away, but Minerva's voice rose to a shout, and his head swiveled back as she screamed at him. "I want to know why you killed those women, Augustus. Why wasn't it enough to flaunt them in my face? Why did you have to kill them?"

Augustus sighed and rose from the arm chair with difficulty. He straightened up slowly and painfully with his hands supporting his lower back, which crackled as he stood. At his full height, he still had to tilt his head up to look directly into his wife's eyes as she stood straight and tall before him. Quietly but clearly, enunciating each word, he said, "I had to kill them, my dear, to take what I needed." He began walking away in the direction of the kitchen. Over his shoulder, he said, "Now, do you have anything to eat and drink? I've had a long journey and I could use a decent meal before bed."

"You're not staying here tonight!" Minerva reached out and grasped his stooped shoulder to prevent him from venturing further into her home and sanctuary. He spun around with a speed that belay his apparent frailty and clenched a gnarled hand around her throat. His face was so close to hers as she gasped for breath and tore at the bony fingers encircling her neck that she could smell his breath, stale and sour like the end of an old cigar, chewed between rotten teeth.

"Oh, but I am. Tonight and tomorrow night and as many more nights as I please. I'm still your husband, and you're still my wife, even if you neglected to mention me to your new friends in this charming little town, *Miss Latham*." He said her maiden name with a sneer as he tightened his grip around her throat. He gave it a sharp squeeze, then released her and resumed walking towards the kitchen.

Minerva stood with her hands to her throat, massaging away the pain and taking in deep, panicked breaths. Her heart pounded in her chest. She could hear Augustus in the kitchen, opening and shutting cabinet doors and clattering dishes together. She said a silent prayer and waited for her heartbeat to return to a more normal pace before following him.

"Are you going to finish those pies?" he asked conversationally as she appeared in the doorway. He was holding a plate of cold roast beef and new potatoes with chives and forked large bites into his mouth as he leaned against the counter. A teapot emitted thin wisps of steam as it heated on the stovetop. Through a bite of potato, he added, "This isn't bad. I missed your cooking."

"They're for a little girl," she answered. He looked at her quizzically. "For a little girl's funeral, that is," she added. He turned his attention back to his plate. The death of a child was of no concern to him. Minerva watched him eat for a moment, then began to busy herself with putting the pies into the oven. "Although I suppose one pie would be enough, if you want to eat the other. The grieving parents aren't likely to be very hungry." She heard him scraping the last of his meal from the plate and then dropping the plate and silverware into the sink with a clatter.

The teapot's low whistle turned into a shriek. Minerva automatically moved to take the teapot away from the flame, but when she turned toward the stove, Augusts was already stirring sugar into his cup of tea and watching her with cold amusement in his black eyes.

"There's a spare room down the hall and to the right," she said, keeping her voice neutral. "The bed linens are fresh. I just changed them and aired the room on Friday. You can put your things in there. I'll just be cleaning up in here and waiting for the pies to finish baking." She turned her back on him but could still feel his malignant stare burning twin holes into the back of her head. Her hands shook as she filled the sink to wash the dishes.

Over the splash of water and clink of china, Minerva listened for the sound of shoes on tiled floor. She was desperate for him to leave the room, to break the tension that had built up in her body like a coiled spring, barely contained, but she heard nothing. When finally she stole a glance over her shoulder, Augustus still was standing exactly where he had been, sipping his cup of tea and looking steadily at her. A shiver ran up her spine, and she whipped her head back around, dropping the pan she had been washing into the sink and splashing sudsy water onto her tear-streaked face.

After several more minutes, a hand came around Minerva's waist from behind, and she nearly jumped out of her skin. She uttered a small, frightened yelp before registering that the hand held an empty tea cup and spoon on a saucer. She heard a low chuckle inches from her ear as the hand gently lowered the cup and saucer into the dishwater. She closed her eyes and held her breath until she heard footsteps moving away and out the kitchen door.

Minerva released her breath slowly through her mouth and willed herself to be calm. She remained perfectly still with her eyes tightly closed for a long moment, then clasped her hands in front of her and said a silent prayer. This time, it was not for guidance. She knew what she needed to do. This time, she said a prayer of thanks for this opportunity for redemption. A smile twitched at the corners of her mouth, and she began to hum softly.

After emptying the dishwater and wiping down the countertop, Minerva placed the clean dishes on a drying rack, except for the rolling pin, which she left on the counter near the stove. The pleasant odor of baking pastry began to fill the room. Minerva opened the oven door with a quilted mitt and checked the progress of the pies. Molten sugar bubbled on the surface, and the crust was only just beginning to turn golden. She pushed the pie pans towards the back of the oven and closed the oven door. Still holding the mitt, she cleared her throat and called out, "Augustus, could you please come back to the kitchen? I need your help."

She clutched the mitt with shaking hands and waited. An eternity later, Augustus appeared in the doorway with an amused expression on his face. "Well now, I've only been here an hour or two and already you've found use for your beloved husband. What is it you need?"

"The pies are ready," she said. "Would you mind taking them out of the oven for me? I'm afraid it's rather harder than it used to be for me to lift anything heavy, and I would hate to drop them." She opened the oven door and stepped to the side, then offered him the oven mitt with an outstretched hand.

Augustus bent over with a creaking back and reached far into the depths of the still hot oven with his mitted hand to grab the edge of the pie pan. Minerva watched as he struggled to reach the pan and grasp it with the bulky mitt. Finally, he uttered a muffled "Got you!". He took a step back as he pulled the pie forward. Before he could straighten up from his stooped position, Minerva brought the rolling pin down hard on the back of his head.

"No, Augustus," she said. "I got you."

The cherry pie slid from Augustus's hand and fell face-up on the floor. Augustus remained upright, still bent over the oven, until a second blow from the rolling pin brought him to his knees. A third blow sent him toppling over, his face landing squarely in the pie and sending scalding hot cherries flying up around his body like buckshot. Minerva hit him again – a fourth time, a fifth time, again and again until she could hear the crunch of his skull each time she struck and see the blood spurting from his ruined head to intermingle with the red juice of the cherries.

Finally, as the adrenalin-fueled strength began to leave her tired arms, Minerva set the rolling pin down in the sink and wiped her bloody hands on a dish towel. She carefully retrieved the oven mitt from Augustus's hand and, pushing his body out of the way with her foot, reached into the oven to remove the second pie, which she placed on a drying rack near the open window. "One pie will just have to do," she said.

She turned to look down on her husband's crumpled body and crushed, bloody head. She studied him silently for a moment as she straightened her drenched and spattered skirt and patted an errant wisp of hair back into her bun, then spoke calmly to the bleeding corpse, as if reasoning with a willful child.

"I'm sorry, Augustus. I really am, but it's your own fault, you know. It wasn't right that I let you get away with murder. I've known that all along, and it has bothered me ever since I left you. At least now, the weight of that sin is off my conscience. And besides, I did warn you that if you ever laid your hands on me again, I would kill you. Did you forget? Or maybe you thought I didn't really mean it. But I did mean it. I guess you found that out, didn't you? Once I said it, it was like a commitment – a promise – and breaking a promise is the same as bearing false witness, you see, and that's a sin."

Minerva suddenly felt very tired. She felt bad about leaving Augustus's body where it lay, still dripping into the splattered remains of the pie, but the thought of trying to move him and clean up the mess was just too much. She took off her blood-soaked apron and hung it on a hook on the kitchen wall, then moved slowly and wearily to her bedroom where she quickly undressed, collapsed onto the bed, and fell immediately into a deep, dreamless sleep.

33

Confession

"Oh God, whose beloved Son took children into his arms and blessed them: Give us grace to entrust Sarah to your never-failing care and love, and bring us all to your heavenly kingdom; through Jesus Christ our Lord, who lives and reigns with you and the Holy Spirit, one God, now and forever. Amen."

"Amen," the mourners repeated. Reverend Palmer looked out at the congregation gathered before the tiny grave. It was a gray, overcast morning, and a chill wind rustled the leaves in the trees and stirred the hem of the Reverend's cassock and the veil of the grieving mother's black silk hat. She held a lace handkerchief to her face and sobbed into it while her husband stood rigidly at her side, his arm around her shoulder.

"Let us turn to the Gospel of John," the Reverend continued, "which tells us, 'Him that cometh to me, I will in no wise cast out. And this is the Father's will which hath sent me, that of all which he hath given me, I should lose nothing, but should raise it up again at the last day'."

From the corner of his eye, Reverend Palmer noticed Minerva Latham, dressed in black from head to toe and standing apart from the others. She clutched a prayer book in her gloved hands close against her chest. He could not see her face for the heavy veil that covered it, but he easily recognized her tall, straight stature. There was something about her solitary and unmoving figure that reminded him of the stone statues of weeping angels standing guard over the dead in the old cemetery by the church he attended as a child. Rather than bringing comfort, the image was strangely unsettling. A cold sweat trickled down between his shoulder blades.

The Reverend tore his gaze away from the old woman and turned back to face the huddled mourners. He raised his voice to the heavens and completed the burial ritual. The tiny white coffin gleamed briefly in a ray of sunlight that broke through the overhanging clouds, then disappeared into shadow as it was lowered into the ground.

Minerva waited until the others had walked away from the grave toward the church before she approached and tossed a handful of rich, black earth upon the coffin. Somewhere overhead, a single crow cawed three times, sharp yet distant like the laughter of a witch riding the wind on a broomstick. She hurried to catch up with the Reverend, who was trailing behind the congregation as they made their way from the churchyard to the open door of the sanctuary.

"Reverend Palmer." He turned at the sound of his name to see Minerva striding toward him. "I must speak with you."

"Of course, Miss Latham." He waited for her with his hands tucked into his cassock sleeves against the persistent, biting wind. He smiled at her when she stopped a pace in front of him and pushed back her veil, but his smile faltered when he saw the tears running down her face. Her voice had been strong, and he was surprised to see that she was crying. "It is always the hardest to bear when a child is taken from us," he said gently.

"Yes, it is, Reverend, but that's not what I need to talk to you about," she replied. "I have a confession to make – a quite serious one, I'm afraid."

"We are all sinners, as the scripture tells us, and I can't imagine that you have done anything so terrible that couldn't be understood and forgiven by a merciful God." He gave her an encouraging smile. "Little

Sarah's family will be waiting for me in the church. Is this something we could talk about after the funeral luncheon?"

"I would rather we spoke now. I'm going to have to call in the police as soon as possible today, and after that, I doubt we will get another chance to speak." Her voice remained steady, but her hands were in constant motion, gripping and twisting the prayer book she held in front of her like a shield. "To get straight to the point, I killed my husband last night, Reverend Palmer. It wasn't in self-defense, not in any immediate sense, although I do think he had it coming."

The Reverend gaped at her. When he recovered the power of speech, he sputtered, "You killed your...I'm sorry, Miss Latham, but I don't think I heard you correctly. Did you say you killed your husband?"

"Yes, that is what I said."

"But, Miss Latham, you live alone. You have no husband!"

"I'm afraid I haven't been entirely honest with you, Reverend Palmer. I do, or I should say, I did have a husband. I left him five years ago right before I came to live here. He showed up at my house last night quite unexpectedly, and then I hit him over the head with a rolling pin until he was dead. He's lying on my kitchen floor right now, which is why I needed to speak with you now instead of later. I really should be getting on with summoning the police before he starts attracting insects."

"You, uh, you beat your husband to death with a rolling pin, and he's...he's on the kitchen floor, and, um, uh, you don't want him to attract insects, and um..." Reverend Palmer had gone very pale and was starting to totter slightly. "Miss Latham, perhaps we should go inside now."

"Yes, I think that might be best. Here, Reverend, let me help you." Minerva put her arm around the Reverend's narrow waist, and he put his around her shoulder, and together they walked back to the church, the elderly murderess supporting the young clergyman from collapsing in a dead faint.

****

Through the intersession of Reverend Palmer and the kind heart of the judge who heard her case, Minerva Short, née Latham, was spared a jury trial and sent to live out her remaining days in the lunatic asylum in Columbus, Ohio. There, on the night of November 18, 1868, she, along with five other female inmates, died of smoke inhalation as a small fire that started in a linen storage room quickly escalated into a massive inferno that consumed most of the facility and reduced it to a smoldering ruin.

As the fire raged out of control and moved inexorably toward her small cell, Minerva lay on her cot, breathing in searing ash and smoke, and thought about Joan of Arc. People thought her insane too when she was alive, but after her death, they made her a saint. Minerva didn't think of herself as a saint, but she had always tried to serve God, and she had suffered much in her life. Perhaps, like Joan of Arc, it was all in preparation for fulfillment of God's greater purpose for her. Maybe her own usefulness wasn't ending here in flames but only just beginning.

"Please, God," she prayed silently, *"forgive me for letting those women lie there in that unhallowed grave without anyone to mourn them. Forgive me for letting Augustus continue his evil deeds for so long, when I had the power to stop him. I know now that running away was selfish. I shouldn't have waited so long to bring an end to his wickedness. The women who died at Augustus's hand after I left – and only You know how many more there were – I accept that their deaths are as much my fault as his."*

The smoke filled her lungs and burned her eyes. With her last breath, she had one final plea. *"If I'm not worthy of heaven, oh Lord, then let me prove myself worthy. Let me be your vessel on Earth. Let me bring your divine justice to those who suffer at the hands of wicked men like my husband."*

Minerva's world dissolved into sooty darkness, and she descended into the sleep of death. When she awoke again, it was not to the glory of heaven or the eternal despair of hell. When she opened her eyes and looked upon a changed but changeless world, her spirit was bound through her dying plea to that nameless space that is neither life nor death. Her sorrow for those she could not save and her wrath, born of a twisted and rigid faith, were tethers to the living world, and she would not leave it until her burning thirst for vengeance was quenched.

34

Searches

Oscar had one more thing to do before he got on the highway for the long drive down to his cousin's house in Hermosillo. No matter how cliché it might be, he was going to have to return to the scene of the crime. The cops might not have any suspicions about him or they might already be looking for him. He had no way of knowing. The TV news report didn't mention suspects, but that didn't mean anything. The cops could be holding back information to see if the people who called the Crime Stop number were legit or just nut jobs looking for attention.

As far as he knew, no one had figured out exactly where the assault had occurred. That night, after he left Lorena lying there on the ground by the overpass, he had driven to a bar a few miles away and had a couple of beers to calm his nerves. Once his anger had cooled, he realized it had been a mistake to leave her like that.

He tried to convince himself that she was going to be fine. She would probably just get up and walk away on her own, pissed as hell, and then she wouldn't speak to him for a few days or weeks. He would let her be mad for a while, and then he would coax her back – he knew just what to say to break down her resistance, and the makeup sex would be so fine. The thought brought a twitch of a smile to his lips.

On the other hand, maybe she would stay passed out until someone else came along and raped her or something. He would feel really bad if that happened. He loved her, but she was just so hot-headed and independent that sometimes he couldn't help but put her in her place. That line of thinking ultimately won the mental battle, and so he had left the bar and climbed back in his truck.

Lorena was still lying in the same place when he got back. It was almost 2:00 AM, and the streets were dark and empty. He picked her up and carried her to the truck. She was a dead weight in his arms and limp as a rag doll. She showed no signs of regaining consciousness, her head lolling on a neck as weak as a newborn's. When he opened the passenger door, the interior light shining through it revealed the extent of her injuries, and Oscar was suddenly afraid.

He had intended to take her home and put her to bed, or at least hand her off to that fag roommate of hers, but instead he drove to a park just down the road from the overpass. Once he was certain no one was around, he lifted her from the passenger seat and carried her to a grassy area far from any lights, then hid her behind some bushes where no one would be likely to see her, at least not until daylight.

She hadn't moved, hadn't so much as fluttered an eye lid, from the time he found her. Not during the drive over, and not since he laid her down in the grass and folded her long legs under her to better conceal her from view. Her skin felt cold to the touch despite the warm night. As he bent over her to kiss her closed eyelids, Oscar whispered a prayer and reached for the St. Christopher medal he had worn since he was ten years old, when his abuela gave it to him for protection from harm. The silver chain was no longer around his neck.

Oscar felt his heart rate accelerate with panic as he patted down his shirt front. He felt around his neck as though the medal would suddenly reappear, but it was gone. The chain must have broken during the fight with Lorena, or maybe it fell off while he was carrying her from the truck. Either way, it was a problem. A big problem. Anyone who knew him would without a doubt recognize that medal as his. It was as much a part of him as the tattoos on his skin.

He looked around in the grass and dirt, straining to see in the dark. He retraced his steps to the truck without finding the medal. Should he go back to the overpass and look for it there? He had been lucky so far. No one had driven past him while he parked his truck, and there had been no pedestrians lingering in the park at this late hour, looking for drugs or a quick rendezvous in the men's room, or maybe just a place to sleep. There was a good chance that no one would see him if he went back and looked around, but what if they did, and what if that someone made a connection between him searching for something under the overpass and the dying girl in the park, just a short distance away?

It was a lot of "if's", and Oscar wasn't about to push his luck any further tonight. He had been trying not to think about it, trying hard to believe that it wasn't real, but the truth was that Lorena looked very close to death. There was no way she was just going to bounce up and walk away from this. She might even be dead already. The thought made him turn around to look behind him, certain someone would be there watching. He couldn't take the chance of being seen anywhere near her.

And so, Oscar had left the park and driven straight home and sponged the spots of blood from the passenger seat of his truck. And he had waited. He waited anxiously for a news report about a dead body found in a park, but as the hours ticked away without a word on the TV or social media, he began to relax. Maybe she was okay after all. Somebody would have found her body by now if she were dead, so that must mean she had woken up and gone home. She was probably there now, punishing him by not calling.

But what if she really was dead and no one had found her yet? It was possible. He had hidden her pretty well. The fear started to creep back in, and he was contemplating going back to the park one more time to have a look around when he got the call from Lorena in the hospital. She was alive and about to meet with the police. From that moment on, his path was clear.

After he left the hospital, Oscar made preparations to cross the border and lay low for as long as necessary. He called his uncle Martín in

Tucson, who in turn called his cousin Julio in Hermosillo to arrange for a place to stay. That way, he figured, no one would be able to trace him directly to Julio. Even his own mother didn't know where he was going, just in case the police tried to question her. Plausible deniability – isn't that what they called it in the movies?

He had everything he needed now: a place to stay, provisions for the road, a full tank of gas. His handgun was loaded and concealed in the compartment between the front seats. He just needed to make that one last stop before heading out of town. Oscar eased the truck into the right-hand lane and took the exit that would lead him back to the place where this whole mess started. Soon, he could put it all behind him, but for now, he had to find that damn medal before someone else did.

****

"Richie?" Lonny kept his voice calm and chose his words carefully. The look in his partner's eyes was a look he had never seen there before, and it scared him, not for himself because he knew with an iron-clad certainty that Richie would never hurt him, but for Richie himself. That look practically shouted violent intent – a no-holds-barred, reckless, erupting violence that, once unleashed, would not be restrained until either the target of his rage or Richie himself were rendered powerless to fight any longer.

"Yeah?" Rich kept his eyes locked on the red truck a few car lengths ahead of him, moving south on the freeway.

"What exactly is the plan?"

Rich risked taking his eyes off the truck long enough to shoot Lonny an exasperated look. "Haven't we been over this already? I'm going to stop Oscar from fleeing the country. Once he makes it to the border crossing, I'll give you the wheel and I'll get out of the car. The traffic at the boarding crossing is always at a complete standstill at this time of day, so I should be able to run ahead of the line and warn the authorities that an armed murderer is coming toward them in that vehicle."

"Oh," Lonny said, momentarily at a loss for words. "Wow, Richie, that's actually a pretty good plan."

"Thanks. What did you think I was going to say? That I was going to have you climb into the backseat, get the rifle from the trunk through that opening behind the armrest, and then I was going to tell you to drive while I hang out the side window and shoot Oscar in the back of the head through his back windshield?"

"Maybe. Something along those lines anyway. I'm very relieved to hear that isn't actually the plan." Lonny took a deep breath and let it out again. He hadn't realized that he had been holding his breath for much of the way since they left the barrio in pursuit of Oscar's truck.

"Yeah, that's Plan 'B' – just in case Plan 'A' doesn't work."

Lonny's head swiveled back toward Rich fast enough to cause whiplash. He searched for signs of humor in Rich's expression but saw only the same grim determination. He opened his mouth to speak, but Rich spoke first.

"Looks like we're making a side trip. Now, I wonder where he's going…" Rich followed the red truck to the off-ramp, being careful to keep a couple of vehicles between them. The mid-day traffic was heavy enough to conceal their pursuit as long as they kept to the main roads, but when the truck turned onto a side street, Rich had to stay farther behind to keep from being seen. He lost track of it altogether in a series of twisting roads alongside a neighborhood park.

The tension inside the car was as taut as a tight-rope over a fiery pit, with Rich focused on finding his quarry, and Lonny trying and failing to form an argument in his head that would convince Rich to stop this madness. Finally, they spotted the truck parked several yards ahead on a dirt pull-out near an overpass. Rich parked behind another car on the other side of the street and opened his door.

"Where are you going?" Lonny whispered.

"I need to get closer. I can't see anything from back here, and I want to know what he's up to," Rich said. "And why are you whispering? He can't hear you, you know. He's like a quarter of a mile away." Lonny reached for the passenger door handle. "No, Lonny, you stay here. It's easier for one person to hide than two."

"Yes, it is," Lonny shot back, still in a whisper. "And it's also easier for a somewhat petite person to hide than a colossal hulk who looks like a circus strongman in pastels. Why don't *you* wait here, and *I'll* go see what he's doing?"

"Lonny, for once, could you please not argue with me? Just stay here, alright? I'll be back." Rich closed the door behind him before Lonny could say anything else.

The landscape of aging warehouses and neglected houses, some boarded up and covered in layers of graffiti, offered little in the way of cover. A few rain-starved trees and dried grass and weeds were scattered across dirt yards, and a miasma of heat hovered over the surface of the street's cracked asphalt. Rich kept to the sidewalk, strolling at a casual pace in hopes that if Oscar looked in his direction, he wouldn't see him as anything other than just some guy walking down the street.

As he got closer, Rich could see Oscar bent at the waist and feeling around in the weeds and trash just beyond the cleared area where his truck was parked. His body was turned away and slightly to the left, blocking Rich's view of the handgun he had last seen shoved into his belt. Rich crouched down and kept the truck between himself and Oscar as he crossed the street. His flipflops slapping rhythmically as he walked were a percussion solo turned up to the highest volume in his ears. He held his breath, sure that Oscar must have heard him approach, but a few yards away, his search through the roadside debris continued uninterrupted.

Oscar straightened up and brushed his hands against his jeans. This was the right spot; he knew that for certain, but it looked so much different by the light of day. Beyond the gravel-strewn dirt pull-out, there was an expanse of yellowed grass and tumbleweed, littered with crushed beer cans and old cigarette butts. About ten feet from the road, the grassy area sloped sharply downward into a dry ravine that ran through the concrete and steel pylons of the overpass.

Oscar replayed the fight with Lorena in his mind and tried to match up the images with the view in front of him. The fight had begun as soon as she got out of the truck, so on the near side of the downward slope. He had searched the area carefully already, every patch of weeds and gopher hole, and had come up empty.

In the back of his mind, a tiny worm of fear began to squirm and wiggle its way into his consciousness. What if the police had already been here and found his medal? What if they were somewhere nearby, waiting for him to show up and search for it as he was doing right now, right on cue?

He quickly swiveled around to look behind him. On either side of the truck, the yards and windows of the buildings across the street were empty and quiet, other than the squabbling of a pair of sparrows in a sickly mulberry tree and the distant yapping of small dogs, excited by the mail carrier or a passing car.

Oscar looked down one side of the street, then the other, squinting through the glare at the parked cars dotting the curb along the blocks leading back to the main roads for signs of occupancy. The movie reel in his head rolled on to the next scene. Suddenly, he recalled Lorena walking away from him, heading the wrong way in her determination to end their conversation and find her own way home. He had gone after her, struggled with her, struck her down, not here by the truck, but half a block away.

He started off, almost at a run, down the road in the direction Lorena had gone when she had made the fateful decision to walk away from him. He scanned the ground around him closely as he strode toward the place where he had caught up with her that night. Only a couple of nights ago. It seemed like a lifetime.

A glint of sunlight on an object in the grass caught his eye and momentarily diverted him from his path, but it proved to be nothing more than a broken beer bottle with a silver label. As he turned again to the road ahead, a sound behind him, like a shout cut off prematurely followed by a muffled gagging, caused him to whirl around and reach for his gun. His hand grabbed at his belt but grasped only air. His gun was still in the truck, and between him and it was a scene so bizarre as to stop him dead in his tracks. He stood frozen in place and gawked open-mouthed, his lost medal forgotten.

35

Confrontations

Rich dropped into a crouch behind the truck, nearly falling backward onto his ass when Oscar suddenly turned around and looked behind him. His brief glimpse of the gangster's front side showed that the gun was missing from his belt. He must have left it in the truck. "*Good,*" Rich thought. "*Now I can stop hiding here like a wuss and take care of business.*"

He waited until Oscar was almost half a block away to come out from behind the truck and follow stealthily after him. Better to put as much distance between them and the truck as possible before confronting him, just in case things didn't go his way and Oscar decided to go for his gun. Up ahead, the gangster had slowed his pace and was bending down and shielding his eyes from the glare to peer at something on the ground. Rich opened his mouth to shout Oscar's name, but his voice was cut off at "ahh..." by a sudden blow to the throat.

In the blink of an eye, the Guardian was there, nearly transparent in the bright sunlight, her eyes depthless white holes in her malign face. Her figure flickered in and out of view, like a TV image in a thunderstorm. She drew back a gnarled fist encircled by a tattered black lace cuff and moved with impossible speed through the hazy distortion that surrounded her to strike Rich's throat a second time.

Still gagging from the first blow, Rich dodged the second one just in time. He jumped backward, tripping over his flipflops and falling to the ground. She was instantly upon him, snarling in her rage and grabbing for his throat with her clawed hands. Now barefoot and on his back, Rich kicked out wildly and somehow managed to knock the Guardian off him long enough to regain his feet.

The sunbaked sidewalk seared the soles of his feet, and Rich had to dance in place like a boxer in the ring. Just out of reach, the Guardian hovered. Her form flickered in and out of sight, but her eyes burned into him without ceasing. She seemed to have paused in her attack to observe him. Hoping to distract her long enough to give himself a chance to think of some way to escape with his life, Rich spoke to the fiend.

"Why are you doing this?" he rasped through the pain of his nearly crushed larynx. "What have I done to piss you off anyway? Whatever it is, I'm sorry. Really, really sorry. Please, just go away and haunt somebody else." He took a tentative step backwards as he spoke, but the Guardian matched his move by taking a step toward him. To his surprise and horror, she answered in a voice like dry branches scratching against a mausoleum wall.

"It isn't what you've done to me, young man. It's what you did to the girl, Lorena. Such a pretty little thing, and so defenseless against a muscle-bound brute like you, Richard."

At the sound of his name, Rich cringed and seemed to shrink into himself as the Guardian loomed over him.

"Did you think you could beat her and toss her aside as though she had no worth?" she went on. "Did you think there would be no consequences for your wickedness?" She laughed, a hollow and joyless cackle, and took a step forward. "You will pay for her death with your life. An eye for an eye, a tooth for a tooth." She smiled at him with a hideous grin that revealed blackened, sharp teeth between gray, leprous lips. Then she took another step forward.

****

At first, Oscar wondered if he was hallucinating. The sun was hot and glaring, and he had been out in it for quite a while without a hat or any water. He blinked his eyes rapidly several times to clear his vision, but the spectacle before him went on. No more than five or six paces in front of him stood, or rather staggered, Rich Wright, the last person he expected to see here or anywhere else today. He must have sneaked up on him somehow, but now the dumbass *maricón* was making weird choking noises and flailing around like he was trying to repel an invisible bear attack.

As he watched, Wright tripped and fell on his back, kicking his legs in the air like a child having a temper tantrum. Then he leaped up and started talking in a strangled voice, too low for Oscar to hear, and backing away, one step at a time, with his hands held up defensively in front of him. He was looking straight ahead with wide, terrified eyes, but there was no one else around, and he wasn't looking in Oscar's direction. In fact, he seemed not to know that Oscar was even there.

"Hey, *puta*, what is wrong with you, man?" Oscar called out to get his attention. "Are you on acid or something? What are you doing here?" Wright appeared not to hear him, but kept up his strange monologue, his hands still held up as if to shield his body. He seemed to be pleading with someone.

Oscar began walking slowly toward him. The man was clearly out of his mind, and Oscar didn't have time for crazy right now. Screw the medal; the day was slipping away, and he needed to get the hell out of here and across the border as soon as possible. If he could just get around Wright and get to his truck, the crazy fag could stand here all day talking to himself for all he cared.

He took another step, then heard the unmistakable sound of a gun being cocked. Pivoting swiftly in the direction of the sound, Oscar saw a small-framed Latino man in madras shorts and a teal polo shirt standing in front of a black compact car and pointing an antique rifle at him. He stood with a wide stance like a gunslinger in an old Western movie, but his narrow knees and the hands holding the gun were visibly shaking.

"Hold it right there," Lonny said in a higher and less authoritative voice than he had intended. Across the street, Oscar stopped and put his hands up, but his facial expression showed amusement rather than fear. He glanced over at Wright, who was still focused on his invisible foe, and took a step toward the little man with the gun.

"Hey, man, take it easy, okay? You must be Wright's boyfriend. Larry or Lorie or something like that, right? What have you two been smoking today, eh man – loco weed?" He chuckled at his own joke and lowered his hands. He stepped closer.

"It's Lonny, and I said to hold it. Don't take another step or I'll shoot you."

Oscar stood still but continued to smile at Lonny in an amused, unconcerned way. "That's a nice rifle you have there, Lonny. It looks old. Are you sure it even works?"

"Do you want to find out?" Lonny held the gun higher, tried to look menacing, but doubted he looked anything other than scared to death, which he was. "I want you to back away from Rich, right now. Put your hands back up and keep them there. And don't try anything. I *will* shoot you."

Off to the right, Rich stumbled backward, almost falling down again but recovering his balance in time. There was a wild look in his eyes, and he shouted, "Can't you see you've got the wrong guy?"

Lonny turned in bewilderment to look at Rich. "What? What do you mean I've got the wrong guy? This is Oscar, isn't it?"

Oscar saw his opportunity the moment Lonny took his eyes off him. He cleared the distance between himself and Lonny in three steps and lunged forward, grabbing the rifle from the startled man's hands. He pointed it at him and shook his head, amused.

"Look, I don't know what is going on with you two *loco* fags right now, but I've had enough." He gestured toward the black car behind where Lonny now stood as still as a statue. "Is that your ride?" Lonny nodded. "Good. Go sit in the back of the trunk where I can see you, and put your hands on your head, just like in the cop shows."

Much to Oscar's surprise, Lonny ignored his directive and started edging his way closer to where Rich was hopping up and down on his bare feet. "Hey, are you deaf?" Oscar shouted. He pointed the rifle in the air and pulled the trigger to fire a warning shot. Nothing happened.

Lonny heard the click of the rifle firing on an empty chamber and saw the look of angry disbelief on the gangster's face. He bolted toward Rich, but not fast enough. He heard a single, loud crack and simultaneously felt intense pain in the back of his head. He dropped to his knees and teetered there. "I've been shot", he said, but he couldn't hear his own voice. "I've been…," he tried again, but then he fell forward, landing face-down on the blistering asphalt, and lay still.

Oscar tossed the rifle aside and headed for his truck. He looked over at Wright just to make sure he kept his crazy ass at a safe distance and was surprised to see that he was no longer air-fighting, talking to himself, jumping up and down, or doing anything crazy at all. He was simply standing there looking toward Oscar but not at him. In fact, he seemed to be looking right through him, and on his face was an expression of relief and something else. Triumph? Oscar looked at him in disgust, then shook his head and kept walking.

36

Al

Just as the dying sun began to melt in a red and gold spill beneath the heat-blurred horizon, Al DeLeon dropped from the freeway overpass for the first time this night. He landed on his back, one arm broken and twisted under his body, and his head battered and bloody. He lay still with his eyes closed, resigned to his fate but in no particular hurry. He had relived the same night thousands of time. He knew how it ended. Al listened to the familiar hum of the traffic overhead and sighed.

When a new and unexpected sound traveled down the slope from the far side of the ravine, Al's eyelids snapped open. It was the sound of voices.

It was rare for people to come to this isolated place. The last time was when that *monstruo* had hurt that poor little *chica* and left her lying there bleeding into the hard ground. Curious, Al got up and shuffled on his ruined legs through the ravine and up the hill, following the voices. There were three of them, two male and one female. The female voice chilled Al's already-lifeless body to the core, and he hesitated before proceeding more cautiously up the steep slope, staying in the shadows as he went. He wasn't concerned about the men. They wouldn't even know he was there. But *she* would.

The source of the voices came into view as he cleared the summit of the small hill, and he observed that there were three men present, not two. One of them lay crumpled on the street, his face turned downward onto the pavement. Al could feel the warmth of the man's body, even from a distance, and he could see his heart beating in his chest. It was a soft red, the color of rose petals. This was a good man; Al was glad that he still lived.

A second man was standing at some distance. He had been turned away from the man lying in the street, but as Al watched, he caught sight of him. He called out "Lonny!" in an anguished voice, then sprinted toward the prostrate man and dropped to his knees in front of him. He sobbed and called the man's name over and over as he knelt over him. He turned him onto his back with the utmost tenderness and kissed his face.

The crying man was big, well over six feet tall, and lean, all muscle, with a powerful upper body that seemed incongruous with his gentle touch and the tears that continued to stream down his cheeks. Looking deeper into the man's soul as he grieved for his fallen friend, Al saw that this too was a good man with a humble and tender heart, the color of new violets. His torn and dirt-smudged clothes and the angry red marks on his neck and arms showed that he had been in a fight very recently and with a formidable opponent. Al had no doubt as to who or what that opponent was.

As Al looked on, the man on the ground stirred and opened his eyes.

"I think he shot me in the head," Lonny said.

The big man had been sobbing into his hands and rocking back and forth. At the sound of Lonny's voice, he froze. He dropped his hands from his face and stared.

"Oh my God, Lonny! You're alive! I thought you were dead. You scared me so much. I didn't know what to do, but now you're alive. Oh my God." Rich paused to catch his breath and allow his pounding heartbeat to subside. He clutched Lonny's hand and held it against his heart.

"Wait a minute. What did you just say about getting shot in the head? With my grandpa's rifle?"

"It's okay. I don't blame you, even though bringing the gun was a stupid idea."

"No, you don't understand. The rifle wasn't loaded. I didn't have any ammunition for it, and I didn't know how to load it anyway. I was only going to try to scare him with it. Anyway, what I'm trying to say is that he can't have shot you in the head with an unloaded rifle. Besides, you wouldn't be talking to me right now if he did. He must have just hit you with it."

"Which makes bringing the gun even more of a stupid idea. Richie, do you think you could help me get up out of the street and into the car before *El Chapo* over there gets his own gun and shoots us both?"

Lonny tried to sit up. A thousand white lights bloomed in his vision, and intense pain erupted in the back of his head. He fell back and closed his eyes. "Are you sure he didn't shoot me?"

Al turned his attention to the third man, the *monstruo*. He was back, the evil man he last saw attacking the young woman and leaving her for dead. His eyes were frost-rimmed windows looking dimly into a shriveled soul, and his heart was hardened and selfish and the color of old, rusted iron. Al could feel his anger and the self-centered fears that overruled his intellect. This man was dangerous and a real and present threat to the other two men. Al dragged his broken limbs and hobbled toward him, ready to protect Lonny and his companion if necessary.

The man was reaching for the door handle of his truck when, swift as a brush fire, the Hag rushed at him. She grabbed him by the back of the neck and wrenched him away from the door, then tossed him like a ragdoll into the street. Al shrunk back into the shadows.

Oscar lay spread-eagled on the asphalt. He propped himself up on his elbows and looked wildly around, expecting to see Wright standing nearby, ready for a fight, but Wright was yards away, kneeling over the little guy's body. Shaken and confused but not badly injured, Oscar started to pull himself up. He froze, still sitting in the middle of the street, when an overwhelming stench invaded his nostrils. It smelled like charred, rotten meat with an overlay of decaying flowers. He wretched. Rancid breath stirred the hair on his face, and a voice from his childhood nightmares of *La Llorona* whispered in his ear.

"You killed her," the voice said. "Now, you will die. Vengeance is mine, sayeth the Lord."

It was the last thing Oscar heard before a powerful blow struck him in the head, knocking him unconscious. He fell back on the asphalt and lay still. In the distance, the engine of a black Dodge Charger roared to life. The car spun around and sped off toward the main road.

Al watched as the Hag climbed into the truck. She sat in the driver's seat for a while, an incongruous old woman in nineteenth century clothing at the wheel of a modern vehicle, and studied the instrument panel. A key on a ring with a studded leather strap hung from the ignition. She turned it, and the engine started up. Methodically and unhurriedly, she tested the pedals on the floor and the gear shift to her right until she was confident that she understood how the machine operated. Then she delicately straightened her skirt, adjusted her hat, and placed the truck into gear. She turned the steering wheel to point the truck toward the figure lying motionless on the street.

By the time Al realized what the Hag's intentions were, he had no more than a split second to decide what he should do. In that fleeting window of time, he tried to weigh the value of a human life, even a life as wasted and destructive as this man's life, against the justice of allowing the man to be punished for what he had done to that poor girl. He wasn't sure if he even had the power to stop the Hag, and he was equally unsure of whether he wanted to stop her. The man had a wicked heart and he had done terrible things. He didn't deserve to be saved. Al would take pleasure in watching him die. With that thought, he knew which choice was the right one.

In an instant, Al stood in front of the prostrate man and in the path of the approaching vehicle. He waved his good arm over his head and called out, "*Señora*, please stop!" The truck continued toward him, then stopped with a squeal of brakes just inches from where he stood. The old woman behind the wheel glared angrily at him through the windshield. He held up his hand in a supplicating gesture and spoke to her.

"Please, *Señora,* don't do this, I beg you. It is wrong to kill a man. He is of no threat to you, certainly, and I can protect these other innocents from him. You don't need to do this. Please, show mercy."

The truck rolled forward.

37

Hag

In the end, Minerva had reluctantly concluded that the big man Richard was being truthful. It wasn't his pleading tone or that he clung tenaciously to his story. Many of the powerful, abusive men to whom she brought her righteous retribution broke down and sobbed, begging her for forgiveness or swearing their innocence with their blood-stained hands clasped in supplication.

This was different. Once he started talking, he surprised her by voicing a compulsion to avenge Lorena's murder that was almost equal to her own. She could see the anger beneath the fear on his handsome face. He claimed he had been following the man who was the real killer and that he was intent on bringing him to justice one way or another. This could be nothing more than a diversion, a way to save his own skin, but Minerva didn't think so.

She had stifled her doubts about Richard as the girl's killer, but the doubts had lingered. He had been at the same hospital where Lorena had been taken, but he had not gone to her room. Instead he had visited the strange old man and then went home. She had assumed he had gone back later and killed the girl, but that made no sense. Why not do the deed while he was already there? So, when he had so boldly dared to speak to her, she had listened, and much to her surprise, his explanation had rung true.

She had nothing to lose in believing Richard's story. If she found herself still stuck in this place and time after executing Oscar, she would know that he had tricked her and kept her from fulfilling her mission. She would not hesitate again to punish him for it.

For the present, Minerva pushed Richard aside and turned her full attention on the other man, Oscar. She caught up with him just in time. He had been about to mount his vehicle and leave. She reached out one bony hand and wrenched him away from the truck, then threw him to the ground effortlessly, like tossing a ball.

It was then that she got the idea of running him over with his own vehicle. Driving a motor car would be an interesting novelty. She had never done such a thing before, and the idea brought a mischievous smile to her face. It was a bit theatrical, she had to admit, and quite different from her usual methods. She was typically more hands-on and focused on results instead of showing off, but this had been a challenging mission, and it seemed fitting to end it with a flourish.

She climbed inside and aimed the steering wheel so that the king-cab truck's oversized wheels would crush the unconscious man's skull. After a few false starts, she figured out the gears and shifted into drive. Her smiling face shifted into a death's head grin as she accelerated toward the body in the road.

Then the Guardian appeared.

He was tall and powerfully built, but his face was gentle and compassionate. He had wings, golden-brown like the wings of a great eagle, and they spread out behind him as if to shield the motionless figure on the ground. A warm light surrounded him and softened the immediate landscape so that objects and colors blended into each other like an Impressionist painting. Where cracked, baking asphalt had been, there was a smooth, glassy surface dotted with the silvery-blue fire of a million marcasite. The dried grass was fresh and green, and the yellowed weeds blossomed into a profusion of wildflowers. Even the stars directly above the Guardian shined with a light clearer and purer than any other celestial objects in the night sky.

The Guardian positioned himself in the path of the vehicle and raised a hand, commanding it to stop. "Please, *Señora,* don't do this," he said.

Minerva ground her sharp teeth with rage and frustration. This was *her* mission. She had been called to do this work – God's work. The guilty must be punished. The wicked must be brought down. There had been too many delays already. She would tolerate no further interference. She took her foot off the brake and pressed the gas pedal.

Al saw the chrome grill of the truck lunge forward like a predatory beast. There was no time to think. He threw himself on top of Oscar's body, and the three-quarter ton vehicle rolled over them both. He felt the weight and heat of the truck as it rolled over him, and he spread out his body as much as he could to shield the man beneath him from the crushing, hot metal. He heard the engine rumbling as the truck passed over and continued down the street. There was a loud crash as it hit something solid enough to stop its progress.

The sound of the engine died and was replaced by an alarm that pierced the night with its shrill and relentless wail. Al rose from the ground and looked down at the man he had tried to protect. His eyes were wide open and terrified, but his gaze was unfocused, and he showed no sign of registering Al's presence. Physically, he appeared unharmed. It figured. The man was reprehensible and he had come away without a scratch.

"You're on your own from here, *pendejo.*" Al gave a swift kick to the man's knee with the tip of his soiled Stacy Adams wingtip and walked away.

****

Oscar awoke with a stabbing pain in his temple and the pressure of a body draped over him. He opened his eyes just in time to see a broad expanse of black tire tread and the undercarriage of a vehicle heading right for him. There was no time to react, even if he had not been pinned down by someone or something he couldn't see. He struggled against whatever force held him captive and screamed until all of the air in his lungs was gone.

As the vehicle rolled inexorably toward him, he squeezed his eyes shut and waited for the sound of his own bones being crushed into fragments. He felt the heat of the engine and smelled exhaust fumes and hot rubber, but when he risked opening his eyes a sliver, the vehicle already had passed over him and was gone. He heard the crunch of metal against solid wood when it crashed into a telephone pole a block away. The alarm system blared. It was a familiar sound. It dawned on him then that it had been his own truck that had nearly ground his body into the pavement.

The weight of someone holding him down had been lifted. Through watering eyes, Oscar scanned the area all around and could see no one. He searched through the failing light for Wright or his partner, but the black Charger was no longer parked along the street. Suddenly, a sharp pain erupted from his right knee, as if he had been stabbed. He clutched his knee and attempted to stand up, but his leg buckled under him. The world around him seemed to spin in a cloudy haze, and his head throbbed. He fell backward on his ass and had to crawl to the curb. He sat in the dirt by the pullout where his truck had been before someone used it to try to run him over. It had to be Wright or his plucky little friend, but where were they now?

Oscar looked over at his truck. Its front end was caved in where it wrapped around the telephone pole. The wail of the siren finally sputtered and died, and the silence that followed was unbroken. If anyone in the neighborhood had heard or seen anything, they had not bothered to come out and investigate. No one got out of the truck, and Oscar could see through the open door hanging crookedly on its hinges that the driver's seat was unoccupied.

Oscar turned his head at a sound like bicycle wheels passing over ruts in the pavement. A block away, an old man in a wheelchair was pulling himself down the sidewalk with the aid of two rusted iron fenceposts which he wielded like ski poles. His legs were bandaged in thick layers of gauze, and he moved slowly, as if in pain. He seemed preoccupied with negotiating his route over broken concrete and pot holes to cross the street toward the sloping greenbelt and the distant overpass. He didn't seem to notice Oscar and didn't even glance at the wrecked truck. Oscar wondered if the old man intended to go down the hill and how he would manage it without toppling out of his wheelchair, but it was a passing thought, and he quickly lost interest. There were far more pressing matters to deal with.

He fought against his aching head to see and think clearly. Night had fallen, and he would never make it to the border before it closed for the night. He didn't dare go back to his mother's place. The cops were almost certainly looking for him by now, and that's the first place they would go. Besides, he doubted he could drive. His head hurt too much, and his eyes still weren't working right. Then there was the matter of his truck, which was smashed against a pole and likely undrivable. Any way he looked at it, he was screwed.

He stood up from the curb with difficulty and staggered toward the truck, which seemed to jump from one side of the street to the other and back again like a ping-pong ball. The illusion of motion and the act of walking, or more accurately, weaving his way down the street made him dizzy and nauseous. When he finally reached the vehicle, he grabbed a hold of the hanging door frame and vomited on the ground before climbing into the cab and leaning back against the head rest until the pounding in his skull began to subside.

****

Minerva climbed out of the driver's seat of the crashed vehicle just as the Guardian was walking away from the man who he had chosen to protect from her. The murderer still lay motionless on the ground. He could wait, she decided; he wasn't going anywhere. First, she would deal with the intruder.

She watched him as he trudged wearily away from her in the direction of the overpass, his wings folded crookedly behind him. The warm light that had emanated from his body when he stood against her was dimmed now and flickering, but it was powerful enough still to bring fresh green shoots from the dried grass with each footfall. His head was down.

Minerva flew at him, covering the distance between them with the speed of a bullet and a stench like gunpowder. Her veneer of piety and righteous purpose was gone, along with the remnants of her sanity. Bobby had been wrong about her. She was different from his fellow soldier back in the jungles of Vietnam. She was not now, nor had she ever been, a Guardian. The creature that launched itself with burning eyes and bared teeth at the true Guardian was a Hag.

Not far away, Bobby watched in terror and realized his mistake.

38

Loose Ends

Rich watched the gurney bearing an unconscious and bleeding Lonny being wheeled away by a team of doctors and nurses toward the surgery wing. A fractured skull and probable cerebral edema, the doctor had said. He was an older man with bushy eyebrows jutting out like gray caterpillars above kind but tired eyes, and he had patted Rich on the shoulder and pointed him in direction of the family waiting room before striding quickly away to attend to the next patient in the crowded emergency room.

Rich didn't go to the family waiting room. Instead, he remained standing in the corridor, looking in the direction Lonny had been taken, although the gurney had turned a corner and passed out of view several minutes ago. Someone, probably a nurse, gently grasped his shoulder and pushed him to the side. He didn't look to see who it was. He allowed himself to be moved, like a cardboard cutout of himself, but he didn't take his eyes off the corridor. The image of the man he loved, helpless and possibly dying, lingered in his head. Another gurney wheeled by, this one carrying an elderly woman with an oxygen mask over her nose and mouth. He glanced at her, and her eyes were open wide and frightened.

The doctor bought his story, or appeared to, about an errant base-ball hit that had traveled at high speed and accidentally struck Lonny on the back of the head while he was turned to check the man on first base. Rich wasn't sure why he made up this story. He could have told the truth, and then the hospital would have contacted the police. Just maybe, the police would have reacted quickly enough to catch Oscar before he got to the border and passed beyond their reach.

It was almost certainly what Lonny would have wanted him to do, but Lonny had lost consciousness on the way to the emergency room almost as soon as he was buckled into his seat. Rich had come up with the story about the baseball as they hurtled through the late evening traffic like a guided missile aimed at the hospital. Some subconscious part of his brain must have already known what he was going to do.

Surgery would take a minimum of three, or as many as six, hours. Then Lonny would be moved to a recovery room where he would awaken from the anesthesia. Rich needed to be there when he did. For Lonny to wake up alone was unthinkable. He might never forgive him, and Rich wouldn't blame him. He wouldn't be able to forgive himself.

And there was also the matter of what Lonny would tell the hospital staff when they asked him how he had been injured. Dear, sincere, maddening Lonny would tell the truth without a second thought, right down to the part about being the first one to point a gun at Oscar. Still, he would have to risk it. He had unfinished business, and it couldn't wait.

Rich turned his back on the corridor and walked purposefully to-ward the sliding doors of the emergency room exit, only looking back once before leaving the brightly-lit lobby for the semi-darkness of the parking lot. He would just have to get the job done quickly and make it back in time. He owed it to Lorena to act decisively this one time, after all the times he had failed to act at all, and the time that mattered the most when he had acted too late to save her. And now she was gone forever.

"Hold on, Lonny," he whispered. "I'll come back soon. Please be here when I do. I can't lose you too."

Rich remembered nothing about the drive back to the lonely road alongside the overpass. He might have run over the tops of other vehicles and sent pedestrians flying right and left for all he knew or cared. Only when he spied the battered truck wrapped around the telephone pole at the end of the block did he allow himself to breathe freely. Oscar hadn't gotten away after all. He hadn't realized until this moment that he had been practically holding his breath the entire mad race from the hospital.

He had to be here somewhere, maybe still inside his truck, unless the Guardian had killed him. That would explain the crash. Rich pictured the hideous old woman suddenly appearing in Oscar's headlights as he tried to make his getaway. That would be enough to make even the toughest gangster swerve into a pole, and maybe piss his pants while he was at it.

Rich felt an unexpected twinge of guilt at the thought of the Guardian killing Oscar. He had wanted to kill him himself, had even brought along his grandpa's gun as part of his fantasy of bringing the bastard down like an outlaw in some old western movie. He hadn't admitted it to himself at the time, but he probably would have beaten the man to death right there if not for the Guardian appearing and miraculously believing him when he told her about Oscar. When she let him go and took off after Oscar instead, Rich had stood by and let it happen. He had been pleased to know that she was going to kill him.

What kind of man is happy to see another man murdered, even a terrible man like Oscar? Rich didn't know, but he knew he didn't want to be that kind of man.

He parked his car in almost the same spot as before and approached the vehicle with caution, remembering the evil-looking gun Oscar had taken with him when he left his mother's house. When he was still several yards away, he stopped suddenly and listened. Some kind of commotion was happening just out of sight, down the slope that led to the concrete pillars of the overpass. He heard voices raised in anger and sounds of a struggle. A flash of light illuminated a cloud of particles, like ashes, rising above the slope. Rich had seen a cloud like that before. The

Guardian! He ran toward the sounds and then dropped to his hands and knees to peer over the slope without being seen.

Directly below him, the now familiar figure of the old woman kneeled over the body of a strange creature lying supine on the ground. It looked like a man but had huge wings that spread out in a span of twelve feet or more beneath its back. It was surrounded by a soft golden glow that appeared to emanate from its body and illuminate the scene against the backdrop of nightfall. This light flared brighter when the creature attempted to fight off its assailant, but its strength was flagging, and the golden glow dimmed incrementally with each diminished effort. The tawny wings flapped weakly against the ground as the creature struggled to free itself from her iron grip. It seemed to be losing the battle.

As Rich looked on in horror, the old woman leaned over to within an inch of the creature's face and breathed a thick cloud of blackened ashes from her gaping jaws into its nose and mouth. The creature abruptly ceased its struggles and lay still. Then the hag inhaled deeply, and a vapor began to rise from the creature's lips and stream into her cavernous mouth.

As the light surrounding it flickered out, the creature's body began to change. Its wings folded and dwindled to stubs that disappeared beneath its prostrate form. Its legs became bent and broken, and gaping wounds oozing blood and gore appeared on its head and torso. One arm lay in pieces, tenuously held together by tendons and flesh.

At the end of this transformation, Rich was looking down at the battered body of a middle-aged Hispanic man in outdated clothes reminiscent of late 1970's disco-wear. Rich thought he saw the man's eyes flutter open and then shut again.

"Well, if that don't beat all," whispered a voice from just behind Rich's left ear.

Rich nearly jumped out of his skin. He whirled around to see a haggard-looking man in a wheelchair, leaning forward to see what was happening beyond the slope. He was keeping himself from tumbling over the hill by holding tight to two metal posts he had thrust into the dirt on either side of his chair.

"Sorry, friend, but I guess I was wrong," the old man continued. "That ain't no Guardian. It's something much worse. As to what that other thing is, well you got me. If I had to guess, I'd have said it was an angel, but then it turned into what looks more like a beat-up *cholo*, so I'm done guessing."

"Bobby?" Rich managed to keep his voice to a whisper, although his heart was pounding in his chest. "What are you doing here? Wait, never mind. Just keep quiet and let me get you away from here before she sees us." Rich stood up as quietly as he could. He pulled up the metal posts and placed them in Bobby's lap before turning the wheelchair around and pushing him back toward the street.

When they were a relatively safe distance away, Rich set the brake on Bobby's wheelchair and sat down beside him on the curb. He covered his face with his hands and spoke through his fingers. "What just happened? And what the hell are you doing here, Bobby? Why aren't you in the hospital?"

"Like I said, I'm done guessing about the crazy shit that seems to be following you around for some reason that I sure as hell don't understand. To be honest with you, I'm relieved that you were seeing the same things I was seeing. They gave me some meds in the hospital to get my head straight, and I was wondering if they were making me worse instead of better. But if you seen all that too, then I guess it must be real.

"That thing over there, the one that I thought was a Guardian like Mighty Mouse turned into, well, now I think maybe it's something else my granny used to talk about. She would tell me stories about these things called Hags. Used to give me nightmares. She said they look like old women, and they like to sneak up on you while you're sleeping. They climb up on your bed, Granny said, and breathe death into your lungs. Then they suck the life out of you to keep themselves alive. That's what it reminded me of when I saw what that old gal was doing over yonder to that poor Mexican guy."

"That poor Mexican guy, as you call him, had wings and glowed like a nightlight," Rich said wearily. "I must be losing my mind." He took his hands from his face and looked over at the old man in the wheelchair. "You still haven't told me why you're here and not in the hospital where you belong."

Bobby looked sheepish. "Let's just say that there was a little difference of opinion between the doctors and yours truly about where I should go when the time came to let me loose. They wanted to transfer me to the psychiatric unit and then to some kind of extended care facility or some such bullshit. That little discussion you and me had when you visited me in my room didn't do much to help my case." Bobby glanced over at Rich with a frown. "So, to make a long story short, I hijacked this wheelchair and rolled on out of there when the nurse's back was turned. She was a pushy old dame anyway. Reminded me of my ex-wife."

"Jesus, Bobby. But, why did you come here?"

"This is where I live! Down that hill and to the other side of the overpass. I got me a nice, comfortable little place down there. Not much good when it rains, but I've got some shade during the day and the traffic overhead to sing me to sleep at night. That's where I was heading, or trying to – it wasn't going to be easy in this chair – when I saw you crouched down here. Got my curiosity up enough to come check out what you were looking at. I wish I could have seen that Mexican guy with the wings before the Hag got to him. That would have been a sight worth seeing. Too bad she was already killing him when I got here."

"I think he's still alive," Rich said.

"Well, hell man, why didn't you say so? Here we sit lollygagging while there's a Hag sucking the life out of the poor dude! Don't you think we ought to do something?" Bobby looked down at his bandaged legs and the spots of blood soaking through the gauze and sighed. "Maybe I should say, don't you think *you* ought to do something? The best I could do right now would be to fall on her."

"You're right. I've sat back and let too many people get hurt already." Rich stood up and started walking back toward the slope.

"Wait a minute," Bobby called after him. "Take this with you." He handed one of the metal posts to Rich. "My granny said you can kill evil spirits with iron. Seems to be she was right about a few things, so maybe she was right about that too. Of course, she also used to tell me that if you let a lizard count your teeth, you'll die, so I'm not sure she wasn't just about as crazy as I am. Anyway, it's better than nothing. Just in case, you know."

Rich accepted the iron post with a nod and turned back toward the slope. He crouched down and jogged with light, quiet steps to a spot where he could peer over the edge without being seen.

A few yards below, in a spot partially lit by the glow of the lamp posts dotting the overpass, the Hag stood over the fallen man. She held her hands in front of her chest and wrung them one over the other as she looked down at the man's bloodied face. From his vantage point, Rich heard her dry and crackling voice and caught a glimpse of the silvery light in her eyes as she gazed at the broken body lying still on the ground.

"I had no choice," he heard her say. "He wouldn't listen to reason. The guilty must be punished. It is God's will."

Rich sensed movement on the ground near his feet. He looked down just as a two-inch scorpion crawled onto the strap of his flip-flop. A squeal escaped his lips, and he flung his shoe off and immediately stepped down on a sharp piece of gravel. He cursed, hopping on one foot until he stumbled and fell over the slope. He rolled and landed a few feet away from the Hag and her victim.

She turned with a hiss, her claws extended. Wisps of ash-filled smoke issued from her open mouth, and her eyes flared with an inner fire as she glared at Rich. He clamored to his feet and stood his ground, looking into her burning eyes, even as his knees threatened to buckle under him with fear. To his surprise and relief, she transformed in a blur of swirling ashes back to her guise as a harmless, though deathly pale, old woman, clad in the mourning dress of a century ago. She pursed her lips, and without another word, began to walk away.

She made no move to intervene as Rich came forward to kneel beside the body in the dirt. He checked for vital signs and could find no pulse, neither at the neck nor the wrist, and when he leaned his ear over the man's mouth, he could detect no breathing and no rise and fall of the chest. The body felt cold, as though long dead. With a shudder he could not repress, Rich positioned himself to begin CPR. Out of the corner of his eye, he saw the Hag walking toward the street where Bobby waited, vulnerable in his wheelchair.

"Hey!" Rich called out. "Where are you going?"

The Hag looked back only briefly before continuing on her course. "To finish my mission," she said primly.

"Mission?" Rich called after her. "What mission?" She continued on without answering, taking long strides up the hill and vanishing into the darkness that surrounded her.

He looked down at the dead man stretched out on the ground in front of him. Whoever, or whatever, this man was, the Hag had sucked the life out of him and left him there as though his life had no meaning, no importance at all. Whatever her mission was, anyone who got in the way of it was expendable. Rich thought about Bobby waiting for him at the top of the hill – sitting directly in the Hag's path. What if she decided he too was in the way of her mission?

He leapt to his feet and went after her. He had to run to catch up with her, and it was a certainty that she would get to Bobby before he could stop her. He felt the iron fence post still clutched in his hand and forgotten since Bobby had given it to him. What had he said about iron?

Rich was right behind the Hag when she turned suddenly and confronted him. He held the iron post like a javelin and drew back his arm to thrust it at her.

So swiftly that Rich's brain couldn't register the transition, the Hag went from standing a yard in front of him to standing inches from his face and grabbing his arm. She clenched her bony fingers around his wrist and shook it, sending the iron post flying out of his hand and into the dark. She grabbed him by the shoulders, and her sharp nails penetrated his shirt and punctured his flesh like hooks in a slab of meat. She dug deeper as he screamed, and she pulled him close to her face.

"Enough," she said in a voice like the crackle of twigs in a brush fire. Her face transformed again into a monstrous death mask, and her jaws opened impossibly wide. She breathed a thick, ashen miasma into Rich's face.

His mouth was open already from screaming, and now he gasped in terror and drew the deadly vapor into his mouth and nose. He tried to pull way, but the pain of her talons in his shoulders was too much. He gagged once, soundlessly, and then his eyes rolled up into his head, and he dropped like a rock to the ground.

He landed on his back with his face pointed toward the sky, and he lay still as though peacefully star-gazing.

39

Endings

Minerva adjusted her lace cuffs, straightened her skirt, and walked briskly away from Rich. She did not give him another thought. Her mind was focused on one aim only – to ensure the final payment of his sins from the man Oscar, who had sealed his fate by killing the young woman she had been called to save.

She glided past the old man in the wheelchair without a glance. His presence was unimportant. She didn't notice that his eyes widened and followed her as she passed, close enough for him to smell her sickening perfume of rancid flowers and burnt flesh. She made her way purposefully toward the crashed truck, her feet seeming to tread on a thin layer of smoke that hovered just above the ground. As she moved farther away, instead of disappearing into the darkness that surrounded her, she gave off a dim fluorescence like rotting sea creatures in a dark ocean.

Bobby turned around in his wheelchair to watch the Hag as she walked away. He gripped the wheels of his chair to back it up and grimaced at the sharp pain that shot through his legs and up through what seemed like every nerve in his body. Dark spots had begun to blossom and spread through the bandages that glowed white on his legs against the faded night-tinged colors of surrounding objects.

Bracing himself with his remaining iron fence post, Bobby ignored the pain and leaned over to search for some sign of movement from the two bodies that now lay a few yards apart at the bottom of the hill. All was still and silent. Rich and the man-angel-thing below looked like shallow mounds of stone set into the dry, grassy landscape.

Bobby swore under his breath, but this time it had nothing to do with the voices in his head. He wiped away tears that had begun to trickle down his weathered cheeks. "Goodbye, young man," he whispered. "I liked you. You were alright for a rich kid." He turned his attention to trying to navigate the wheelchair through the rough terrain in the direction of his ravine.

Three shots rang out behind him at close range, piercing the silence with their explosive intensity.

****

Inside the cab of his truck, Oscar leaned back in the driver's seat with his eyes closed. His thoughts drifted on the edge of unconsciousness like wispy clouds in a light breeze. At first, the sound of the door hinges creaking barely registered in his brain, but as the door was thrown wide open, he shot up in the seat so fast that spears of pain punctured his head, and stars danced before his eyes. He reached blindly for his gun just as something grabbed him around the throat and pulled him with unnatural strength out of the truck.

He was thrown against the side panel of the vehicle with enough force to knock the air from his lungs. He tried desperately to see through the darkness and the pain in his head, but he couldn't see his assailant, only an indistinct fog that smelled faintly of charred, damp wood and spent flowers. Someone or something hissed like a cat. He sensed that someone was standing there, right in front of him, and he felt a pair of burning eyes and a puff of hot, foul breath against his face.

"Who's there?" he croaked. "Get away from me or I'll kill you!"

"Like you killed her?" The words, spoken in a raspy whisper, came from inches away.

Oscar cowered against the unyielding metal of the vehicle behind his back. He pointed his weapon in front of him with both hands shaking and fired three shots wildly before the gun was ripped from his grasp and tossed away.

The Hag reached out and grabbed Oscar by the collar. She drew close to him, her gaze locked on his terrified eyes as they darted unseeing in all directions. That he couldn't see her was no surprise to Minerva. It was that way sometimes with men too worldly and self-assured to acknowledge the existence of a power outside of their egocentric understanding. It was of no consequence. He wouldn't be seeing anything much longer.

She opened her mouth and inhaled deeply. Then she leaned closer until her lips nearly brushed his. She pulled the man's lower jaw down with one gnarled hand. A tunnel opened from her gaping mouth down into the dark depths of her throat. With a sound like a roaring fire drawn up and into a hungry chimney, she began to exhale. A thick rope of dense smoke shot out of the tunnel and invaded the man's mouth with irresistible force, down his throat and into his lungs.

As ashes poured from her mouth and swirled around the two figures like a windstorm in hell, Minerva felt a sudden stab of cold piercing her body, starting at her back and traveling through her long-stilled heart and out of her chest. She shut her mouth, cutting off the miasmic flow, and tilted her head to look down at her body. A thin cylinder of rusted black metal protruded from a hole in her black crepe dress, just below the bosom.

There was no blood, and Minerva felt no pain. She experienced a strange sensation of wonder and confusion and reached down to touch the metal object that had so suddenly appeared. The iron post burned her finger tips with an icy blue flame. She shrieked once, a jagged, crackling screech, and then she dissolved into a cloud of ashes and smoke that drifted away in the gentle night breeze.

The fog instantly began to clear from Oscar's vision. At the same time, he felt a stabbing pain in his body. He looked down and saw a metal rod plunged into the right side of his abdomen, just below the ribs. Blood was oozing from the wound and already had begun to drip from the hem of his drenched shirt.

His head snapped up at the sound of something close by. It sounded like a squeaky bicycle wheel. Sitting in the shadows in front of him was an old man in a wheelchair.

"Oops," the old man said. Oscar slid to the ground, and his eyes fluttered closed.

****

"Rich! Rich! Hey, man, if you ain't dead, you gotta wake up!"

Rich opened his eyes and lay still for a moment, staring up at the starry sky. Awareness slowly returned to him, and he had a vague impression that someone was calling his name. He wondered where he was, how he had got there, and why he was sleeping outdoors. As the questions floated around in his head, he heard his name again.

"Rich! Hell, maybe he really is dead."

Memories came flooding back: The Guardian or Hag or whatever she was, the slaughter of the winged creature that turned into a man, then the attack – claws tight around his throat, the hideous face so close to his, the eyes like a glimpse into the eternal pit. He remembered suffocating, the terror of fighting to take in air, but instead feeling only the burning sensation of his lungs filling with smoke.

Rich pulled himself up onto his elbows and looked around. Where the body of the Hispanic man had been, there was nothing now but dirt and weeds. There was no sign of the supernatural struggle that Rich had witnessed. Could he have dreamed the whole thing?

"Hey, Rich, over here!"

"Bobby?" Rich looked up the hill and spotted the old man in his wheelchair, waving his arms and calling down to him. He held something in his right hand that looked like a gun.

"If I ever wake up from this nightmare, I'm going straight to a psychiatrist," Rich muttered as he pulled himself up from the ground and trudged up the slope.

He was greeted at the top by an agitated Bobby clutching what was indeed a firearm. He seemed unaware that it was still in his hand, but his grip on the weapon was practiced and confident, like the trained soldier he once had been. Even though night had fallen completely now, Rich could still see the patches of blood on Bobby's bandaged legs.

"Bobby, what's going on now? Where's the Guardian, or the Hag, or whatever the fucking thing is? And where did you get that gun?"

"The Hag is gone," Bobby said breathlessly. "She's dead...46, 47, 48, 49, 50...I killed her. 51, 52, 53, 54, 55...I guess my granny was right. Iron worked after all. I'm never grinning at another lizard as long as I live. 56, 57, 58, 59, 60."

"What about the gun, Bobby? Where did it come from? It looks like Oscar's gun. Where is he now? Did the Hag get him?"

"Would you just shut the fuck up and give me some breathing room? 61, 62, 63, 64, 65..."

"Bobby, just calm down, okay? You're hurt and you've been through a shock. Maybe you should give me that gun." Rich slowly extended his hand, palm up. "Just hand it to me, okay? Everything's going to be alright."

"What?" Bobby looked at Rich's outstretched hand and up again at his face. "66, 67, 68, 69, 70...Oh, I wasn't talking to you. I was talking to the other guy – Beelzebub. The hospital meds must be wearing off 'cause he's back and trying to talk my ear off again. Insulting bastard. 71, 72, 73, 74, 75...You can have the gun if you want it. It's his." Bobby handed the gun to Rich and pointed a thumb to where Oscar sat on the asphalt, propped against the side of his truck with an iron post sticking out of his stomach. Rich handled the gun gingerly, as if it might spontaneously fire without warning. He carefully tucked it into the back of the waistband of his shorts.

"That part was an accident," Bobby went on, looking over at Oscar with an expression of disgust on his face. I'm trying, but funny thing is I'm not really sorry about it. Guy seemed like a first-class asshole."

"Oh my God." Rich gasped, finally registering the presence of the fence post in Oscar's middle as reality and not a trick of the dim light or his own overtaxed imagination. He rushed over to where the injured man sat breathing in shallow gasps and clutching his bleeding abdomen.

Oscar looked up at Rich as he approached. He opened his mouth as if to speak, but at first only his lips moved, as though he didn't have enough air in his lungs to push the words out. His eyes had a glassy, unfocused look.

In the background, Bobby continued his count, now in the two hundred's, interspersed with curse words and pleas for Beelzebub to shut up and let him think.

"Get it out of me," Oscar finally managed to say in a choked voice, his words slurred and barely audible. "Please, you gotta get it out of me!"

The site of the metal rod in Oscar's flesh, and the blood oozing out around his fingers as he clutched his body, made the bile rise up from Rich's stomach until he had to look away to keep from vomiting. He found himself almost feeling sorry for man until he remembered what he had done.

"No, that would be a bad idea," Rich said in as neutral of a voice as he could manage. "I saw it on a cop show on TV. If I pull it out, you could bleed to death. I probably should just walk away and let you bleed to death, but I'm not like you." Rich pulled off his t-shirt and wrapped it around the post where it protruded from Oscar's flesh.

"Here, hold this against the wound. Put as much pressure on it as you can to slow down the bleeding."

Oscar groaned in pain as he pressed the shirt against the hole in his abdomen, but the blood flow did seem to slow. He held it in place, and breathed in short, measured puffs, in and out though his nose until his breathing became more regular. His jaw was clenched and he fought to stay alert, to regain control of his violated body.

"Is your phone in the truck?" Rich asked. Oscar nodded without looking up. Rich leaned into the open cab, found the phone in a cup holder, and returned to the injured man. He sat down on ground and faced him, with the phone in one hand and the gun now held firmly in the other.

"Okay, I'm going to call for an ambulance, but first, you and I need to talk. I have a deal for you, and the sooner you take it, the sooner you get to have that piece of metal out of your worthless body" Rich said. The look in his eyes seemed to invite argument, just enough to give him an excuse to push the iron the rest of the way out through his back.

"What...deal?" Oscar growled through gritted teeth.

"Well, the main thing is that you are going to confess to murdering Lorena." Oscar began to shake his head. "I'm sorry, but this isn't really a negotiation," Rich continued. "You are going to agree to my terms – all of them – or I'm going to smash this phone to pieces and drag your ass over that hill to die slowly and painfully where no one will even know you're there."

Oscar stopped shaking his head and glared at him.

"Do you understand?" Rich asked. Oscar nodded once and said nothing, although the hatred in his eyes spoke volumes. "I'm going to take that as a 'yes'," Rich said. "Now, where was I? So, number one, you confess. You tell the whole truth about what you did to her. No excuses, no shifting the blame. Number two, you tell them that the homeless guy over there stabbed you in self-defense after you shot at him. I don't know why you shot at him, and I don't really care, as long as you make it clear that it was your fault and not his. You got that?" Oscar nodded.

"Sss...something tried to kill me," Oscar wheezed. "Something invisible. I shot at it, and then that guy stabbed me, and it went away."

"You know, if I was you, I would leave that part out when you talk to the cops, but that's up to you," Rich said. "Have we got a deal?"

Oscar nodded and drew in his breath as a wave of pain went through him. "Deal," he said.

"Good. Because if you break your word in any way, I'm going to bring the invisible man back, and this time, I'm going to make sure he kills you." Rich returned the gun to his waistband and leaned forward to catch the light of the nearest street lamp. He began to thumb "911" into the phone.

With strength and speed born of adrenaline and desperation, Oscar reached out with one bloodied hand and yanked the gun from Rich's pants. He pointed it at Rich and smiled, then winced in pain. The effort it took to grab the gun and hold it steady was costing him, but at such close range, it would be impossible to miss.

"Give me the phone," Oscar said, his voice weaker now but his intention unmistakable. Rich backed away a couple of paces and held up both hands, one still clutching the phone. "Give it to me now, or I'll shoot you and take it from your dead, fucking body."

Rich lowered his hands and started to hand over the phone, but instead swung wide and tossed the phone as far as he could in the direction where he hoped Bobby still waited.

"Bobby!" he shouted, his eyes on the barrel of the gun pointed at his chest. "I threw a phone somewhere close to you. Can you see it? I need you to dial 911 and tell the cops there's been a murder. Tell them to hurry because there's going to be another one."

For the first tense seconds that hung in the air like the interminable pause before a giant wave crests and falls on the helpless ship below, there was silence. Rich stared into the gun barrel, watched it shake slightly from side to side but never away from his pounding heart.

"Bobby, can you hear me?"

A voice carried from the distance. The words were spoken conversationally, but the conversation was one-sided. "Six hundred and sixty-fucking-six, you little shit. Now, go away. A deal's a deal. Right now, I got things to do. Don't you have any other souls to torment?"

"Bobby!"

"I don't think he's listening, *puto*. It's just you and me, and now I'm making the deals." Oscar's face had gone deathly pale, and his breathing was becoming labored, but he maintained his grip on the gun, and the expression on his wan face was determined. "You're going to walk straight over there, slow like you're walking your blushing bride Lenny down the aisle, and you're going to bring back my phone. If you stop and talk to the crazy *viejo*, or if you try to dial the phone or go anywhere but straight back here, I'll shoot you. You got that?"

Rich stood up slowly with his hands raised. Without a word, and with one last glance at the shaking gun (was it shaking more than before?), Rich turned and began walking slowly in the direction of where he remembered throwing the phone.

Finding a phone in a black case in the dark wouldn't be easy under any circumstances, and it was even harder while walking with his hands up, afraid to stoop over too much and evoke Oscar's suspicion. An object loomed just ahead. Rich could just make out a spoked wheel.

"Bobby?" Rich whispered, but as he drew closer to the wheelchair, he saw that it was empty.

****

The blinding pain in his legs was both a curse and a blessing. The last time he had scuttled across a field in the dark on his elbows, trying to avoid detection by an armed adversary, he had been a young man in prime physical condition with a pair of strong legs and a mind only slightly touched by the aftereffects of too much pot and too little sleep. Now, he was an old man with two broken legs and a broken mind. *Looking on the bright side,* Bobby thought, *at least the pain keeps the voices away.*

He stopped just outside the glow of the streetlamp. No more than five yards ahead, the man with the gun, the man he had saved from the Hag, a decision he now regretted ruefully, still sat on the asphalt and leaned against the side of the truck. His back was turned to Bobby, but the position of his arms indicated he still held the pistol out in front of him, pointed toward where Rich was shuffling along, head bowed and concentrating on the ground.

Bobby considered his options. Five yards seemed like fifty to an old man who couldn't even rise up on his knees, let alone get up and run. He tried to calculate how long it would take him to drag his body the rest of the way to get close enough to try to wrestle the weapon from the injured man. He would have to do it quietly, without alerting the man to his approach, or he could simply turn and shoot him, and that would be the end of it. He needed a distraction, but couldn't think of a single thing he could do that wouldn't draw attention to himself too soon and blow the whole plan.

He was still crouched motionless on the ground when a sudden outburst from the gunman made him jump and almost shout out loud and give himself away.

"Hey, *puto*! What are you doing? Just get the phone and get your ass back over here!" The effort it took to raise his voice and still keep a hold of the gun was too much. Oscar began to wheeze and cough. He laid down the gun beside him and clutched his abdomen with both hands.

Bobby saw his chance, and he took it. He pulled himself up on his hands and launched himself forward, the pain in his legs screaming through his body as his knees made contact with the hard ground. He ignored the pain and thrust himself forward the last few feet and reached for the gun.

Movement in the corner of his eye caught Oscar's attention, and he turned his head just in time to see the old man's hand reaching toward the gun that lay on the ground at his side. He lunged for it, sending an excruciating jolt of white-hot pain through his body.

Rich had forgotten to keep his hands in the air and was searching the area, desperately looking for any sign of what had happened to Bobby, when he heard Oscar shouting something at him from a distance. He couldn't quite make out what he was saying. Then, a single shot rang out, stark against the stillness of the neglected park at night.

He dropped to all fours, certain that Oscar had shot at him but not yet sure of whether he had been hit. He felt around his body. Nothing hurt, and there was no blood and no sign of a gunshot wound. He froze, waiting for another shot to follow the first, but nothing happened. He waited a full five minutes, then cautiously stood up and peered through the darkness toward where Oscar was last sitting and pointing the gun at him.

At first, he felt tremendous relief. Oscar lay twisted on the ground, his body kept from lying flat against the pavement by the iron rod that still protruded from his middle. He didn't appear to be moving. Rich began to jog across the distance to where the prostrate form lay. Then he spotted the second body. "Bobby!" he shouted.

Bobby lay stretched out on his back with the gun still in his hand. He cradled it against his body like a baby. His legs were drenched in blood below the knees, and the ground beneath him glistened with an expanding pool of blood like a black river flowing away from his body toward the gutter. His eyes opened at the sound of Rich's approach, and a weak smile played across his face.

"Got 'im," he said. He chuckled, then gasped for air.

Rich rushed forward and saw the blood. So much of it. "I've got to get you back to the hospital." He dropped to his knees and pulled off his shirt, preparing to use it as a tourniquet for the second time today.

Bobby watched him. "Too late for that, I think," he whispered. His eyes looked into Rich's and then lost focus, staring into nothing. Bobby's face slackened into an expression of peaceful repose.

"Oh, Bobby, no. Oh, no." Rich leaned over him and touched his wrinkled face. He felt for a pulse, then gently closed the old man's eyes. Tear's streamed down Rich's face as he gave Bobby's hand a parting squeeze. "Thank you, my friend," he said.

He looked over at Oscar only long enough to confirm he was dead. The gangster's eyes stared up toward the starry sky. Rich left them that way. It was the only glimpse of heaven he was likely to get.

"By the way," he said, "his name is Lonny".

Rich held back the urge to spit on the body. He looked down at his watch. It was time to go. He walked to his car and drove away without looking back.

40

Beginnings

Lonny opened his eyes. At first, he didn't know where he was, but then he remembered Rich helping him into the car to take him to the hospital. He remembered nothing after that. "Richie? Where are you?"

A pile of blankets fell away from a lump on a small sofa across the room, and Rich's head appeared. "I'm right here," Rich said, instantly awake. "I was just dozing off for a minute. How do you feel?" Rich moved to sit on the side of the bed and took Lonny's hand.

"My head hurts," Lonny said. He reached up to feel the bandages surrounding his head and began frantically patting at them. "Richie! I think they shaved my head! Oh my God, I'm bald!"

"Shh...," Rich stroked Lonny's hand. "Calm down. It's okay. You just had surgery on your skull, you know. They had to shave your head to save your life. Your brain was swelling. Do you think I care about your hair right now?"

"Maybe you don't, but I do," Lonny said through tears. "I'm going to look terrible bald. My uncle José is bald, and he looks like brown-skinned naked mole rat."

"*You* are not going to look like a naked mole rat, and even if you did, I would still love you." Rich kissed him gently. "Now, try to rest and don't get so upset. Your hair will grow back before you know it, and in the meantime, I'll buy you as many hats as you want."

"I look stupid in hats," Lonny pouted. His brow wrinkled for a moment, then he said, "Hey, I wonder what happened after we left. Do you think Oscar got away, or do you think the Guardian got him?"

"I think Oscar got exactly what he had coming to him. Now, about what happened back there. I need you to stick with the story I told them about how your head got hurt. I said I hit you with a baseball on accident and…"

"A baseball? Are you out of your mind? Do I look like I play baseball? What's wrong with the truth, huh? The truth will set you free, you know. Haven't you ever heard that? Baseball! Are you kidding me?"

"Shh, Lonny," Rich said with a smile. "We'll figure something out, okay? Just rest." He planted another kiss on Lonny's lips, and Lonny stopped talking, at least for a little while.

****

Al DeLeon lay on his back and listened to the hum of the traffic going by overhead. His many injuries caused him no physical pain, but he felt a bone-aching weariness from head to toe. He hadn't wanted to wake up. He had hoped the Hag would finish him off and end the perpetual loop of his existence, but here he remained. The Hag was gone now, along with the men.

There was no one else around, just Al and the overpass and the constant flow of traffic. Even the old man who used to sit in the nearby ravine and talk to himself at night was gone. Dead, like the Hag and the murderer. Dead like the young woman in the car all those years ago. Al felt a tear slide down his wasted cheek.

Wearily, he pulled himself up, first to his knees and then to his feet, and started trudging slowly toward the overpass. When he reached the concrete pillar and was about to begin climbing, a figure came around from the side of the pillar and stood before him.

It was a young woman with dark hair and luminous eyes. She was dressed in something white that seemed to fade into the soft luminance that surrounded her. She was smiling at him. Al recognized at once that this was not another Hag, but until she started to speak, he didn't know what, or who, she was. As soon as her lips parted and she spoke the first word, he knew instantly, even though he had never before heard her voice.

"Francisco Alfonso Veracruz-DeLeon," Genevieve said in a soft voice like the coo of a dove. "You are forgiven."

Al dropped to his knees and bowed his head. He closed his eyes and wept into his hands. "I am so sorry."

When he raised his head, she was gone. He looked down and saw that his body had been made whole and clean, down to the shine on his silver belt buckle and his Stacy Adams wingtips. He turned away from the overpass and started walking. After a few steps, he vanished.

In two beats of golden-brown wings, the Guardian reappeared on a busy street in an unknown city at an unknown time. A teenage boy with his eyes locked on his phone screen stepped into the street. Al pulled him back just as a city bus whooshed past. "Damn!" the boy said.

"Not anymore," Al said with a smile.

* * * * * * *

A woman lay on the couch, pretending to sleep while the TV blared some late-night re-run of a comedy show. Her body ached too much for sleep, and her busted lip throbbed. Her husband would be home soon, and he would be drunk again, just as sure as the sun comes up in the morning. If he found her awake, he would pick up where he left off, or worse yet, decide that makeup sex would be just the thing to make her forget all about the beating. Never mind that he would be too drunk to complete the act before passing out with his sweaty, beer-reeking body pressed against her. No, much better to feign sleep and hope for the best.

The front door rattled as someone outside struggled to fit a key into the lock.

In a corner of the room, beyond the reach of the light from the TV, an old woman in an old-fashioned dress opened her eyes and took a deep breath.